PENGUIN CLASSICS

THE LOST ESTATE

ALAIN-FOURNIER, christened Henri Alban, was born in La Chapelle d'Angillon (Cher) in 1886, the son of a country school-master. He was educated at Brest and in Paris, where he met and fell in love with the original Yvonne, who influenced his whole life and work. *The Lost Estate* (*Le Grand Meaulnes*) was published in 1912. *Les Miracles* appeared posthumously in 1924. Alain-Fournier's important correspondence with Jacques Rivière and his letters to his family were published in 1926 and 1930 respectively. Alain-Fournier was killed in action on the Meuse in 1914.

ROBIN BUSS translated a number of works for Penguin Classics, including a selection of writings by Sartre, Henri Barbusse's *Under Fire* and Albert Camus' *The Plague* and *The Fall*. He also wrote books on French and Italian cinema. Robin Buss died in 2006.

ADAM GOPNIK has been writing for the *New Yorker* since 1986, and is the author of *Through the Children's Gate: A Home in New York* and *Paris to the Moon*. He is a three-time winner of the National Magazine Award for Essays and for Criticism and the George Polk Award for Magazine Reporting. From 1995 to 2000, he lived in Paris; he now lives in New York City with his wife and their two children.

ALAIN-FOURNIER

The Lost Estate

Le Grand Meaulnes

Translated by ROBIN BUSS
with an Introduction by ADAM GOPNIK

PENGUIN BOOKS

PENGUIN BOOKS

Published by the Penguin Group
Penguin Books Ltd, 80 Strand, London WC2R ORL, England
Penguin Group (USA) Inc., 375 Hudson Street, New York, New York 10014, USA
Penguin Group (Canada), 90 Eglinton Avenue East, Suite 700, Toronto,
Ontario, Canada M4P 2Y3 (a division of Pearson Penguin Canada Inc.)
Penguin Ireland, 25 St Stephen's Green, Dublin 2, Ireland (a division of Penguin Books Ltd)
Penguin Group (Australia), 250 Camberwell Road, Camberwell,
Victoria 3124, Australia (a division of Pearson Australia Group Pty Ltd)
Penguin Books India Pvt Ltd, 11 Community Centre,
Panchsheel Park, New Delhi – 110 017, India
Penguin Group (NZ), 67 Apollo Drive, Rosedale, North Shore 0632, New Zealand
(a division of Pearson New Zealand Ltd)
Penguin Books (South Africa) (Pty) Ltd, 24 Sturdee Avenue,
Rosebank, Johannesburg 2196, South Africa

Penguin Books Ltd, Registered Offices: 80 Strand, London WC2R ORL, England

www.penguin.com

First published 1913
This edition published in Penguin Classics 2007
This My Penguin published 2007
1

Translation copyright © Robin Buss, 2007
Introduction copyright © Adam Gopnik, 2007
All rights reserved

Set in 10.25/12.25 pt PostScript Adobe Sabon
Typeset by Rowland Phototypesetting Ltd, Bury St Edmunds, Suffolk
Printed in England by Clays Ltd, St Ives plc

978-0-141-03346-4

Contents

Introduction

*New readers are advised that this Introduction
makes details of the plot explicit.*

Part Hans Christian Andersen tale – a poor boy brought to a
fairy castle – part grimly lyrical study of provincial manners
and landscape in a still-rural France, and in part the model of
all the adolescent novels which marked so much of twentieth-
century literature, Alain-Fournier's 1913 novel *Le Grand
Meaulnes* is a keystone of modern French literature which is,
oddly, less well-known among English-speaking readers than
many French books less famous and foundational. Among
French readers, particularly those of a certain age, *Le Grand
Meaulnes* is as much part of life as *Catcher in the Rye* is in
America and shares some of the same slightly intense glamour
that *Brideshead Revisited* has in Britain (both novels which it
in certain crucial ways resembles). In a poll of French readers
taken as recently as a decade ago, it came sixth among all
twentieth-century books, not far behind Saint-Exupéry and
Proust and Camus' *L'Etranger* – but it seems likely that many
English-speaking readers who have been alienated alongside
Meursault and longed along with Swann (and been impatient
in the desert with the Little Prince) will have only a vague sense
of the action and purpose of this book. (Although the ones
who do care, care a lot: as early as the 1920s Havelock Ellis
wrote a rhapsodic appreciation of Fournier's novel for English
readers.)[1]

Some of the trouble has been laid to its supposedly untranslatable title: *Le Grand Meaulnes* has appeared over the years in
English as *The Wanderer*, as *The Lost Domain*, and even as
Big Meaulnes. 'No English adjective will convey all the shades
of meaning that can be read into the simple word "grand"

which takes on overtones as the story progresses,' one translator has written[2] – but in fact its title is exactly equivalent, in its combination of sardonic irony and appreciative applause, to that of Fitzgerald's *The Great Gatsby* a decade later, one more brief classic of the same resonant kind (and yet one more Anglo-American novel which *Le Grand Meaulnes* resembles and must have influenced). And some other small part of its difficulty lies in the oddity of its author's name, a pseudonym which is not pseudonymous; the author, who died in the first weeks of the Great War, a year after the novel's publication, was actually named Henri-Alban Fournier; the Alain was adopted, and no one is entirely sure where, or whether, to place the hyphen.

The apparent matter of the book is simple and myth-like. François Seurel, the fifteen-year-old narrator, is living in the provincial village of Sainte-Agathe, in the snowy, bleak Sologne, in central France, around the turn of the last century. He is the son of the village schoolmaster, and one day a new, slightly older boy, Augustin Meaulnes, arrives at the school. His size, natural charisma and sheer physical presence leads him to be called 'the Great Meaulnes' and sometimes, in a similar spirit, 'Admiral Meaulnes'. He's big in spirit and size – a country boy, at once innocent and oddly blessed, whom François recognizes quickly as a kind of romantic fool, a knight errant in schoolboy overalls. One day, not long after his arrival at the school, Meaulnes mysteriously disappears for three days. When he comes back, suddenly, to the schoolroom, he is at first closed-mouth about his absence. Eventually, though, he confides to the star-struck François the true story of his disappearance.

Lost in a country road in the snow, Meaulnes had wandered into an old château, a 'lost domain', a vast and beautiful country house and garden complete with stables and outbuildings. Far from being abandoned, he discovers, it is weirdly alive with children and young people, who have gathered together there for the wedding of Frantz de Galais, a member of the aristocratic family who seem still to own the run-down place; Meaulnes, for some inexplicable reason, is warmly welcomed by the celebrants, as an old friend. Following a strange Pierrot figure in a dance through the old rooms, he sees a beautiful young girl playing the piano, and the next day sees her again, near a silver lake on the grounds. She turns out to be Yvonne de Galais, Frantz's sister, and Meaulnes instantly falls in love with this frail and lovely girl. But the wedding is mysteriously cancelled, and quickly the entire party abandons the château; Meaulnes is taken away and then roughly deposited back on the highway near Sainte-Agathe.

The rest of the book tells of Meaulnes' attempt to understand what has happened to him – to return to the lost domain, the enchanted castle, to find and win Yvonne and to make the vision which has changed his life part of others' lives, too. He does all of this, with results at once predictably disillusioning and oddly re-enchanting. At the end, he marries Yvonne, but he flees her side – perhaps from guilt, perhaps from a feeling of unworthiness – for another woman, returns and is left with the daughter that she has given him before dying in childbirth. That daughter, we understand from the wiser but not disenchanted François, at the end, will become for Meaulnes the repository of another set of romantic desires.

If the matter is romantic, the treatment of it is often peculiar. At moments, *Le Grand Meaulnes* is a novel that may seem very hard to 'understand' in conventional terms – in places stilted and sentimental seeming; in other places unduly bitter and prematurely soured. Some of this is simply 'French', reflecting the way that French life prolongs adolescence while accelerating sex: at moments the protagonists, having school-yard snowball fights, seem as innocent as the schoolboys we are told they are; at other moments, frequenting fast women and contemplating suicide, as hard cases as Baudelaire or Rimbaud, who was, after all, hardly more than a schoolboy himself.

Even the most Francophile of English-speaking readers is likely to throw up their hands, however, at the sudden roller-coaster turns of the narration, at what Dr Johnson might have called the improbability of the incidents and the extremity of the experiences. In the middle of the book, for instance, after Meaulnes' mysterious sojourn at the château, the reader is

stopped cold by a long incident involving a 'Bohemian' gypsy
and wandering player, who turns out to be Frantz, the son of
the mansion, in disguise – a bit of melodrama that might have
struck even Balzac as far-fetched. In some places the details of
provincial life – the cold and snow, the chestnuts gathered –
are as calmly beautiful as a Sisley, and then we are off into a
fantasy world where long, moony trips to Paris take place with
no visible means of support. Meaulnes himself is never entirely
credible as a character, an odd and empty vessel: at moments
he is a gawky schoolboy, at others as receptive and enchanted
a hero as Dante seeing Beatrice. Although the appeal of Yvonne,
the just glimpsed fairy princess, to him is apparent, *his* instant
appeal to her is very hard to understand.

But if the novel's incidents are improbable, its images are
unforgettable. Hard to enter, it is still harder to abandon. Once
read, *Le Grand Meaulnes* is forever after *seen*. Seen rather than
remembered: I have noticed that most French readers who are
devoted to the book hardly notice or recall, or even brood much
on, the somewhat improbable entanglements of the second part
of the book – any more than Fitzgerald-lovers are likely to
recall the just as sordid and improbable workings of the adulter-
ous affair that leads to Gatsby's shooting. The force of the
imagery – the lost château, the green light – is in both cases so
strong that it blissfully erases the apparent point of the story.

As with any book that lasts, it is the quality of Alain-
Fournier's line that counts, the writing and the imagery and the
wit, and, even where translation cuts off some of the wit, it
doesn't eclipse the images. What readers have recalled, and
cherished, for a century, is the force and simplicity of that
fable – the lost domain of happiness, the abandoned château
brought to life again by the presence of children, the perfect
fairy princess found within it and then pursued at the cost of
common sense and grown-up sexuality – and the way in which
the fable is made credible by what Fournier called his 'nervous,
voluptuous prose' surrounding the dream. By placing what
is essentially a medieval allegory of love in the terms of the
late nineteenth-century realist novel, Fournier, in his one completed book, created a story whose elements – the great, good

place glimpsed in the snow; the girl seen once at a distance, after which life becomes simply an attempt to seek her out again – are part of the way we see and the way we sing now, part of pop culture.

The story is simple, but not without tension. At the heart of *Le Grand Meaulnes* Fournier placed two parallel but counterpointed impulses: the first towards Yvonne, that idealized erotic love, one glimpsed briefly and pursued for ever after, and the second towards the recapture of childhood, evoked by the lost domain where Meaulnes first sees her. The hero, like so many teenagers who will come after him (cf. David in Scott Spencer's *Endless Love*), is torn between the two – between a desire to retake the lost domain, to go back to the good place, and a desire to conquer the beautiful unknown, to get the girl and keep her. Sexual conquest is identified with romantic recuperation; the erotic world leads back to a state of childhood bliss. *Le Grand Meaulnes* is not a coming-of-age story – though the hero marries and even fathers a child – but, like *Catcher in the Rye*, a *refusal*-to-age story, a story of a fight, seen by the narrator as quixotic and noble, to remain within the enchanted world of childhood and at the same time to make that enchanted world continuous with the post-adolescent world of romance and erotic love. *Le Grand Meaulnes* is both a kid who refuses to grow up, Peter Pan in provincial France, and a Parsifal, pursuing his love to the ends of the earth even as she proves to be merely another girl. It is this double movement that gives the book its persistent poetic intensity, even in the midst of its strangely dated and mannered atmospherics.

The intensity of *Le Grand Meaulnes* as imagery and fable seems due in large part to the immediacy of such emotions for the author. Hardly more than a schoolboy himself when he wrote it, Henri-Alban Fournier drew on a set of adolescent erotic experiences – 'crushes' one could call them, fairly enough – that were still close enough to recall, just distant enough to become literature. Fournier was born in 1886 in the Sologne, and his father really was a schoolteacher, though, rather than staying in the village school as he got older, Fournier was sent away to Paris, where he studied at the elite Louis-Le-Grand. In

1903, he went away briefly to a preparatory school in Sceaux, where he met Jacques Rivière, who would later become the founder of the great periodical the *Nouvelle Revue Française*, as well as Fournier's brother-in-law. They exchanged letters on literature for the rest of Fournier's life, and Rivière seems to have encouraged him to become a novelist; in a sense, in his novel Fournier cast himself in the Rivière role, the wise watcher, while actually being a kind of Meaulnes himself.

On 1 June 1905 – Ascension Day – Fournier walked out of an exhibition at the Grand Palais on the Right Bank and, like Freddy in *My Fair Lady*, saw a girl who seemed to be the most beautiful and haunting he had ever seen. He followed her down along the Cours la Reine and across the Seine, until eventually she turned into a house on the Boulevard Saint-Germain. He haunted the street and was eventually rewarded with another glimpse of her, and, after some time had gone by, actually got her into a conversation. Her name, it turned out, was Yvonne de Quievrecourt; she asked him, perhaps flirtatiously, to please never follow her again, as she was engaged. A year later, he went back to the Boulevard to look for her again, but couldn't find her. 'Even if she had been there,' he wrote to Rivière, 'she would not have been the same girl.' (Eventually, he would meet her once again, just before the publication of his book, when she was already the mother of two children.)

The dry-eyed critic is duty-bound to doubt both the truth and the force of the famous anecdotal meeting of Fournier and the original Yvonne – but anyone who has seen a photograph of Yvonne as she was when Fournier saw her will not doubt it for a minute, any more than anyone who recalls seeing a beautiful small girl as a boy will doubt the truth of Dante's feelings about Beatrice. The force of this revelation – of perfect beauty, the one true love, revealed in a glimpse and then lost, or never even held – stayed with him through the next few years, as he did two years of military service and then eventually became an aide to the French statesman Jean Casimir-Périer. When his book was published, it was an instant hit – coming second in that year's Goncourt competition – though it was published, of course, on the brink of catastrophe.

Fournier fought with the French army in that terrible August and died on the front in September. He wasn't yet twenty-eight years old.

But on the other hand, it does not require a faith in Freudian dogma – though, perhaps, it requires an understanding moulded by Freudian insight – to see that in the intricate and seductive fabric of romance as Fournier made it for himself there is some plain sheer fear of sex. We have a sense, reflecting on Fournier's life and art, that what is being fabulized is in part an ambivalence about sexual intercourse; we want to sleep with the girl in a fairy-tale castle and still live there, remain children and get laid at once. The intensity of the romance of childhood and the attempt to marry it, literally, to an erotic-romantic dream glow bright for Fournier with the light of something not quite real, a flare not a fire. Fournier's dream is at once erotically charged and sexually neutered (we can no more imagine the act of sex that produces the child in *Le Grand Meaulnes* than we can imagine Gatsby penetrating Daisy).

This makes the dream, of course, unreal, as dreams must be, and easy to condemn. The rose has her thorns, but eventually there must be little roses. But unreal though it may be, the fantasy remains essential to the novel of adolescence that Fournier invented. The novel of adolescence is very different from the novel of arrival: the novel of arrival taking as its subject the growth of the youth into a man; the novel of adolescence, the rejection of apparent maturity for youth. The great novels of arrival – *Lost Illusions* or *Phineas Finn* or, in another way, *David Copperfield* – are about the romance of growing up. (*Great Expectations* is perhaps, in this as in so many other ways, what professors call a key transitional work: Pip grows up by going back to the heartfelt intuitions and loyalties of his childhood. David grows up; Pip gets back.) Meaulnes' final image in the narrator's mind is of the same big schoolboy with a taste for adventure, not a man tempered by experience; it is the resilience of his romantic nature, not its instruction by experience, that makes him matter to François, and to us.

A line of robust critical counter-reading of *Le Grand Meaulnes* insists, first, that Fournier's epiphany in Paris was

constructed, as most such literary epiphanies so often are, retro-
spectively, in light of the book he later wrote and had
in mind to write. (Real though she was, Beatrice doubtless
shone brighter to Dante once he started writing his poem and
needed her image more.) More important, the movement of the
book can be understood, without too much strain, as really
counter-romantic; Meaulnes, after all, impregnates his fairy,
leaves her to die in childbirth and is left not with the persistence
of his adolescent fantasies but with the physical consequence
of his animal and adult nature: his daughter, not his dream.
(The vengeful fantasy of seeing a woman who has, in real life,
rejected you die while bearing your child is one that Hemingway
indulged in, too, a few years later, in *A Farewell to Arms*, an
adolescent novel pretending to be a war book.) It is possible to
draw a cold, sardonic moral from *Le Grand Meaulnes* just as,
once again; it is possible to draw an anti-idealist and anti-
romantic moral from *The Great Gatsby*. Gatsby, after all, is
not an avatar of the American dreamer, but a victim of the
American dream – a decent man brought down by the false
pursuit of an unworthy object and a sordid and debased and
meretricious set of values; all those shirts are not a worthy
object of a grown man's desire.

Yet to say this is to deny the manifest spell both novels cast.
It is left to ordinary books, of which there are many, to teach
realistic lessons and point out morals; good books cast spells
and cast out demons. If *Le Grand Meaulnes* offers a kind of
day-dream, it has lasted for a very long day. Part of the power
of the novel is that Fournier was among the first to see that this
form of erotic attachment – which in one way is not erotic
attachment at all, but merely adolescent fantasy – can be as
powerful as any other. Fournier's fantasy persists into our own
day as a pattern in books as stirring (and unlike) as *A Separate
Peace* and *The Secret History*. Alain-Fournier was the first to
give form to one of the most powerful of twentieth-century
myths, which continues to illuminate life.

A flare more than a fire . . . with one of those dreadful sym-
metries that are too much for fiction, this novel of a lost,
enchanted world was published just as the lights were about to

go out all over Europe, and real flares would take their place.
Yet perhaps it was the tragedy that awaited poor Meaulnes,
and poor Fournier (as it awaited Wells and the boys in the Peter
Pan house, for that matter), that helped give this day-dream its
resonance. Poor Meaulnes? Poor Fournier? Lucky Meaulnes,
lucky Fournier, perhaps, for all that they foresaw, and for all
that they were not forced to see. There are worse things in the
world to be prisoners of than childhood.

Adam Gopnik

NOTES

1. Havelock Ellis, Introduction to *The Wanderer* (New York: New Directions, 1928).
2. Frank Davison, Translator's Introduction, *Le Grand Meaulnes* (Harmondsworth: Penguin, 1966).

A Note on the Translation

Translators of Alain-Fournier's novel have come across several difficulties, starting with the title. 'Le Grand Meaulnes' is both the title of the book and the name given to its central character, the schoolboy whose fellows are impressed by his presence and his height: *grand* can mean 'tall' as well as 'great'. Some, like the translator of the previous version in Penguin Classics, decided to skirt round the problem by keeping the French title, with an alternative, 'The Lost Domain', as a subtitle. Another translator tried 'The Wanderer' and, as a subtitle, 'The End of Youth'. There are, in fact, more titles of this book in English than there are translations of it.

My own solution is to take a phrase from the novel, 'le domaine perdu', to translate it literally as 'the lost estate' and to use that as the title, taking advantage of the fact that in English the word 'estate' can be used to mean both a property in the country and a period of life ('man's estate', 'youth's estate'): this is a book about the passing of adolescence – and nostalgia for it – in which the central character comes across an isolated country house and estate, has a strange adventure and is later unable to find his way back there. But I do not imagine that everyone will approve of my choice of title. This is a work that has passionate admirers who will defend it against any meddling.

The novelist John Fowles was one such admirer. In his Afterword to Lowell Blair's translation he described Alain-Fournier's novel as a 'poignant and unique masterpiece of alchemized memory'.[1] He also remarked that, in his opinion, the book was 'very nearly untranslatable': 'Just as certain great French wines like Montrachet and Sancerre . . . have defeated all attempts by foreign vineyards to imitate them, so do Fournier's style, tonality, and charm refuse transposition into another language.' He was not, he said, suggesting that Lowell Blair had made a bad job of it, 'but simply underlining the insoluble problems that face the brave man who tried the task'.[2]

Fowles is not the only person to suggest that Alain-Fournier's book is, in many respects, untranslatable. Frank Davison, the translator of the previous Penguin Classics version, has two lengthy footnotes early in the book explaining his difficulties with two crucial problems of translation: the first is the title of the book; the second is the designation of the isolated house and grounds that Meaulnes discovers, for which Fournier uses the French word *domaine*.[3] As Davison points out, both terms, *grand* and *domaine*, here carry overtones and shades of meaning that are not conveyed by any single word in English. As a result, he decided, first, to retain the French expression 'Le Grand Meaulnes' both as the title of the book and as the name of its central character; and secondly, to use the English word *domain*, while describing it as 'a literal, if not exact, translation'.

There are, clearly, difficulties in translating any literary work, but I think that both Fowles and Davison have tended to exaggerate the problems in this case. As I said, *Le Grand Meaulnes* is a novel that has attracted a cult following. For those who read it in French, the language of the book, the atmosphere of the book, the very words of the book acquire a peculiar resonance, an indefinable poetry that seems to exclude any form of re-expression. 'Le domaine mystérieux', 'l'étrange domaine' and, most of all, 'Le Grand Meaulnes' are beyond translation: read Davison's first note, in which he finds not only 'tall' and 'great' in this particular *grand*, but also 'the big, the protective, the almost grown-up . . . in schoolboy parlance, good old Meaulnes' and, 'in retrospect', the image of someone 'daring, noble, tragic, fabulous[4] . . . No wonder he throws up his hands in despair and decides not to translate the phrase at all, using the French word throughout his version.

Yet, as Davison himself admits, some of the meanings evoked

by the words *grand* and *domaine* only attach to the phrase 'in retrospect', after one has read the Alain-Fournier's book. Similarly, for some readers of F. Scott Fitzgerald, the mere phrase 'The Great Gatsby' may have a powerful connotative charge. So if these everyday words, *grand* and *domaine*, have acquired such a charge in the context of this book, to the extent that they appear untranslatable, this must be because they are part of a whole in which the narrative and the language it uses combine to move the reader in a particular way. The words that designate the hero and the place where he had his adventure acquire their poetic charge from the context of the novel, not the other way around.

For that reason, I have decided to translate these expressions into plain English: Meaulnes is 'The Great Meaulnes', the *domaine* is the 'estate'. I assume that my English readers will be able to get over the tendency to call the central character The Great Moan, and that they will realize that a country estate in the Sologne is not the same as one in Hampshire or Shropshire. In short, though, I have decided simply to ignore these two cruxes that seemed such a problem to Davison and to hope that the rest of my translation will, at least to some extent, convey what Fowles calls Fournier's 'very simple, poetic manner'.[5]

In fact, Fowles goes on to mention certain negative characteristics of Fournier's style: his simplicity which is at times naivety, his repetitions . . . He might have added Fournier's fondness for suspension points, as well as for sentences and even paragraphs beginning with 'and'. There is also the typical Fournier sentence, with its subordinate clauses separated by commas, giving a nervous feel to the writing:

> Meaulnes, hiding behind the firs, so that no one could see him, was looking at this clutter when he noticed, on the other side of the yard, just above the seat in a tall charabanc, a half-open window in one of the outbuildings (p. 48)

– one result of which is to give a sense of anxiety, unease, disturbance – words that recur over and again to describe

the feelings of the characters and particularly of The Great
Meaulnes himself.

Every translation represents a series of compromises; no
translation can convey the whole of the original. The most I
can hope is that, for some readers at least, I shall have suggested
a little of the charm of Alain-Fournier's 'untranslatable' novel.

Robin Buss

NOTES

1. Alain-Fournier, *The Wanderer, or The End of Youth (Le Grand
    Meaulnes)*, translated by Lowell Blair with an Afterword by John
    Fowles, Signet Classic, New American Library, 1971, p. 223.
2. Ibid., pp. 221–2.
3. Alain-Fournier, *Le Grand Meaulnes*, translated by Frank
    Davison, Penguin Books, 1966, pp. 18 and 47. This translation
    was originally published by Oxford University Press in 1959.
4. Davison, *Le Grand Meaulnes*, p. 18.
5. Fowles, Afterword to *The Wanderer*, p. 221.

To my sister, Isabelle

PART ONE

I

THE BOARDER

He came to our place one Sunday in November 189–.

I still say 'our place', even though the house no longer belongs to us. It will soon be fifteen years since we left the neighbourhood, and we shall certainly never go back.

We lived on the premises of Sainte-Agathe upper school. My father (like the other pupils, I called him 'Monsieur Seurel') was in charge of both the upper school, where they studied for the teaching certificate, and the middle school. My mother took the junior class.[1]

A long red house, with five glazed doors shrouded in Virginia creeper, at the far end of the little town; a huge courtyard with shelters and washing places which opened at the front towards the village through a large gateway; on the north side, the road beyond a little barred gate leading to the railway station, three kilometres away; to the south and at the back, fields, gardens and meadows, with the outskirts of town beyond them ... There you have a sketch plan of the dwelling in which the most poignant and anguished days of my life were spent, the dwelling where our adventures ebbed and flowed, breaking like waves on a solitary rock ...

The transfer lottery – a decision by a school inspector or a departmental préfet[2] – had brought us there. One day, towards the end of the holidays, long ago, a peasant's cart, going on ahead of our goods and chattels, set my mother and me down in front of the little rusty gate. Some kids who had been stealing peaches from the garden fled silently through gaps in the hedge. My mother, whom we called 'Millie', and who was the most methodical housewife that I have ever known, went directly into the rooms full of dusty straw and immediately announced in despair – as she did at every move we made – that our furniture would never fit into such a badly designed house. She came out to confide her troubles in me and, as she spoke, gently wiped my little face, blackened by the journey. Then she went back to make an inventory of all the doorways and windows that would have to be replaced if the quarters were to be made habitable ... And I, meanwhile, under a large straw hat with ribbons on it, stayed back on the gravel of this unfamiliar courtyard, waiting, ferreting around in a tentative way by the well and under the shed.

At least, this is how I imagine our arrival today; because whenever I try to recapture the distant memory of that first evening, waiting in our courtyard at Sainte-Agathe, what I remember are, in fact, other times of waiting, and I see myself with both hands resting on the bars of the gate, anxiously looking out for someone coming down the main street. And if I try to visualize the first night that I had to spend in my garret, between the first-floor storerooms, what I recall are actually other nights: I am no longer alone in the room; a great, restless, friendly shadow wanders back and forth along the wall. This whole, peaceful landscape – the school, Old Martin's field with its three walnut trees and the garden, filled every day from four o'clock onwards by visiting women – is forever enlivened and transformed in my memory by the presence of the person who caused such an upheaval in our adolescent years and who, even after he had gone, did not leave us in peace.

Yet we had already been there for ten years when Meaulnes came.

I was fifteen. It was a cold Sunday in November, the first day of autumn, suggesting the winter to come. All day, Millie had been waiting for a carriage from the station that was to bring her a hat for the cold weather. In the morning, she missed Mass, and I, sitting in the choir with the other children, had looked anxiously towards the bell tower, right up to the sermon, expecting to see her come in with her new hat.

In the afternoon, I had to go to Vespers by myself.

'In any case,' she said, to cheer me up, brushing my child's outfit with her hand, 'even if the hat had arrived, I would certainly have had to devote Sunday to adjusting it.'

In winter, that was how we often spent our Sundays. In the morning, my father would set off for some distant pond shrouded in mist, to fish for pike from a boat, and my mother, retiring until nightfall to her dark bedroom, would darn her simple clothes. She shut herself up in that way because she was afraid that someone or other, one of her friends as poor as she was, and as proud, might catch her at it. So, after Vespers, I would wait in the cold dining room, reading, until she opened the door to show me how the clothes looked on her.

That particular Sunday, an event in front of the church kept me outside after the service. The children had gathered to watch a christening in the porch. On the town square, several men, dressed in their firemen's jackets, had formed columns and were stamping their feet in the cold as they listened to Boujardon, the fire chief, getting entangled in the complexities of drill . . .

The baptismal bell stopped suddenly like a peal of festive bells that had mistaken the time and place. Boujardon and his men, their weapons slung across their backs, were jogging away with the fire-engine, and I saw them vanish round the corner followed by four silent boys whose thick soles crushed the twigs on the frosty road down which I did not dare follow them.

The only life left in the village was in the Café Daniel, where you could hear the customers' muffled voices rise and fall. As for me, hugging the wall of the great courtyard that separated our house from the village, I came to the little iron gateway, a little anxious at arriving late.

It was half open and I saw at once that something unusual was afoot.

At the dining-room door – the nearest of the five glazed doors opening on to the courtyard – a woman with grey hair was leaning forward and trying to peer through the curtains. She was small, and wearing an old-fashioned black-velvet bonnet. She had a sharp, thin face, now looking worn with anxiety. I am not sure what premonition made me stop on the first step in front of the gate when I saw her.

'Where has he gone? Oh, my God!' she was muttering. 'He

was with me just now. He has already been all round the house.
Perhaps he has run away.'

And between each sentence she tapped three times on the
window, so lightly that you could hardly hear it.

No one came to open to the unknown visitor. No doubt,
Millie had got her hat from the station and was shut in the red
room, oblivious to everything, in front of a bed strewn with old
ribbons and flattened feathers, sewing, unsewing and remaking
her poor hat ... And, sure enough, when I did come into
the dining room with the visitor right behind me, my mother
appeared, both hands holding lengths of brass wire, with ribbons and feathers on her head, not yet quite assembled. She
smiled, her blue eyes tired from working at close of day, and
told me:

'Look! I was waiting to show you ...'

Then, seeing the woman sitting in the large armchair at the
back of the room, she stopped in embarrassment and quickly
took off her hat which, for the remainder of what followed,
she held pressed to her bosom, like a nest turned over in the
crook of her right arm.

The woman in the bonnet, who was hugging an umbrella
and a leather handbag between her knees, began to explain,
gently nodding and making a polite clicking sound with her
tongue. She had fully regained her composure and even,
when she started to talk about her son, acquired a superior,
mysterious air that intrigued us.

They had come together by car from La Ferté-d'Angillon,
which was fourteen kilometres from Sainte-Agathe. A widow –
and, as she gave us to understand, very rich – she had lost the
younger of her two children, Antoine, who had died one day
on coming home from school, after bathing with his brother in
an unhealthy pond. She had decided to give us the elder boy,
Augustin, as a boarder in the upper school.

At once, she began to sing the praises of this new boy she
was bringing us. I no longer recognized the grey-haired woman
I had seen bending over by the door a minute earlier, with the
imploring, fraught look of a mother hen which has lost the wild
one of her brood.

The admiring account that she gave us of her son was quite surprising: he loved to please her and would sometimes walk for miles along the banks of the river, barefoot, to find moorhens' and wild ducks' eggs for her hidden among the reeds . . . He also set snares for birds and a few nights ago had found a pheasant in the woods, caught by the neck.

I gave Millie a look of astonishment: I would hardly dare go home if I had a tear in my smock.

But my mother was not listening. In fact, she motioned to the lady to keep quiet and, carefully putting her 'nest' down on the table, got up silently as though trying to surprise someone.

Above our heads, in a storeroom piled high with the scorched fireworks from the last Fourteenth of July,[3] a stranger was walking backwards and forwards, with a confident step, shaking the ceiling and then moving on through the vast, murky lofts on the floor above, the sound finally fading as he reached the disused assistant teachers' rooms where we kept drying lime leaves and ripening apples.

'I heard that noise just now in the downstairs rooms,' said Millie, in a low voice. 'I thought it was you, François – that you'd come home.'

No one spoke. All three of us were standing, with hearts beating, when the door from the loft leading to the kitchen staircase opened and someone came down the stairs, walked across the kitchen and stood in the dark doorway of the dining room.

'Is that you, Augustin?' the lady asked.

He was a tall boy of around seventeen. All I could see of him at first, in the evening light, were the peasant's felt hat pushed back on his head and the black smock with a belt around it, like schoolboys wear. I could also see that he was smiling . . .

He noticed me and, before anyone could ask him anything, said:

'Are you coming into the yard?'

I hesitated for a moment. Then, as Millie didn't stop me, I took my cap and went over to him. We left through the kitchen door and crossed over to the shelter, which was already in darkness. As we went along, in the last of the daylight,

I examined his angular features, his straight nose and the down on his upper lip.

'Look,' he said. 'I found this in your attic. Have you never looked there?'

He had a little wheel of blackened wood in his hand, with a chain of tattered rockets running round it: it must have been the Catherine wheel from the Fourteenth of July fireworks.

'Two of them haven't gone off, so we can still light them,' he said calmly, like someone who expected something better to turn up later.

He threw his hat down, and I saw that he had a peasant's close-cropped hair. He showed me the two rockets with their bits of paper fuse that had been cut, blackened, then abandoned by the flames. He planted the stick of the firework in the sand and – to my great astonishment, because we were strictly forbidden such things – took a box of matches out of his pocket. Cautiously bending down, he lit the touchpaper. Then, taking my hand, he pulled me sharply back.

A moment later, my mother came out on the doorstep with Meaulnes' mother, after discussing and settling his boarding fee and saw, under the shelter, two sprays of red and white stars bursting – and for a second she could see me, standing in the magical light, holding the hand of the tall, newly arrived boy and not flinching . . .

Once again, she did not dare say anything.

That evening, there was a silent companion to dinner round the family table, who ate, head bowed, untroubled by the looks that the three of us turned on him.

AFTER FOUR O'CLOCK

Until then, I had seldom been to play in the street with the town children: I had suffered from a problem with my hip up to that year, 189–, and this had left me timid and withdrawn. I can still see myself running behind the nimbler boys in the streets round our house, pitifully hopping on one leg.

So they would hardly let me go out. I remember that Millie, who was very proud of me, more than once dragged me back home, under a hail of blows, when she had come across me hobbling around with the urchins from the village.

The arrival of Augustin Meaulnes, coinciding with my being cured of the disability, was the start of a new life.

Before that, when lessons ended, at four o'clock, a long, lonely evening would begin for me. My father took the fire from the stove in the classroom to the fireplace in our dining room, and the last stragglers would leave the now cold school along with the billowing wisps of smoke. There were still some games and chases round the yard. Then night would fall, and the two pupils who had been sweeping the classroom looked for their capes and hoods in the shelter and hurried off, their baskets on their arms, leaving the main gate wide open . . .

After that, as long as there was any light, I would stay in the part of the building that comprised the town hall, shut up in the records room full of its dead flies and flapping posters, and read, sitting on an old weighing-machine near a window overlooking the garden.

When it was dark and the dogs on the farm next door would start to bark and the window of our little kitchen lit up, I would finally go home. My mother would have started to make dinner.

I would go up three steps on the staircase to the loft and sit there, silently, my head pressed against the cold banisters, watching her as she lit the fire in the narrow kitchen by the flickering light of a candle.

But someone came and swept me away from all these tranquil, childish joys – someone who snuffed out the candle that had cast its light on my mother's gentle face as she prepared our evening meal; someone who turned off the light around which we gathered as a happy family on those evenings, after my father had closed the wooden shutters across the French windows. And that someone was Augustin Meaulnes, soon to be called by the other pupils 'The Great Meaulnes' – '*Le Grand Meaulnes*'.

As soon as he came to board with us, that is, from the first days of December, school was no longer empty in the evening, after four. Despite the cold coming through the open door and the shouts of the sweepers with their buckets of water, there were always some twenty of the older boys after school in the classroom, boys from the country as well as from the village, pressing around Meaulnes. And there were long debates and endless arguments, and I would slip into the group, with a feeling of pleasurable anxiety.

Meaulnes would say nothing, though it was always for his benefit that one of the more talkative would push to the front of the crowd and, calling on each of his companions in turn to bear witness, which they noisily did, tell some lengthy tale of marauding and pillage that the others followed open-mouthed, with silent laughter.

Sitting, swinging his legs, on a desk, Meaulnes pondered. At the best moment in the story, he too would laugh, but softly, as though saving his bursts of laughter for a better story that he alone knew. Then as night fell and the classroom windows no longer gave enough light to the jumbled mass of boys, Meaulnes would suddenly stand up and shout, 'Come on, off we go!' as he walked through the crowd pressing around him.

Then they would all follow, and you could hear them shouting in the darkness from the far end of town . . .

*

I now used to go with them sometimes. With Meaulnes, I would go to the doors of the village stables where the cows were being milked. We would go into shops and, out of the darkness, between two creaks of his loom, the weaver would say, 'Here are the students!'

Usually, at dinner time, we would be not far from school, with Desnoues, the wheelwright, who was also a farrier. His workshop used to be an inn, with big, double doors that we left open. From the street, you could hear the bellows of the forge squeaking and, by the light of the fire, in this murky, clanging place, you could sometimes make out countryfolk who had stopped their carts to chat for a while; or occasionally a schoolboy like ourselves, leaning against a door, watching and saying nothing.

And that is where it all began, roughly a week before Christmas.

'I USED TO TAKE GREAT DELIGHT IN STANDING AT A BASKET-MAKER'S'

The rain had been falling all day long and only stopped in the evening. It had been a deadly boring day. At break times, no one went out, and you could hear my father, Monsieur Seurel, in the classroom constantly shouting: 'Now then, boys, stop stomping around with those clogs!'

After the last break of the day – or, as we said, after the last 'quarter hour' – Monsieur Seurel, who for some time had been striding thoughtfully up and down, stopped, banged his ruler down on the table to quell the incoherent buzz that comes at the end of a boring class and, in the expectant silence that followed, asked, 'Who's coming to the station in the trap tomorrow with François, to meet Monsieur and Madame Charpentier?'

These were my grandparents: Grandfather Charpentier, the man with the big grey wool burnous, a retired forest warden who wore a rabbit fur hat which he called his *képi*.[4] The small boys knew him well. In the morning, he would wash his face by drawing a bucket of water from the well and sploshing around in it like an old soldier, giving his goatee beard a splash or two. A circle of children would watch him, with their hands behind their backs, respectfully curious. They also knew Grandmother Charpentier, a little peasant woman with a knitted bonnet, because Millie would take her at least once into every infants' class.

Every year, a few days before Christmas, we would go and fetch them from the station on the 4.02 train. In coming to see us, they would have crossed the whole *département*, laden with bundles of chestnuts and Christmas fare wrapped in towels. As soon as the pair of them were over the threshold of the house, warmly clad and smiling, slightly bewildered, all the doors would be closed behind them and a whole week of fun would begin . . .

Someone was needed to drive the trap with me and bring them home, someone reliable who would not tip us into the ditch and also someone fairly easy-going, because Grandfather Charpentier swore freely, and my grandmother was quite a chatterbox.

A dozen voices answered Monsieur Seurel's question, all shouting together, 'Meaulnes! The Great Meaulnes!'

But Monsieur Seurel pretended not to hear.

So some shouted, 'Fromentin!' And others, 'Jasmin Delouche!'

The youngest of the Roy lads, who would gallop across the fields on a sow, yelled, 'Me! Me!' in a piercing voice.

Dutremblay and Moucheboeuf just raised their hands shyly.

I should have liked it to be Meaulnes. This little trip in the donkey cart would have become a more significant event. He wanted it, too, but he affected a disdainful silence. All the big boys were sitting, as he was, on the table, backwards with their feet on the benches, as we used to at times of special leave or celebration. Coffin, his blue smock raised and tucked into his belt, was clasping the iron pillar that supported the ceiling of the classroom and began to climb up it to show how happy he was. But Monsieur Seurel brought us all down to earth by announcing, 'Right! It will be Moucheboeuf.' And we went back to our places in silence.

At four o'clock, in the great icy courtyard, streaked with gullies from the rain, I was alone with Meaulnes. Neither of us spoke as we looked out at the gleaming village drying in gusts of wind. It was not long before little Coffin, with his hood up and a slice of bread in his hand, emerged from his house and, hugging the wall, arrived, whistling, at the wheelwright's door. Meaulnes opened the gate, called out to him, and, shortly after that, all three of us were sitting in the hot, red workshop where, from time to time, brisk gusts of ice-cold wind would blow:

there were Coffin and I, sitting by the forge, our muddy boots in the white wood shavings, and Meaulnes, with his hands in his pockets, saying nothing and leaning against the front door. Out in the street, now and then, a village woman would go by, head down against the wind, coming back from the butcher's, and we looked up to see who it was.

No one said a word. The farrier and his man, the latter on the bellows while the farrier struck the hot iron, cast long, sharp shadows on the wall. I remember that evening as one of the greatest of my adolescent years. I felt a mixture of pleasure and anxiety, afraid that my companion might deprive me of the meagre joy of going to the station in the trap and, yet, at the same time, without daring to admit it even to myself, waiting for him to perform some spectacular feat that would alter all the arrangements . . .

From time to time, there would be a momentary halt in the peaceful, regular work of the forge. The farrier would let his hammer ring clear on the anvil with brief, sharp blows, then bring the piece of iron that he had worked close to his leather apron to examine it. And, looking up, he would say to us, 'Well, lads, how's it going?' – as a chance to catch his breath.

His assistant would stay with his raised hand on the chain of the bellows, put his left fist on his hip and look at us, laughing.

Then the heavy, noisy thumping would resume.

It was in one of these breaks that we saw Millie through the double door, wearing a tight scarf against the strong wind and going by, carrying lots of small parcels.

The farrier asked, 'Is Monsieur Charpentier coming soon?'

'Tomorrow, with my grandmother,' I replied. 'I'm going to meet them in the trap from the 4.02 train.'

'In Fromentin's trap, is it?'

I answered, 'No, Old Martin's.'

'Well, now, you'll never be back.' And both of them, the farrier and his man, began to laugh.

For the sake of saying something, the assistant said, slowly, 'With Fromentin's mare, you could have fetched them from Vierzon. The train stops there for an hour. It's fifteen kilometres. You'd have been home before Old Martin's ass was even harnessed up.'

'Now that,' said the farrier, 'is a mare that covers some ground.'

'And I'm sure Fromentin would be happy to lend it.'

That's where the conversation stopped. The forge was once more a place full of sparks and noise where everyone thought his own thoughts.

But when the time came to leave, and I got up to signal to Meaulnes, he didn't notice me at first. Leaning back against the door, head bowed, he seemed to be thinking deeply about what had been said. Seeing him there, lost in meditation and peering, as though through a deep bank of fog, at these people intent on their work, I suddenly thought of the picture in *Robinson Crusoe* where you see the English boy, before his great adventure, 'standing at a basket-maker's'.[5]

I have often thought of it since.

IV

ESCAPE

At one o'clock in the afternoon on the following day, the classroom of the Upper School is as distinct against the frosted landscape as a boat on the surface of the sea. It doesn't smell of brine and sump oil, like a fishing boat, but of grilled herrings on the stove and the scorched wool of the boys who have come in and warmed themselves too close to the fire.

The end of the year is getting closer and the essay books have been handed round. While M. Seurel is writing up the questions on the blackboard, there is a partial silence, broken by whispered conversations, little, stifled cries and sentences cut short which are meant to terrify the boy next to the speaker: 'Sir, sir! So-and-so has . . .'

As he writes out his questions, M. Seurel is thinking of other things. From time to time, he turns round, giving all of us a look that is at the same time stern and vague. The furtive whispering and shuffling stop dead for a moment, then resume, subdued at first, like a gathering drone.

I alone am silent in the midst of all this agitation. As I am at the end of a table in the section reserved for the youngest in the class, near the large windows, I have only to sit up a little to see the garden, with the stream at the bottom, and then the fields.

From time to time, I stand on tiptoe, looking anxiously towards the farm of La Belle-Etoile. As soon as the class started, I noticed that Meaulnes had not come back after the midday break. The boy who shares his desk must of course have noticed it too. So far he has not said anything, because he has been taken up too much with his work. But as soon as he looks up, the news will spread through the whole room and someone, as usual, will certainly shout out the first words of the sentence: 'Please, sir, Meaulnes . . .'

I know that Meaulnes has gone. Or, to be more precise, I suspect him of having escaped. As soon as lunch was finished, he must have jumped over the little wall and struck out across the fields, over the stream at La Vieille-Planche as far as La Belle-Etoile. He would have asked for the mare to go and fetch Monsieur and Madame Charpentier. He would be getting it harnessed up at that moment.

La Belle-Etoile is a large farm on the side of the hill, over beyond the stream. In summer, it is hidden by elms, by the oaks in the yard and by hedgerows. It stands on a little track that leads, in one direction, to the station road, and in the other to a village. The vast farmhouse, dating from feudal times, is surrounded by high walls with buttresses that rise out of a bed of manure; in June, it vanishes among the leaves, and all that you can know of it from school is the sound of carts rumbling and cowmen shouting as night begins to fall. But today, between the leafless trees, I can look through the window and see the tall, greyish farmyard wall, then the gateway and, between two lengths of hedge, the line of the track, white with frost, running alongside the river and leading to the station road.

So far, nothing is moving in this clear winter landscape. As yet, nothing has changed.

Here, Monsieur Seurel is just finishing writing out the second question. Usually, he gives us three, but what if, by some chance, today, he were to give us only two . . . He would immediately go back to his desk and notice that Meaulnes is not here. Then he would send two boys to look for him in the village, and they would surely find him before the mare was harnessed up.

For a moment, after copying out the second question, Monsieur Seurel lets his tired arm fall. Then, much to my relief, he goes to a new line and starts to write, saying, 'Now this one is child's play!'

Two small black shapes which earlier rose above the wall of La Belle-Etoile have vanished: they must have been the two raised shafts of the trap. I am sure that preparations are being made over there for Meaulnes' departure. Now we have the mare: her head and neck emerge between the posts of the gate, then stop, no doubt while a second seat is being fixed at the back of the trap for the travellers that he claims to be meeting. Finally, the whole team slowly leaves the yard, vanishes for a moment behind the hedge, then proceeds at the same leisurely pace along the length of white track that you can see through a gap in the hedge. It is then that, in the dark shape holding the reins, casually leaning as the peasants do with one elbow on the side of the cart, I recognize my friend Augustin Meaulnes.

Shortly after that, everything disappears behind the hedge. Two men who have remained standing at the gate of La Belle-Etoile, watching the cart leave, are now involved in an increasingly animated discussion. One of them finally puts his hands to his mouth, like a megaphone, and calls out to Meaulnes, then runs a little way towards him along the track. But at that moment, as the little cart slowly reaches the station road and must now be invisible from the little farm track, Meaulnes suddenly changes position. Rising up like a Roman charioteer, with one foot resting on the footplate and shaking the reins with both hands, he urges the animal on at full speed, and in a second has vanished over the brow of the hill. The man on the farm track who was shouting at him starts running again, while the other has set off at full speed over the fields and appears to be coming towards us.

In a short while, at the very moment when Monsieur Seurel has left the board and is rubbing the chalk off his hands, at the very moment when two or three voices are calling from the back of the class: 'Monsieur! Meaulnes has gone!', the man in the blue smock has reached the door, which he suddenly throws open and, from the doorway, raising his hat, asks, 'Excuse me, Monsieur, but did you authorize that boy to request the trap to go to Vierzon and fetch your parents? Because we were starting to wonder . . .'

'Certainly not!' Monsieur Seurel replies.

And instantly there is the most frightful commotion in the room. The first three boys next to the entrance, whose usual task is to chase away the pigs and goats by throwing stones at them when they come into the school yard to munch the alyssum leaves, rush through the door. Outside, the loud crashing of their hobnailed clogs on the flagstones gives way to the dull sound of their footsteps hurrying across the sand in the yard and skidding around the corner at the little gateway opening on to the road. All the rest of the class is crowding around the garden windows, and some have climbed on the tables to get a better view.

Too late: Meaulnes is gone.

'Go to the station with Moucheboeuf even so,' Monsieur Seurel tells me. 'Meaulnes doesn't know the way to Vierzon. He will get lost at the crossroads and never meet the three o'clock train.'

Millie puts her head round the door of the little classroom to ask, 'What on earth's going on?'

In the village street, people have started to gather. The farmworker is still there, stubbornly, not moving, with his hat in his hand, like someone asking for justice.

V

THE CARRIAGE RETURNS

When I had brought my grandparents back from the station and after dinner, seated around the tall fireplace, they were starting to give a detailed account of everything that had happened to them since the last holidays, I soon realized that I was not listening to what they were saying.

The little gate into the courtyard was close to the dining-room door. It would squeak as you opened it. Normally, at nightfall, on our country evenings, I would secretly wait for that squeaking of the gate. It would be followed by the sound of clogs tapping or being wiped on the threshold, and sometimes by whispering, like that of people conferring before they came in. Then a knock. It was a neighbour, or the women teachers, or in any case someone to amuse us in the long evening.

Now, that evening, I was not expecting anything from outside, because all my loved ones were inside the house, yet I was constantly straining my ears for all the sounds of the night and expecting someone to open our door.

My old grandfather, with his shaggy appearance, like a large Gascon shepherd, his two feet fairly and squarely in front of him and his stick between his legs, was there, leaning over to knock out his pipe against his shoe. His kindly, moist eyes agreed with what my grandmother was saying about the journey and her hens and their neighbours and the peasants who had not yet paid the rent for their farms. But I was no longer listening.

I was thinking about the sound of a carriage suddenly stopping in front of the door. Meaulnes would leap down and come in as though nothing had happened. Or he might perhaps go first of all to take the mare back to La Belle-Etoile, and I would shortly hear his footsteps on the road and the opening of the metal gate.

But nothing happened. Grandfather was staring ahead, and his eyelids began to droop as though sleep was coming. Grandmother, a little annoyed, repeated her last remark, which no one had heard.

'Are you worried about that boy?' she asked eventually.

In fact, I had questioned her at the station, but in vain. She had not seen anyone at the Vierzon stop who was like The Great Meaulnes. My friend must have taken a long time on the journey. He had failed. Coming home in the trap. I thought over my disappointment, while my grandmother talked to Moucheboeuf. The little birds were fluttering around the hooves of the donkey as it trotted along the white, frosty road. From time to time, breaking the deep peace of a wintry afternoon, came the distant shout of a shepherdess or a boy calling his friend from one copse to another. And every time, these long cries over the empty downs made me shudder, as though I had heard the voice of Meaulnes in the distance inviting me to follow him.

While I was going over all this in my head, bedtime arrived. Grandfather had already gone to the red room, the bed-sitting room, which was damp and cold after being shut up since the previous winter. To make room for him, the lace antimacassars had been removed from the armchairs, the rugs had been taken up and any fragile objects put to one side. He had put his stick on one chair and his boots under another, and just blown out his candle; we were standing saying goodnight and getting ready to go off to our beds when we were silenced by the sound of someone driving into the yard.

It sounded like two vehicles, one following the other, at a slow trot. They slowed still further and finally came to a halt under the dining-room window, which overlooked the road, but couldn't be opened.

My father had got the lamp and, without waiting for a knock, he opened the door, which had already been locked. Then, pushing the metal gate and going up the steps, he held the light above his head to see what was going on.

There were, indeed, two carts which had stopped, the horse of one harnessed to the back of the other. A man jumped down and stood there, hesitating . . .

'Is this the town hall?' he asked, coming over. 'Could you point me to Monsieur Fromentin, the farmer at La Belle-Etoile? I've found his trap and his mare going along without a driver, near the road to Saint-Loup-des-Bois. My lantern showed me his name and address on the metal plate, and, as it was on my way, I brought the trap back here to avoid accidents. But I may tell you it's made me very late.'

We stood there in amazement. My father came across and shone his lamp on the carriage.

'There's no sign of a passenger,' said the man. 'Not even a blanket. The animal's tired, and she's limping a bit.'

I had gone over with the others and was looking at this lost carriage that had come home to us like a wreck from the sea: the first and last wreck, perhaps, of Meaulnes' adventure.

'If it's too far to Fromentin's,' the man said, 'I'll leave the cart with you. I'm already very late, and they must be getting worried at home.' My father agreed; in that way, we could take the carriage back to La Belle-Etoile that same evening without having to explain what had happened. Afterwards we could decide what to tell the people in the village and what to write to Meaulnes' mother . . . And the man whipped up his horse, refusing the glass of wine that we offered him.

From the bedroom where he had relit the candle, my grand-father called out, as we were coming back inside, in silence, while my father took the trap back to the farm: 'So what? Has the wanderer returned?'

The women exchanged a brief look, then said: 'Yes, yes, he went to his mother's. Go to sleep and don't worry.'

'That's good. Just as I thought,' Grandfather said, in a grati-fied voice, before putting out his light and turning over to sleep.

We gave the same explanation to the village people. As for the fugitive's mother, we decided to wait before writing. And we kept our anxiety to ourselves, for three whole days. I can still see my father coming back from the farm at eleven o'clock, his moustache damp from the night air, and talking in a low whisper to Millie, in a voice full of unease and anger.

VI

A KNOCK ON THE
WINDOW PANE

The fourth day was one of the coldest that winter. Early that morning, the first boys to arrive warmed up by making a slide on the ice around the well. They were waiting for the stove to be lit in the school so that they could rush to it.

Inside, there were several of us waiting and watching for the country boys to come. They would arrive still dazzled after marching through landscapes of frost, from seeing frozen ponds and the copses where the hares scamper. There was a smell of hayloft and stable on their smocks that thickened the air of the classroom when they clustered around the glowing stove. And that morning one of them had brought a frozen squirrel in a basket, having found it on his way. I remember how he tried to hang the long, stiff carcass of the creature by its claws from a beam in the playground shelter.

Then the sluggish winter lessons began . . .

Suddenly, a knock on the glass made us look up. Standing behind the door, we saw The Great Meaulnes, shaking the frost off his smock before he came in, holding his head high and with a look of wonderment!

The two pupils on the bench closest to the door rushed to open it. There was a sort of conclave in the doorway which we could not hear, and the fugitive at last made up his mind to come inside.

The rush of cold air from the deserted courtyard, the wisps of straw clinging to Meaulnes' clothes and above all his appearance – like a weary, hungry but marvelling traveller – all of these gave us a strange feeling of pleasure and curiosity.

Monsieur Seurel had stepped down from the little lectern on

its platform, at which he was in the middle of giving us dictation, and Meaulnes walked towards him with an aggressive look. I still remember how fine my older friend looked at that moment, despite his air of exhaustion and his bloodshot eyes, the result no doubt of nights spent in the open.

He walked over to the teacher's desk and said, in the confident tones of someone with a piece of information to impart, 'I'm back, Monsieur.'

'So I see,' Monsieur Seurel replied, examining him curiously. 'Go and sit down in your place.'

The boy turned round towards us, his back a little bent, smiling ironically, as unruly older children do when they are being punished; and, taking a corner of the table in one hand, he slid on to his bench.

'I'll give you a book,' the teacher said – all heads were by now turned in Meaulnes' direction. 'You can read it while your comrades are finishing their dictation.'

So the lesson resumed. From time to time, The Great Meaulnes would turn towards me, then look out of the windows through which you could see the still, fluffy, white garden and the fields empty except for the occasional crow. The atmosphere in the classroom was heavy, next to the glowing stove. My friend, with his head in his hands, was leaning on one elbow to read. Twice I saw his eyelids closing and I thought he was about to fall asleep.

'I'd like to go and lie down, Monsieur,' he said at length, half raising his hand. 'I have not slept for the past three nights.'

'Go on, then!' said Monsieur Seurel, anxious above all to avoid a scene.

All of us were looking up with our pens poised, regretfully watching him go, with his smock crumpled at the back and his muddy shoes.

How slowly the morning passed! At around midday we heard the traveller upstairs in the attic getting ready to come down. At lunchtime, I found him sitting in front of the fire, near my grandparents, who were quite speechless, when the clock was striking twelve and the big boys and little ones who had scattered across the snow-bound school yard started filing past the dining-room door.

All I can remember of that lunch was deep silence and deep embarrassment. Everything was icy: the waxed tablecloth with no linen one covering it, the wine cold in the glasses, the red tiles beneath our feet. It had been decided that, to avoid driving the fugitive to open rebellion, no questions would be asked – and he was taking advantage of this truce to give nothing away.

When at last the dessert was over, we could both go and play around in the yard: a school yard, in the afternoon, with snow trampled away by clogs, a blackened yard where the thawing snow was streaming from the shelter roofs, a yard full of games and loud shouts! Meaulnes and I ran along beside the wall. Already, two or three of our friends from the village had left their games and were running after us, shouting with joy, the slush spurting out under their clogs, hands in their pockets and scarves flying loose. But my friend dashed into the main classroom, where I followed him, and we closed the glazed door just in time to fend off the attack from the boys behind us. There was a sharp, violent din of rattling windows, clogs thumping on the doorstep, and a shove that bent the iron bar across the double doors; but already Meaulnes, risking injury on its broken ring, was turning the little key in the lock.

We used to consider such behaviour very annoying. In summer, those who were left at the door in this way would run round by the garden and often succeed in climbing through one of the windows before they could all be closed. But it was December and everything was already shut tight. For a short time, they pushed at the door and shouted insults at us; then, one by one, they turned around and left, heads hanging, wrapping their scarves around them.

In the classroom, now smelling of chestnuts and coarse wine, there was no one except two cleaners moving the desks. I went over to the stove to get warm and wait at my leisure for the pupils to come back while Augustin Meaulnes was looking through the desks and the drawers in the master's table. It was not long before he found a little atlas and began to peruse it eagerly, standing on the dais with his elbows on the lectern and his head between his hands.

I was just getting ready to go over to him. I would have put my hand on his shoulder, and we would doubtless have traced the route that he had taken together on the map, but suddenly the communicating door from the junior class burst open with a violent shove and Jasmin Delouche, followed by a lad from the village and three others from the country, charged in with a shout of triumph. Clearly one of the windows in the junior classroom had been badly closed, so they must have pushed it open and climbed through.

Jasmin Delouche, though quite small, was one of the oldest boys in the Upper School. He was very jealous of The Great Meaulnes, while at the same time pretending to be his friend. Before our boarder had arrived, he, Jasmin, had been king of the class. He had a pale, rather uninteresting face and slicked-down hair. The only son of Widow Delouche, an innkeeper, he acted grown-up and boasted vainly about things he had overheard among billiard players and vermouth drinkers.

When he burst in, Meaulnes looked up and frowned, shouting at the boys as they pushed and shoved to get to the stove: 'Isn't there any chance of some peace and quiet around here?'

'If you don't like it, you should have stayed where you were,' Jasmin Delouche answered, not looking at Meaulnes and feeling he had the support of his companions.

I think Augustin was in that state of tiredness where anger wells up and suddenly sweeps over you.

'You, for a start,' he said, standing upright and closing his book, quite pale. 'You're leaving.'

The other boy sniggered.

'Huh!' he shouted. 'Just because you ran away for three days, you think you're going to be the boss around here now, do you?'

And, bringing the others into the argument, he added, 'Don't think you're going to chuck us out!'

But Meaulnes was already on top of him. First of all, there was a scuffle in which the sleeves of their smocks were ripped and gave way at the seams. Only Martin, one of the country boys who had come in with Jasmin, intervened: 'Leave him alone!' he said, his nostrils flaring, shaking his head like a bull.

Meaulnes gave a brusque shove and threw him staggering back into the middle of the room, with his arms flailing. Then, grasping Delouche by the neck with one hand and opening the door with the other, he tried to throw him out. Jasmin grabbed hold of the tables, and his hobnailed boots grated on the tiles as his feet were dragged across them, while Martin, recovering his balance, strode across the room, head down and furious. Meaulnes let go of Delouche to take care of the other idiot and might have come off the worse for it, when the door to the private part of the house was half opened and Monsieur Seurel appeared, his head turned towards the kitchen because, as he came in, he was finishing a conversation with someone.

The battle stopped at once. Some of the boys clustered around the stove, with lowered heads, having avoided taking one side or the other right to the end. Meaulnes sat down in his place with the tops of his sleeves unpicked and rumpled. As for Jasmin, still very red in the face, he could be heard, in the few seconds before a banging ruler signalled the start of the lesson, proclaiming loudly: 'He's getting really touchy. He's pretending to be so clever. Perhaps he thinks we don't know where he's been!'

'Idiot! I don't know myself,' Meaulnes retorted, in what was by now a deep silence.

Then, with a shrug of his shoulders, he put his head in his hands and started to learn his lessons.

VII

THE SILK WAISTCOAT

As I said earlier, our room was a large attic under the roof –
half attic and half bedroom. There were windows in the other
rooms for assistant teachers, so there was no telling why this
one was lit by a skylight. It was impossible to close the door
entirely because it jammed on the floor. When we went up
to bed at nights, our hands shading our candles from all the
draughts assailing them in that large house, we would try every
time to close the door and every time had to give up the attempt.
So, around us, throughout the night, we could feel the silence
of the three attic rooms seeping into ours.

That is where Augustin and I got together on the evening of
that same winter's day.

In no time, I had taken off all my clothes and thrown them
in a heap on a chair at the head of my bed, but my friend started
to undress slowly and in silence. I was already in my iron bed
with its cretonne curtains in a vine-leaf pattern, and from there
I watched him.

At times, he would sit down on his low, curtainless bed; at
others, he would get up and walk up and down, still taking off
his clothes. The candle that he had placed on a small wicker
table made by the gypsies cast his gigantic shadow on the wall
as he went back and forth.

Unlike me, he was folding and stacking his school clothes
carefully, but with an absent-minded, sour look. I can see him
laying out his heavy belt on a chair, folding his black smock
(which was extraordinarily creased and stained) over the back
of the same chair and taking off a kind of short, dark-blue
jacket that he wore under this smock, then leaning over with

his back turned towards me as he spread it out on the foot of
his bed . . . But when he stood up and turned towards me I saw
that, instead of the little waistcoat with bronze buttons that we
were meant to wear under our jackets, he had a strange, silk
waistcoat, very open, which fastened at the bottom with a
tight row of little mother-of-pearl buttons. It was a delightfully
quaint garment, of a kind that might have been worn by the
young men who danced with our grandmothers at a ball around
1830.

I can remember the tall, peasant boy as he was then, bare-
headed – because he had carefully placed his cap on top of his
other clothes – his face – so young, so brave and already so
hardened. He resumed his pacing across the room and started
to unbutton this mysterious item from a wardrobe that did not
belong to him. And it was strange to see him, in his shirtsleeves,
with his too short trousers and his muddy shoes, fingering this
aristocratic waistcoat.

As soon as he touched it, he was startled out of his daydream
and looked round at me anxiously. I felt like laughing. He
smiled at the same time as I did, and his face lit up.

'Do tell me about it,' I said quietly, encouraged by this.
'Where did you get it?'

But he immediately stopped smiling. He ran a heavy hand
twice over his short hair and suddenly, like someone giving in
to an irresistible urge, put his jacket back on and buttoned it
down over the elegant waistcoat, then put on his smock. After
that, he paused for a moment, looking sideways at me. Finally,
he sat down on the edge of his bed, took off his shoes, letting
them fall noisily on to the floor and, fully dressed like a soldier
on alert, lay back on his bed and blew out the candle.

Some time in the middle of the night, I woke up with a start.
Meaulnes was standing in the middle of the room with his cap
on, looking for something on the clothes rail – a cape, which
he put on . . . The room was very dark, without even the
glimmer of light that you sometimes get with snow. An icy,
dark wind was blowing in the dead garden and across the roof.

I sat up and said, softly, 'Meaulnes! Are you off again?'

He did not answer; so, quite distraught, I went on: 'Right,

then, I'm coming with you. You must take me.' And I jumped
down from my bed.

He came over, took my arm and, forcing me to sit on the
edge of the bed, he told me, 'I can't take you, François. If I
knew the way properly, you could come with me, but first of
all I have to find it myself on the map, or I won't get there.'

'So you can't go either?'

'That's right, it's no use,' he said, dejectedly. 'Come on, go
back to bed. I promise not to go without you.'

He started to walk up and down the room again. I didn't
dare say anything. He would walk, then stop, then set off again
faster, like someone looking for memories or going over them in
his head, comparing and contrasting, calculating, then suddenly
thinking he has the solution . . . Then, once more, he loses the
thread and starts looking again . . .

This was not the only night when, woken by the sound of his
footsteps, I found him like that, walking up and down the room
and the attics at around one o'clock in the morning – like those
sailors who cannot get used to not doing the night watch and
who, in their houses in Brittany, get up and dress at the
appointed hour to go and keep watch over the night on shore.

Two or three times, in this way, in January and the first
fortnight of February, I was woken from sleep. The Great
Meaulnes was there, upright, fully equipped, his cape over his
shoulders, ready to leave; and every time, on the frontier of this
mysterious country into which he had already once escaped, he
paused, hesitating . . . Just as he was about to lift the latch of
the door to the stairs and slip out through the kitchen door
(which he could have opened easily without my hearing), he
shrank back once more . . . Then through the long hours in
the middle of the night, he would stride feverishly through the
abandoned attics, racking his brains.

Finally, one night, around 15 February, he decided to wake me
himself by gently putting a hand on my shoulder.

It had been a day of upsets. Meaulnes, who had entirely
abandoned all the games of his former friends, had spent his

time during the last break of the day sitting on a bench, entirely
absorbed in drawing up some mysterious little plan by following a route, and making long calculations, on a map of the
département of Cher. There was constant coming and going
between the yard and the classroom. Clogs clattered and boys
chased each other around from one table to the next, leaping
over the benches and the master's platform in a single jump . . .
They knew that it was not a good idea to go up to Meaulnes
when he was working like that, yet towards the end of the
recreation, two or three village lads crept up to him as a dare
and looked over his shoulder. One of them was reckless enough
to push the others on to Meaulnes. He slammed his atlas shut,
hid his sheet of paper and grabbed hold of the last of the three
lads while the other two managed to get away.

The unlucky one was the fractious Giraudat, who started to
whine, tried to kick and was finally thrown out by The Great
Meaulnes, shouting furiously, 'You big coward! I'm not surprised they're all against you and want to pick a fight with you!'
And then a shower of insults, to which we responded, without
exactly knowing what he had been trying to say. I was the one
who shouted loudest, because I had taken Meaulnes' side; from
now on, there was a sort of pact between us. His promise to
take me with him, without telling me as everyone else did that
'I wasn't up to walking', had bound me to him for ever. I
was constantly thinking about his mysterious journey and had
convinced myself that he must have met a girl. Of course, she
would be infinitely more beautiful than any in our village, more
beautiful than Jeanne, whom we used to see in the convent
garden through the keyhole, and more than Madeleine, the
baker's daughter, all pink and blonde. And more than Jenny,
the daughter of the lady of the manor, who was splendid, but
mad and kept indoors all the time. He was surely thinking
about a girl in the night, like the hero of a novel. And I had
decided to pluck up my courage and talk to him about it, next
time he woke me up.

The evening after this latest battle, from four o'clock
onwards, we were both busy bringing the tools in from the
garden – spades and picks that had been used for making holes

– when we heard shouting from the road. It was a gang of young lads and kids, marching four abreast, at the double, just like a well-drilled company of soldiers, under the command of Delouche, Daniel, Giraudat and another boy whom we did not know. They had spotted us and were hooting loudly. So the whole village was against us and they were organizing some military game from which we were excluded.

Meaulnes, without a word, put back in the shed the spade and the pick that he was carrying over his shoulder . . . But, at midnight, I felt his hand on my arm and woke up with a start.

'Get up,' he said. 'We're going.'

'Do you know the road now all the way?'

'I know a good stretch of it. We'll just have to find the rest!' he said, through clenched teeth.

'Listen, Meaulnes,' I said, sitting upright. 'Listen to me. There's only one thing to do and that's for us both to look for it in daylight and, using your plan, find the missing bit of road.'

'But that bit is a very long way away.'

'Well, we can take the trap, this summer, when the days are longer.'

There was a lengthy silence, which meant that he had agreed.

'Since we are both going to try and find the girl that you love, Meaulnes,' I said finally, 'tell me who she is. Talk to me about her.'

He sat down on the foot of my bed. In the darkness, I could see his bent head, his crossed arms and his knees. Then he took a deep breath, like someone who has had a full heart for a long time and who is at last about to share his secret . . .

VIII

THE ADVENTURE

That night, my friend did not tell me all that had happened to him on the road. And even when he did make up his mind to tell me everything, during some days of unhappiness that I shall describe later, it was to remain the great secret of our adolescent years. But today, now it is all over, now that nothing is left but dust

> of so much ill, of so much good,

I can describe his strange adventure.

At half-past one in the afternoon, on the Vierzon road, in that freezing weather, Meaulnes was driving his horse along at a good pace, knowing he was not ahead of time. At first, to amuse himself, he thought only of how surprised we would all be when, at four o'clock, he brought Grandfather and Grandmother Charpentier back in the trap – because, at that moment, this was certainly all he intended.

After a while, as the cold chilled him, he wrapped his legs in a blanket which he had refused at first, but which the people at La Belle-Etoile had insisted on putting into the cart.

At two o'clock, he went through the village of La Motte. He had never before been through a small village like this at school time and was amused to see it so deserted and sleepy. Only a curtain or two, from time to time, lifted to reveal the face of an inquisitive old woman.

Leaving La Motte, he paused at a crossroads just after the schoolhouse and thought he could remember that you had to turn left for Vierzon. There was no one to ask. He roused the mare to a trot on the road which was now narrower and badly surfaced. For a time, it ran beside a wood of fir trees, and at last he met a carter: cupping his hands around his mouth, he asked him if he was on the right road for Vierzon. The mare pulled at its reins and trotted on while the man, who probably didn't understand the question, shouted something, with a vague wave of the hand. Taking a chance, Meaulnes carried on.

All around him, once more, was the vast, frosty plain, featureless and lifeless except for the occasional magpie which flew up, frightened by the cart, and settled a little way off, on the stump of an elm. The traveller had wrapped his large blanket around his shoulders, like a cape. Leaning against one side of the cart, with his legs outstretched, he must have fallen asleep for quite a long while . . .

And then, because of the cold, which was now getting through the blanket, Meaulnes came to his senses and saw that the landscape had changed. No longer were there the distant horizons and great white sky as far as the eye could see, but little fields, still green, with high fences. To right and left, in the ditches, water was running under the ice. Everything suggested that he was coming to a river. And between the high hedges, the road was now just a narrow, rutted lane.

The mare had slowed to a walk some time before. Meaulnes gave her a flick of the whip to speed her up, but she continued to walk on very slowly, and the tall boy, looking to one side over the front of the cart, saw that she was lame in one of her rear legs. He immediately got down, full of anxiety.

'We'll never get to Vierzon in time for the train,' he said, under his breath.

He didn't admit that what really worried him was that he might have taken a wrong turning and that he was no longer on the Vierzon road.

He looked carefully at the animal's hoof and could see no sign of a wound. The mare was quite timid. She raised her leg as soon as Meaulnes touched it and scraped her heavy, clumsy hoof along the ground. Eventually, he realized that she had simply got a stone in her shoe. Being an expert at dealing with animals, he bent down, and tried to take her right hoof in his left hand and put it between his knees, but the trap was in his way. Twice, the mare broke loose and moved ahead a few steps. The running board hit him on the head, and the wheel bruised his knee, but he kept on and in the end managed to control the nervous animal. However, the pebble was so deeply embedded that he had to use his peasant's knife to get it out.

When he had finished and finally looked up, dazed by the blow and with a mist in front of his eyes, he was amazed to see that night was falling . . .

Anyone but Meaulnes would immediately have turned back: that was the only way to avoid getting even more lost. But it occurred to him that by now he must be a long way from La Motte. In addition to that, the mare seemed to have taken a side road while he was asleep. And, in any case, this road must eventually lead to some village or other . . . Add to all that the fact that when this impulsive fellow got up on the running board, while the impatient animal was already tugging at the reins, he was irritated by a growing desire to achieve something and to reach somewhere, despite the obstacles in his path!

He whipped the mare, which shied and set off at a quick trot. It was getting darker. Now, in the sunken lane, there was just room for the cart. From time to time, a dead branch from the hedge got caught in the wheel and broke with a dry snap . . . When it was quite dark, Meaulnes felt a pang as he suddenly thought of the dining room at Sainte-Agathe, where all of us must be gathered at that time. Then he felt anger, then pride – and a profound sense of joy at having, unwittingly, broken free . . .

IX

A PAUSE

Suddenly, the mare drew up, as if it had stumbled against something in the dark. Meaulnes saw her head go down, then up, twice; then she stopped dead, her nostrils to the ground as if she were sniffing something. Around the animal's hooves, you could hear a lapping sound, like running water. There was a stream across the lane. In summer, there must be a ford here, but in this weather the current was so strong that ice had not been able to form, and it would have been dangerous to go on.

Meaulnes pulled gently on the reins to bring the horse back a few steps and, very unsure of what to do, stood up in the cart. This is when he saw, between the branches, a light: it must only have been a few feet away from the lane.

The boy got down from the cart and led the mare back, talking to her, to calm her and stop her from anxiously tossing her head: 'Come now, old girl! Come, now! We won't go any further. We'll soon find out where we've ended up.'

Pushing the half-open gate of a little meadow beside the lane, he led the horse into it. His feet sank into the soft grass. The cart was juddering silently and Meaulnes' head was next to that of the mare: he could feel her warmth and the rasping of her breath. He led her right to the far side of the meadow and put the blanket over her back. Then, parting the branches that lay across the further gate, he once more saw the light, which belonged to an isolated house.

Even so, he had to cross three fields and jump over a deceptive little stream in which he almost landed with both feet. Finally, after a last jump from the top of a bank, he was in the courtyard of a cottage. A pig was grunting in its sty. At the sound of his footsteps on the frozen earth, a dog started to bark furiously.

The top flap of the door was open, and the light that Meaulnes had seen came from a wood fire burning in the fireplace. This was the only light in the room. A woman, sitting inside, got up and came over to the door, not seeming to be very much alarmed. At that moment, the upright clock struck for the half hour at half-past seven.

'Excuse me, my dear lady,' he said, 'but I'm afraid that I've trodden on your chrysanthemums.'

Pausing with a bowl in her hand, she examined him.

'It's so dark in the yard,' she agreed, 'you can easily miss your way.'

There was a silence, during which Meaulnes, still standing, looked at the walls of the room, which were papered with cuttings from magazines, like an inn, and the table, on which there was a man's hat.

'The master isn't here?' he said, sitting down.

'He'll be back soon,' said the woman, more confidently. 'He's gone to fetch some wood.'

'It's not that I need him,' the young man went on, bringing his chair up to the fire. 'We're out hunting and I just came to ask you for a bit of bread.'

The Great Meaulnes knew that with country people, especially in an isolated farmhouse, one had to proceed with considerable discretion, even diplomacy, and most of all to avoid revealing that one was not from the region.

'Bread?' she said. 'We haven't any to give you. The baker comes by every Tuesday, but he didn't come today.'

Augustin, who had briefly hoped that he was somewhere near a village, was alarmed at this.

'The baker from where?' he asked.

'Why, the baker from Le Vieux-Nançay,' the woman replied, in astonishment.

'And just how far is Le Vieux-Nançay from here?' Meaulnes inquired, with growing anxiety.

'By the road, I couldn't rightly tell you, but across country, it's three and a half leagues.'[6]

She started to tell him how her daughter was in service there and how she went by foot to see her on the first Sunday of the month and how her employers . . .

But Meaulnes, who was entirely bewildered by now, interrupted her to ask if Le Vieux-Nançay was the nearest village to there.

'No, that's Les Landes, five kilometres away. But there's no shop there or a baker. There's just a little fair every year on Saint Martin's Day.'

Meaulnes had never heard of Les Landes. He realized that he was so completely lost that it was almost funny. But the woman, who had been busy washing her bowl at the sink, turned round, curious in her turn, and said slowly, looking directly at him: 'Does that mean that you're not from hereabouts, then?'

At that moment an old peasant man appeared at the door with an armful of wood, which he threw down on the tiles. The woman explained to him – very loudly, as though he was deaf – what the young man was looking for.

'Why, that's easy,' he said simply. 'But come in close, Monsieur, you're not getting the fire.'

Shortly after that, both of them were sitting down next to the andirons, with the old man breaking up the wood to put it on the fire and Meaulnes eating a bowl of milk with some bread which they had given him. Our traveller, delighted at finding himself in this humble abode after so many uncertainties, thought that his odd adventure was over: he was already planning how he would come back later with his friends to see these good people. He didn't know that this was just a pause and that his journey would shortly resume.

He soon asked if they could put him back on the road to La Motte. And, reverting bit by bit to the truth, he told them how he and his carriage had been separated from the other hunters and that he was now completely lost.

The man and woman were so insistent that he must stay overnight with them and only leave at daylight that eventually Meaulnes accepted and went out to look for his mare to put her in the stable.

'Look out for the holes on the track,' the man told him.

Meaulnes did not dare admit that he had not come by 'the track'. He almost asked the old man if he would go with him. He hesitated for a moment on the doorstep and was so undecided that he almost reeled backwards. Then he went out into the dark yard.

X

THE SHEEPFOLD

To get his bearings, he climbed up the bank off which he had earlier jumped.

Slowly and with difficulty, as he had done the first time, he made his way through the grass and past puddles and across willow fences, towards the trap, where he had left it at the far end of the meadow. But it was no longer there ... His head pounding, he stood quite still and tried to recognize the sounds of the night, thinking at every moment that he could hear the clinking of the mare's bridle not far off. He went all round the outside of the meadow. The gate was half open, half lying on the ground, as though a cart wheel had gone over it. The mare must have escaped through there on its own.

He walked a little way back up the lane and stumbled over the blanket, which must have fallen off the mare's back. He concluded that it had set off in this direction and started to run after it.

His only thought was a mad urge to recover the carriage at any cost, and this furious determination, which was something like panic, sent all the blood rushing to his head as he ran. From time to time, he stumbled over a rut. When the road bent, he stumbled into the hedges in the total darkness and, already too tired to stop in time, fell on the brambles, with his arms outstretched, tearing his hands to protect his face. Sometimes, he stopped, listened and then set off again. Once, he did think he had heard the sound of a carriage, but it was only a noisy cart going by a long way off, on another road, to the left.

Eventually, his knee, which had been hit by the running board, was hurting so much that he had to stop. It also occurred to him that if the mare had not run off at a gallop, he would have caught her up a long time ago. He also thought that a carriage could not get lost in that way and that someone would be bound to find it. So, at length, he retraced his steps, exhausted, angry and barely able to walk.

Eventually, he thought he had returned to somewhere in the vicinity of where he had started and soon saw the lights of the house which he had been looking for. There was a sunken path through the hedgerow.

'This must be the track that the old man mentioned,' Augustin thought.

He set off along it, happy at no longer having to climb over hedges and banks. After a short while, the path veered off to the left, and the light seemed to move to the right, so that when he got to a crossroads, Meaulnes was in such a hurry to get back to the little cottage that he did not think before taking a path that seemed to be leading directly to it. But he had hardly taken ten steps in that direction than the light vanished, either because it was concealed by a hedge, or because the peasants had grown tired of waiting and closed the shutters. The boy bravely set out across country, walking straight towards the place where the light had been shining a short time earlier. Then, after crossing another fence, he found himself on a new path.

And so it was that Meaulnes lost his way and cut the ties that bound him to the people he had just left.

Depressed and almost exhausted, he decided despairingly to follow this new path right to the end. A hundred yards further on, he came out into a wide, grey meadow with what appeared to be juniper trees spaced out in it and a dark building in a fold of the ground. Meaulnes walked across to it. It turned out to be just a sort of large, abandoned cattle shed or sheepfold. The door creaked as it opened. When the wind drove away the clouds, the moonlight shone through gaps in the walls. Everywhere, there was a musty smell.

Without looking any further, Meaulnes lay down on the damp straw with his head cradled in his hands and his elbows on the ground. After taking off his belt, he curled up in his smock, with his knees up to his belly. It was now that he thought of the mare's blanket that he had left on the road, and felt so miserable and annoyed with himself that he had a strong desire to weep . . .

So he tried to think of other things. Chilled to the bone as he was, he remembered a dream, or rather a vision that he had had as a small child – something he had never mentioned to anyone. One morning, instead of waking up in his room where his trousers and his coats were hanging, he found himself in a long green room with tapestries like forest greenery. The light flowing into this place was so sweet that you felt you could taste it. Beside the nearest window, a girl was sewing, with her back turned to him, as though waiting for him to wake up. He had not had the strength to slip out of bed and walk through this enchanted mansion. He had gone back to sleep. But the next time, he swore that he would get up – tomorrow morning, perhaps!

XI

THE MYSTERIOUS ESTATE

As soon as it was light, he set out again. But his swollen knee hurt, so he had to stop and sit down constantly because the pain was so bad. As it happened, this was the most desolate region of the Sologne, and throughout the morning the only person he saw was a shepherdess in the distance bringing home her flock. Even though he called out to her and tried to run, she vanished before he could make her hear.

Despite that, he went on walking in her direction, but with painful slowness. Not a house nor a soul was to be seen. There was not even the cry of a curlew in the marshes. The December sun shone down on this perfect wilderness, clear and cold.

It was around three o'clock in the afternoon when he finally observed the spire of a grey turret rising above some fir trees.

'An old, abandoned manor house,' he thought. 'Or some deserted pigeon loft.' And he continued on his way, without quickening his pace.

Between two white posts, at the corner of the wood, Meaulnes found the entrance to an avenue and started down it. After a few steps, he paused, astonished, overcome by a feeling that he could not explain. Though he had been walking with the same tired legs and the icy wind was freezing his lips, at times taking his breath away, none the less an extraordinary feeling of contentment raised his spirits, a feeling of perfect, almost intoxicating tranquillity: the certainty that he had reached his goal and that henceforth only happiness awaited him. This was how, in earlier times, he had felt on the eve of the great summer festivals, when at nightfall fir trees were being set up in the village streets and the window of his bedroom was obscured by their branches.

'Such happiness,' he thought, 'because I am coming to this old dovecot, home to owls and draughts!'

He stopped, irritated with himself, wondering if it would not be better to turn back and carry on to the next village. He had been thinking of this for a moment, hanging his head, when he suddenly noticed that the avenue had been swept in wide, regular circles, as they used to do at home for great occasions: the way beneath his feet was like the main street of La Ferté on Assumption Day morning! He could not have been more surprised if he had turned a corner of the avenue to see a crowd of people celebrating and raising the dust in the month of June.

'Can there be some festivity taking place in this wilderness?' he wondered.

He went forward to the first corner and heard voices coming towards him. He hurried off to one side, into the bushy young trees, crouching down and holding his breath. They were children's voices. A group of children came by, quite close to him. One of them, probably a little girl, was talking in such measured and sensible tones that Meaulnes could not help smiling, even though he hardly understood the meaning of her words.

'Only one thing bothers me,' she was saying, 'and that is the matter of the horses. You see, we'll never stop Daniel from riding the big yellowish-grey pony!'

'You'll never stop me,' a boy said, in a jeering tone of voice. 'Aren't we allowed to do just as we like? Even if it means hurting ourselves, if that's what we want.'

And the voices faded into the distance, just as another group of children was approaching.

'Tomorrow morning, if the ice has melted,' a girl was saying, 'we can go out in the boat.'

'But will they let us?' asked another.

'You know we're allowed to organize the festivities just as we want.'

'Suppose Frantz were to come back this evening, with his fiancée?'

'Well, he'll do as we tell him!'

'It must be a wedding,' Augustin thought. 'But are the children in charge here? What a peculiar place!'

He thought he would come out of his hiding-place and ask them where he could find something to eat and drink. He stood up and saw the last group going away. They were three little girls with straight dresses down to their knees. They had pretty hats with ribbons, and each of them had a white feather hanging down behind. One, who had half turned round, was leaning over and listening to her friend as she explained something solemnly with her finger raised.

'I'll only scare them,' Meaulnes thought, looking at his torn peasant's smock and the ill-matching Sainte-Agathe pupil's belt he had round it.

Fearing that the children might meet him as they came back down the avenue, he went on through the trees towards the 'pigeon loft', though without much idea of what he could ask for when he got there. He was soon halted at the edge of the wood by a low, mossy wall. Beyond it, between the wall and the outhouses, there was a long, narrow courtyard full of carriages, like an inn yard on market day. There were vehicles of every kind and shape: slim little four-seaters, with their shafts in the air; charabancs; old-fashioned bourbonnaises with ornamented sides and even old berlins with their windows up.

Meaulnes, hiding behind the firs, so that no one could see him, was looking at this clutter when he noticed, on the other side of the yard, just above the seat in a tall charabanc, a half-open window in one of the outbuildings. Two iron bars of the sort that you find behind stable buildings with their ever-closed shutters had once sealed this opening, but with time they had loosened.

'I'll go in there,' the boy thought. 'And sleep in the hay. Then I'll set off at dawn, without scaring those pretty little girls.'

He climbed over the wall, with difficulty because of his wounded knee, and slipping from one carriage to the next and from the seat of a charabanc to the roof of a berlin, he came level with the window and pushed it open silently, like a door.

He found himself not in a hayloft, but in a huge room with

a low ceiling which must have been a bedroom. In the half-dark of the winter evening, you could see that the table, the mantel-piece and even the armchairs were laden with large vases, valu-ables and old swords. At the far end of the room were curtains, no doubt concealing an alcove.

Meaulnes had closed the window, as much because of the cold as because he was afraid of being seen from outside. He walked across to the curtain, raised it and discovered a large, low bed, covered in old books with bindings trimmed in gold, lutes with broken strings and candlesticks, all left in a jumble. He pushed them to the back of the alcove and lay down on the bed to rest and to think over the strange adventure in which he was caught up.

There was a deep silence over the place. Only occasionally could one hear the high wind of December blowing.

Lying there, Meaulnes even began to wonder if in spite of his strange encounters, in spite of the voices of the children in the avenue, in spite of the carriages piled up against one another, this was not, as he had first thought, merely an old estate abandoned to the loneliness of winter.

Soon after that, he thought that the wind was carrying the sound of some distant music. It was like a memory, full of charm and nostalgia. He recalled how his mother, when young, would sit down at the piano in the afternoon, in their drawing room, and he, saying nothing, behind the door opening into the garden, would listen to her until night fell . . .

'Doesn't that sound as though someone is playing the piano somewhere?' he thought.

But he left the question unanswered: overcome by tiredness, he soon fell asleep.

XII

WELLINGTON'S ROOM

It was dark when he woke up. Chilled through, he turned over and over on the bed, creasing and rolling his black smock under him. A dim light shone on the curtains across the alcove.

Sitting up on the bed, he poked his head out through the curtains. Someone had opened the window, and two green Venetian lanterns had been hung up from the frame.

But no sooner had Meaulnes managed to glance at this than he heard the sound of muffled footsteps on the landing and voices speaking quietly outside. He sprang back into the alcove, and his hobnailed boots clanged against one of the bronze pieces that he had pushed back against the wall. For a moment, he anxiously held his breath. The footsteps drew nearer, and two figures slipped into the room.

'Don't make a noise,' said one of them.

'Why not?' the other replied. 'It's about time he woke up.'

'Have you decked out his room?'

'Yes, like the others'.'

The wind shook the open window.

'Look,' the first voice said. 'You didn't even close the window. The wind has already blown out one of the lanterns. We'll have to relight it.'

'Huh!' said the other, suddenly overcome with idleness and a sense of futility. 'What's the point of all these lights facing out into the country, that is, looking at nothing? There's no one to see them.'

'No one? But people will be coming at times in the night. Over there, on the road, in their carriages they will be very glad to see our lights!'

Meaulnes heard a match strike. The last one to speak, who seemed to be the leader, carried on in a drawling voice, like a Shakespearean gravedigger: 'You're putting green lanterns in Wellington's room. Why not red ones, then? You don't know any more about it than I do!'

Silence.

'Was Wellington American? So, is green an American colour? You're the actor, the one who's travelled; you ought to know.'

'Oh, dearie me!' the 'actor' replied. 'Travelled? Yes I've travelled all right. But I didn't see anything! What can you see from a caravan?'

Meaulnes peered carefully through the curtains.

The one in charge was a fat, bare-headed man, wrapped in a vast overcoat. He was holding a long rod hung with many-coloured lanterns and he was calmly sitting with one leg crossed over the other, watching his friend work.

As for the actor, he cut the most pathetic figure you could imagine. Tall, lean, shivering, with dull, shifty eyes and a moustache hanging over his gap-toothed mouth, suggesting the face of a drowned man dripping on a slab. He was in shirtsleeves, his teeth chattering. Both his words and his gestures indicated the most utter contempt for himself.

After a moment's reflection that was at once sour and comic, he went over to his friend and, spreading both arms wide, addressed him confidentially: 'Do you know what? I don't know why they had to bring in filth like us to wait on people in a fête of this kind! That's what I think . . .'

But without taking any notice of this heartfelt declaration, the fat man went on looking at his work, with his legs crossed, yawned, sniffed quietly, and then, turning his back on the other, went away, with his rod over his shoulder, saying, 'Come on, off we go! It's time to get dressed for dinner.'

The gypsy followed, but as he went past the alcove, he said, bowing and in a sarcastic tone of voice, 'Mr Lie-abed, it's about time you woke up and got dressed as a marquis, even though you're just a skivvy like me. And you will go down to the fancy-dress ball, since that is what these little gentlemen and ladies desire.'

And, with a final bow, he added, in the voice of a hawker at a fairground, 'Our friend Maloyau, member of the kitchen staff, will appear in the role of Harlequin and your humble servant in that of the great Pierrot.'

XIII

THE STRANGE FETE

As soon as they had gone, the boy left his hiding place. His feet were frozen and his joints stiff, but he was rested and his knee appeared to have healed.

'Go down to dinner?' he thought. 'I'll certainly do that. I shall just be a guest whose name everyone has forgotten. In any case, I'm not an intruder here: it's quite clear that M. Maloyau and his friend were expecting me . . .'

Coming out of the total darkness of the alcove, he could see quite clearly in the room, lit as it was by the green lanterns.

The gypsy had 'decked it out'. Coats were hanging from the clothes pegs. On a heavy dressing table with a cracked marble top, they had laid out everything needed to transform into a dandy some lad or other who had spent the previous night in an abandoned sheepfold. On the mantelpiece were matches beside a large torch. But they had forgotten to wax the floor, and Meaulnes could feel sand and grit rolling and grating under his shoes. Once again he had the impression that he was in a long-since abandoned house. Going to the mantelpiece, he almost bumped into a heap of large cartons and small boxes. He reached out his hand, lit the candle, then lifted the lids and leant over to look inside.

There were young men's clothes from long ago: frock coats with high velvet collars, stylish low-cut waistcoats, innumerable white ties and patent leather shoes from the start of the century. He did not dare lay a finger on anything, but after cleaning himself up and shivering as he did so, he put one of the large coats over his schoolboy's smock, turning up the pleated collar, and replaced his hobnailed boots with slender,

highly polished pumps. Then, bare-headed, he got ready to
go down.

He reached the bottom of a wooden staircase, in a dark
corner of the yard, without meeting anyone. The icy breath of
night blew on his face and lifted one corner of his coat.

He took a few steps and, thanks to the faint light in the sky,
he managed at once to grasp the layout of the place. He was in
a little courtyard enclosed by the outbuildings of the main
house. Everything here seemed old and in ruins. The openings
at the foot of the stairways were gaping, because their doors
had long since been removed. Nor had anyone replaced the
glass in some windows, which were just black holes in the
walls. Yet all the buildings had a mysteriously festive air. A sort
of coloured glow shone from the low-ceilinged rooms where
lanterns must also have been lit at the windows opposite the
yard. The ground had been swept and grass pulled up where
it had invaded the cobbles. Finally, if he listened carefully,
Meaulnes thought he could hear some kind of singing, like
children's and girls' voices, some way off in the jumble of
buildings where the wind was shaking the branches across the
pink, green and blue openings of the windows.

He was standing there in his big overcoat, like a hunter,
leaning forward and straining his ears, when an extraordinarily
small young man came out of the nearby building, which had
looked empty.

He had a close-fitting top hat which shone in the dark as
though it had been made of silver, a coat with its collar high
into his hair, a very low-cut waistcoat and trousers with stirrups
. . . This dandy, who was perhaps fifteen years old, was walking
on tiptoe as though lifted up by the elastic under his feet, but
with astonishing rapidity. He greeted Meaulnes as he went past,
without stopping, bowing deeply, automatically, then vanished
into the dark towards the main building – the farm, château or
abbey – the turret of which had guided the boy since early that
afternoon.

After hesitating for a moment, our hero followed behind the
curious little fellow. They went across a kind of great garden
court, passed between flowerbeds, skirted a fish pond with a

fence around it, and a well, then finally reached the door into the main house.

The heavy, wooden door, with a rounded lintel and studded like the door of a presbytery, was half open. The dandy disappeared inside. Meaulnes followed and as soon as he stepped into the corridor, even though he could see no one, he was surrounded by laughter, singing, shouts and the sounds of pursuit.

Another corridor crossed the end of this one at a right angle. Meaulnes was not sure whether to carry on right to the end or to open one of the doors behind which he could hear the sound of voices, when he saw a girl chasing another along the corridor at the end. On his pumps, he ran to look at them and to catch them up. He could hear doors opening and see two fifteen-year-old faces, pink with the cool of evening and the heat of the chase, under their wide-brimmed bonnets with laces, all about to vanish in a sudden burst of light.

For an instant, they twirled round, playfully; their full, light skirts lifted and filled with air. He glimpsed the lace of their long, quaint knickers and then, both together, after this pirouette, they leapt into the room and shut the door behind them.

For a moment, Meaulnes stayed there, dazzled and steadying himself in the dark corridor. Now he was afraid of being discovered: his awkward, uncertain manner would surely mean he would be mistaken for a thief. He was about to retreat towards the door when he once more heard the sound of footsteps in the corridor and children's voices. Two small boys were approaching, talking as they came.

'Is it time for dinner soon?' Meaulnes asked confidently.

'Come with us,' the elder boy said. 'We'll take you.'

And with the trust and need for affection that children have on the eve of a big day, both of them took him by the hand. They were probably two little peasant boys. They had been dressed in their best clothes: three-quarter-length trousers that revealed their coarse woollen stockings and clogs, a little blue velvet jerkin, a cap in the same colour and a white tie.

'Do you know her?' one of the children asked.

'What I know,' said the smaller, who had a round head and innocent eyes, 'is that Mum told me she had a black dress and a ruff and she looked like a pretty pierrot.'

'Who's that?' Meaulnes asked.

'Why, Frantz's fiancée, the one he went to fetch . . .'

Before the young man could say anything in reply, all three of them reached the door of a large hall in which a fine fire was blazing. Trestle tables had been set up, with white table-cloths spread over them, and all sorts of people were dining, ceremoniously.

XIV

THE STRANGE FETE

(continued)

It was the kind of meal, in the great hall with its low ceiling, that is given on the eve of a country wedding to relatives who have come from far away.

The two children had let go of the schoolboy's hand and rushed over to a neighbouring room, where you could hear childish voices and the sound of spoons clattering on plates. Meaulnes, boldly and with complete self-assurance, stepped over a bench and found he was sitting beside two old peasant women. He immediately began to eat greedily, and it was only after a short time that he looked up to examine the other guests and listen to them.

Not that much was being said. These people seemed hardly to know one another. Some must have come from the depths of the country and others from distant towns. Here and there along the tables there were a few old men with sideboards, and others, clean-shaven, who might be old mariners. Beside them were other old people dining who resembled them: the same weatherbeaten faces, the same bright eyes under bushy eyebrows and the same ties as narrow as shoelaces . . . But it was not hard to see that these ones had sailed no further than the parish boundaries, and if they had been tossed and rolled more than a thousand times in wind and rain, it was to make the hard but unhazardous voyage that consists in ploughing a furrow to the end of one's field and then turning the plough around. There were few women to be seen: some old peasants with round faces wrinkled like apples under fluted bonnets.

There was not one of these guests with whom Meaulnes did not feel confident and at ease. Later he explained this feeling, saying: when you have committed some grave, inexcusable sin, you sometimes think, in the midst of great bitterness: 'Even so, there are some people in the world who would excuse me.' One thinks of old people, all-forgiving grandparents who are sure in advance that whatever you do is right and proper. The guests in that room had certainly been chosen from among that breed. And, as for the rest, they were adolescents and children . . .

Meanwhile, next to Meaulnes, the two old ladies were chatting.

'The very best we can hope,' the elder of them was saying, in a comical, high-pitched voice that she was vainly trying to moderate, 'the engaged couple will not arrive tomorrow before three o'clock.'

'Be quiet, or you'll get me angry,' the other replied, in the calmest of tones.

This lady was wearing a knitted bonnet on her head.

'Let's work it out,' the first one carried on, taking no notice. 'One and a half hours by railway from Bourges to Vierzon and seven leagues by car, from Vierzon to here . . .'

The discussion continued. Meaulnes followed every word. Thanks to this gentle little argument, the situation was getting a little clearer: Frantz de Galais, the son of the house – who was a student, or a sailor, or perhaps a midshipman, that was uncertain – had been to Bourges to fetch a girl and marry her. The odd thing was that this boy, who must be very young and capricious, organized everything to suit himself on the estate. He wanted the house that would greet his fiancée to look like a palace decked out for a celebration. And to mark the girl's arrival, he had himself invited these children and jaunty old people. These were the points that emerged from the two ladies' discussion. Everything else, they left in obscurity and constantly reverted to the matter of the engaged couple's return. One of them thought it would be the following morning: the other, the afternoon.

'Poor Moinelle, you're as batty as ever,' the younger one said calmly.

'And you, my poor Adèle, are as stubborn as always. It's four years since I saw you last and you haven't changed,' the other replied, shrugging her shoulders, but in the most untroubled voice.

And so they went on opposing one another without the slightest annoyance. Meaulnes broke in, hoping to learn more: 'Is she as pretty as they say, Frantz's fiancée?'

They looked at him, flabbergasted. No one except Frantz had seen the young woman. He himself, on his way back from Toulon, had met her one evening, distraught, in one of those gardens in Bourges called the Marais. Her father, a weaver, had driven her out of his house. She was extremely pretty, and Frantz had immediately decided to marry her. It was an odd story, but hadn't his father, Monsieur de Galais, and his sister Yvonne always given him whatever he wanted!

Meaulnes was cautiously going to ask further questions when a delightful couple appeared in the doorway: a sixteen-year-old girl with a velvet bodice and flounced skirt, and a young man in a high-collared coat and trousers with elastic stirrups. They danced across the room, in a sort of *pas de deux*. Others followed, then still others ran by, shouting, pursued by a tall, pale-faced pierrot, with sleeves that were too long for him, wearing a black hat and laughing with a toothless mouth. He was running in large, awkward strides as though, at every step, he should have made a jump, and he was waving his long, empty sleeves. The girls were a little afraid of him, but the boys shook his hand, and he seemed to be delighting the children who were chasing after him with shrill cries. As he went past, he looked at Meaulnes through glassy eyes, and the schoolboy thought he recognized M. Maloyau's friend, now clean-shaven: the gypsy who a short while before had been hanging up lanterns.

The meal was over. Everyone got up.

Rounds and farandoles were being arranged in the corridors. From somewhere, there was the sound of music: a minuet . . . Meaulnes, whose head was half hidden in the collar of his overcoat, as though in a ruff, felt he was someone else. Caught up in the game, he too began to chase the great pierrot through the corridors of the château, as though in the wings of a theatre where the performance has spread off the stage. In this way,

for the rest of the night, he mingled with a happy throng in
fanciful attire. At times, he would open a door and find himself
in a room where a magic lantern show was going on and
children were applauding loudly . . . at other times, in a corner
of a drawing room where people were dancing, he got into
conversation with some young beau and quickly gleaned some
information about the costumes that would be worn in the
following days . . .

Eventually, rather anxious at the idea of all this pleasure at
his disposal, constantly fearing that his half-open coat would
reveal his schoolboy's smock, he went to take a few moment's
rest in the quietest and most obscure corner of the house. All
that could be heard there was the muffled sound of a piano.

He went into a silent room, which was a dining room lit by
an overhead lamp. There was a party here, too, but a party for
little children.

Some, sitting on poufs, were leafing through picture books
that were open on their knees. Others were crouching on the
ground beside a chair and, very seriously, spreading pictures
out on it. Still others were by the fire, saying nothing, doing
nothing, but listening to the sound of revelry, far off in the vast
estate.

One door to this dining room was wide open. From the
adjoining room you could hear someone playing the piano.
Meaulnes cautiously put his head round the door. There was a
kind of parlour, in which a woman or girl, with a large brown
cloak over her shoulders and her back to him, was very quietly
playing ditties or part songs. Side by side on the divan six or
seven little boys and girls, lined up like in a picture and obedient
as children are late at night, were listening. Just occasionally
one of them, supporting herself on her hands, would slip off
the divan and go to the dining room. Then one of those who
had had enough of looking at pictures would take her place.

After the party, where everything had been delightful, but
crazy and agitated, and where he had so madly charged after
the big pierrot, Meaulnes now found himself in the midst of
the most tranquil happiness imaginable.

Silently, while the young woman carried on playing, he went

back and sat at the dining-room table where, opening one of the large red books scattered around it, he absent-mindedly began to read.

Almost immediately one of the children who had been on the ground came over, clasped his arm and clambered up on his knee so that he could look at the same time, while another did the same from the other side. Then it was a dream like the one he used to have. For a long time, he could imagine that he was in his own house, married, one fine evening. And that the charming stranger playing the piano, close by, was his wife . . .

XV

THE MEETING

On the following morning, Meaulnes was one of the first to get ready. As he had been advised, he wore a simple black suit, in old-fashioned style: a jacket, tight at the waist with sleeves puffed out on the shoulders, a double-breasted waistcoat, trousers so wide at the bottom that they almost hid his elegant shoes and a top hat.

The courtyard was empty when he came down. He took a few steps, and it was as though he had been transported into a spring day. In fact, this was the mildest morning that winter, and the sun was shining as it does in the first days of April. The frost was melting, and the damp grass shone as though sprinkled with dew. In the trees, several little birds were singing, and now and then a warm breeze touched his face as he walked.

He behaved like a guest who has got up before the master of the house. He went out into the courtyard of the château, thinking that a merry, friendly voice would be calling to him at any moment: 'Up already, Augustin?'

But he walked alone for a long time through the yard and the garden. Over in the main house, nothing was moving, either in the windows or in the turret. However, the double doors in the round wooden entrance had been opened, and a ray of sunlight shone on one of the upper windows as in summer at first light.

For the first time Meaulnes found himself looking at the inside of the grounds in daylight. The remains of a wall separated the run-down garden from the courtyard where sand had recently been spread and raked. At the far end of the outbuildings where he was staying were some stables, an amusing jumble of structures with many corners in which unkempt bushes and untended vines ran wild. Fir woods came right up to the edges of the estate, hiding it from the flat countryside, except to the east, where you could see blue hills covered with rocks and more firs.

For a moment, in the garden, Meaulnes leant against the rickety wooden fence around the fish pond: a little ice remained on the edges, thin and wrinkled like foam. He saw himself reflected in the water, as if leaning against the sky, in his romantic student garb. And he thought he saw another Meaulnes, no longer the schoolboy who had run away in a peasant's cart, but a charming, fabled being, from the pages of the sort of books given as end-of-term prizes . . .

He hurried towards the main house: he was hungry. In the great hall where he had dined the evening before, a peasant woman was laying the tables. As soon as Meaulnes had sat down in front of one of the bowls lined up on the tablecloth, she poured out his coffee, saying: 'You're the first, Monsieur.'

He preferred not to say anything, because he was so afraid that he would suddenly be recognized as a stranger. He just asked when the boat would leave for the morning trip that he had heard about.

'Not for half an hour at least, Monsieur. No one has come down yet,' was her answer.

So he went on looking for the landing-stage, walking round the long manor house with its unequal wings, like a church. When he came round the south wing, he was suddenly confronted by a landscape of reed beds, extending as far as the eye could see. On this side, the lake water came right up to the foot of the walls, and there were little wooden balconies in front of several of the doors, overhanging the lapping waves.

The idler wandered for a while along the bank, which was sanded like a towpath. He was looking with curiosity at the big doors with their dusty windows opening on ramshackle or abandoned rooms, on storage rooms cluttered with wheelbarrows, rusted tools and broken flowerpots, when suddenly, from the far end of the building, he heard footsteps on the gravel.

It was two women, one very old and bent, the other a young woman, blonde, slender, whose delightful attire, after all the fancy dress of the day before, at first seemed astonishing to Meaulnes.

They stopped for a moment to look at the scenery, while Meaulnes – with what he would later feel was quite inappropriate surprise – thought: 'This must be what you'd call an eccentric young woman, perhaps some actress brought here for the party.' Meanwhile the two women walked past him, and Meaulnes stood quite still, watching the girl.

Often, later, when he was falling asleep after trying desperately to recall that lovely, vanished face, he would dream that he saw rows of young women like her going by, one with a hat like hers, another with her slightly stooping manner; yet another had her candid expression, another her slender waist, and another her blue eyes; but none of these was ever the tall young woman.

Meaulnes just had time to see a face, under a heavy mass of blonde hair, with features that were rather small, but drawn with an almost excruciating delicacy. And since she had already gone past him, he looked at what she was wearing, which was the simplest and most demure kind of dress . . .

He was puzzled, wondering whether to follow them, when the girl, half turning in his direction, said to her companion: 'The boat will not be long, now, I suppose?'

Meaulnes followed them. The old lady, bent and trembling, carried on chatting merrily and laughing. The girl gently answered her. And when they came down on to the landing stage, she wore that same innocent and serious look that seemed to mean: 'Who are you? What are you doing here? I don't know you – yet I feel as though I do . . .'

Other guests were now scattered among the trees, waiting. And three pleasure boats pulled up, ready to take them on board. One by one, as the two women went by – they appeared to be the lady of the house and her daughter – the young men ceremonially doffed their hats, and the young women bowed. What a strange morning! What a strange excursion! Despite the winter sun, it felt cold, and the women were wrapping around their necks the then fashionable feather boas.

The old lady stayed behind on the shore and, without knowing how, Meaulnes found himself in the same boat as her daughter. He leant on the rail, one hand clasping his hat as it was battered by the high wind, and was able to look as much as he liked at the girl, who had sat down in a sheltered spot. She looked back at him. She would reply to something said by her friends, smile, then gently turn her blue eyes towards him, with a little bite of her lip.

A great silence reigned on the nearest shore. The boat sailed on, to the gentle sounds of engine and water. It was like being at the heart of summer. They would disembark, apparently, at the fine gardens of some country house. The girl would walk through the grounds beneath a white parasol. Until evening time they would hear the doves coo ... But suddenly, an icy gust of wind reminded the guests at this strange party that it was December.

They pulled up beside a wood of firs. The passengers had to wait a moment on the gangway, pressed against one another, while one of the boatmen unlocked the gate ... What were Meaulnes' feelings afterwards as he recalled this moment when, on the banks of the lake, he had so near to his own the face of this girl – a face that was then lost to him! He had stared at that exquisite profile with every atom of his eyes until they were ready to fill with tears. And he remembered seeing, like a tender secret that she had entrusted to him, a little powder remaining on her cheek ...

Once on dry land, everything happened as though in a dream. While the children were running around shouting with glee, and groups were forming and spreading out among the trees, Meaulnes walked along an avenue with the young woman ten paces ahead of him. Before he had time to think, he was beside her, and said simply, 'You are beautiful.'

But she hurried on, without replying, and set off down a side path. Others ran up, playing among the trees, all going off in whatever direction they wished, obeying only their own whims. The young man deeply regretted what he called his clumsiness, his crassness, his stupidity. He was wandering aimlessly, sure that he would not see the delightful creature again, when suddenly he saw her coming towards him and unable to avoid them meeting on the narrow path. She was holding back the folds of her large cloak with her two ungloved hands. She was wearing open black shoes. Her ankles were so slender that they sometimes bent and you were afraid that they would snap.

This time, he bowed and very quietly said: 'Will you forgive me?'

'I forgive you,' she said, gravely. 'But I must go back to the children, since they are in charge today. Farewell.'

Augustin begged her to stay a moment longer. He spoke to her so awkwardly, but with such confused emotion and agitation in his voice that she slowed down and listened to him.

'I don't even know who you are,' she said at last. She spoke each word in an even tone, with the same emphasis on every one, but saying the last in a softer voice . . . Then her face became impassive again; she bit her lip a little and her blue eyes stared into the distance.

'And I don't know your name, either,' Meaulnes replied.

They were now following a path in the open and, some distance away, could see the guests gathering around a house isolated in the open countryside.

'That's Frantz's house,' the young woman said. 'I have to leave you . . .'

She paused, looking at him for a moment with a smile, and said: 'My name? I'm Mademoiselle Yvonne de Galais . . .'

Then she was gone.

Frantz's house was unoccupied at the time, but Meaulnes discovered that it had been invaded from cellar to attic by a host of guests. In any event, he did not have the time to take a good look at the place: they quickly had a cold lunch that they had brought with them in the boats, which was rather unseasonal, but was doubtless what the children had chosen; then they set off again. Meaulnes went up to Mademoiselle de Galais as soon as he saw her come out and, replying to her earlier remark, he said: 'The name I had given you was prettier.'

'What? What name was that?' she asked, with the same seriousness as before.

But he was afraid that he had said something idiotic and didn't answer.

'My own name is Augustin Meaulnes,' he went on. 'And I'm a student.'

'Ah! You're studying?' she said. And they talked for a little longer. They talked slowly, pleasurably, in a friendly way. Then the young woman's attitude changed. Though now less haughty and less grave, she also seemed more worried. It was as though she were anxious about what Meaulnes might say and was taking fright in advance. She was trembling next to him, like a swallow that has landed for a moment and is already quivering with the urge to take flight again.

'What's the use? What's the use?' she replied softly whenever he suggested anything.

But when at last he dared to ask her permission to come back one day to the beautiful estate, she said simply, 'I'll be expecting you.'

They came in sight of the landing-stage. She paused, suddenly, and said pensively: 'We're two children. We've been foolish. This time we mustn't get into the same boat. Farewell, don't follow me.'

For a while, Meaulnes stood there, saying nothing; then he began to walk after her. At this, the young women, far ahead of him and about to be swallowed up again by the crowd of guests, stopped and, turning back towards him, gave him for the first time a long stare. Was it a last farewell gesture? Was she forbidding him to accompany her? Or did she perhaps have something else that she wanted to tell him?

As soon as they were back, pony races began behind the farm in a long sloping meadow. This was the last event in the party. There was every reason to suppose that the engaged couple would arrive in time to take part, and it would be Frantz who took charge of everything.

However, they had to start without him. The boys in jockey
costumes and the girls dressed as grooms brought out, the first,
frisky ponies with ribbons, and the second, docile, very old
horses. As they came there were shouts and childish laughter,
wagers and long peals of bells: it was as though you had been
transported on to the green, close-cropped grass of some minia-
ture racetrack.

Meaulnes recognized Daniel and the little girls with the
feathered hats whom he had heard the evening before in the
avenue under the trees . . . He couldn't follow the rest of what
was going on, because he was so eager to spot the elegant
hat with the roses and the long brown coat among the crowd.
But Mademoiselle de Galais did not appear. He was still looking
for her when a succession of ringing bells and shouts of glee
announced the end of the races. One little girl on an old white
mare had won the event. She rode past in triumph with the
plumes on her hat dancing in the wind.

Then suddenly it all went quiet. The games were over, and
Frantz had not returned. They stopped for a moment and held
an uneasy debate. At last, they went off in groups back to the
house, to await the couple's return in a mood of silence and
uncertainty.

XVI

FRANTZ DE GALAIS

The racing had finished too early. It was half-past four and still light when Meaulnes got back to his room, his head full of the events of that extraordinary day. He sat down in front of the table, with nothing to do, waiting for dinner and the party that was to follow.

The high wind of the first evening was blowing again. You could hear it roaring like a torrent or whistling with the insistent hiss of a waterfall. The hood over the fireplace rattled occasionally.

This was the first time that Meaulnes had experienced the slight feeling of anxiety that comes over you at the end of a too happy day. For a moment, he thought of lighting a fire, but tried in vain to raise the rusted hood. Then he began to arrange the room: he hung his fine clothes in the wardrobe and set up the overturned chairs along the wall, as though trying to get everything ready for a long stay.

At the same time, aware that he should be ready to leave at short notice, he carefully folded his smock and other school things on the back of a chair, like travelling clothes. Under the chair, he put his hobnailed boots, still caked in mud.

Then he sat down again and, feeling calmer, looked around the home that he had arranged for himself.

From time to time, a drop of rain streaked across the window overlooking the yard with the carriages and the fir wood. More at peace now that he had laid out his apartment, the boy felt entirely happy. He was there, mysterious, a stranger, in the midst of this strange world, in the room that he had chosen. What he had far exceeded his expectations. Now it was enough, to lift his heart, for him to recall that young woman's face, in the wind, turning towards him . . .

While he was daydreaming in this way, night fell, and he did not even think of lighting the torches. A gust of wind blew open the door of the adjoining room, which also overlooked the courtyard and the carriages. Meaulnes was about to close it when he noticed a light in this other room, like a candle burning on a table. He put his head round the door. Someone had come in, no doubt through the window, and was walking up and down with silent steps. As far as he could see, it was a very young man. Bare-headed and with a travelling cape thrown over his shoulders, he was walking endlessly, as though driven wild by some unbearable pain. The wind, blowing through the window which he had left wide open, was lifting his cape, and whenever he walked past the light, you could see the glint of gilded buttons on his elegant frock coat.

He was whistling something through his teeth – a sort of sea shanty of the kind that sailors and loose women sing to make merry in harbour bars . . .

Briefly, in the course of his nervous pacing, he stopped and leant over the table, looked in a box and took several sheets of paper out of it. Meaulnes, in the light of the lamp, saw the profile of a very aquiline face, clean-shaven, under a mass of hair parted on one side. The man had stopped whistling. Very pale and with half-open lips, he seemed breathless, as though he had received a sharp blow to the heart.

Meaulnes hesitated: would it be discreet to retire, or should he go forward and put a friendly hand on his shoulder and talk to him? But the other man looked up and saw him. He examined him for a moment, then, with no sign of surprise, came over and, steadying his voice, said: 'Monsieur, I don't know you. But I am pleased to see you. Since you are here, you are the one to whom I shall explain . . . There!'

He appeared totally distraught. When he had uttered the word 'There!' he grasped Meaulnes by the lapels, as through trying to keep his attention. Then he turned towards the window, apparently thinking about what he was going to say, and blinking – Meaulnes realized that he he had a strong urge to weep.

Suddenly, he fought back all that childish unhappiness and, still staring at the window, went on in a strained voice, 'Well, there it is, it's over. The party's over. You can go down and tell them. I've returned alone. My fiancée won't be coming. Whether from principle, or fear, or lack of trust . . . In any case, Monsieur, I'll tell you how it is . . .'

But he couldn't go on. His whole face crumpled. He explained nothing. Suddenly turning away, he went across the room in the dark to open and close some drawers full of clothing and books.

'I'm going to get ready to go away again,' he said. 'I don't want to be disturbed.'

He put various objects down on the table: a toilet case, a pistol . . .

And Meaulnes, in some consternation, left without daring to say a word or shake his hand.

Downstairs, they seemed to have guessed that something was up. Almost all the girls had changed their dresses. In the main building, the guests had begun dinner, but hurriedly and untidily, as though on the point of departure.

There was a continual coming and going from this great kitchen-dining room to the upper rooms and the stables. Those who had finished eating formed groups saying goodbye.

'What's happening?' Meaulnes asked a country boy who was hastily finishing his meal, with his felt hat on his head and his napkin tucked into his waistcoat.

'We're off,' he replied. 'It was all decided quite suddenly. At five o'clock there we were, by ourselves, all the guests together. We had waited until the very last moment. The engaged couple couldn't be coming. Someone said: "Why don't we go?" So everyone got ready to leave.'

Meaulnes said nothing. He might as well go himself now. Hadn't he followed his adventure to the end? Hadn't he now got everything that he wanted? He had barely had time at leisure to go over in his mind the whole lovely conversation of the morning. Now, there was nothing left except to go. And he would soon be back, this time not under false pretences . . .

'If you want to come with us,' said the boy, who was about

Meaulnes' age, 'hurry up and get ready. We're going to harness the horses in a moment.'

He left at full speed, leaving the remains of the meal that he had started to eat, and forgetting to tell the guests what he knew. The park, the garden and the courtyard were plunged in darkness. There were no lanterns at the windows that evening. But since, after all, this dinner was rather like the last meal at the end of a wedding, the less worthy of the guests, who may have been drinking, had begun to sing. As he went off, he heard their cabaret songs rising up across the park that in the past two days had contained so much elegance and so many wonders. And this was where disorder and devastation began. He passed close by the fish pond where he had looked at his reflection that morning. How everything seemed changed already . . . with the song, chanted in unison, which reached him in snatches:

> Where are you coming from, my libertine?
>   Your hat is all torn
>   And your hair's all awry . . .

And this other one, as well:

>   My shoes are red . . .
>   Goodbye, my lover . . .
>   My shoes are red . . .
>   Goodbye for ever!

As he was arriving at the foot of the staircase in his isolated apartment, someone coming down bumped into him in the dark and said: 'Farewell, Monsieur!' And, wrapping himself in his cape as though he was feeling very cold, he vanished. It was Frantz de Galais.

The candle that Frantz had left in his room was still burning. Nothing had been disturbed. However, on a piece of writing paper left in a prominent place, these words were written:

My fiancée has disappeared, letting me know that she could not be my wife, that she was a dressmaker and not a princess. I do not know what will become of me. I am going away. I do not wish to live any longer. May Yvonne forgive me if I do not say farewell to her, but there is nothing that she could do for me . . .

The candle was burning out: its flame flickered, flared up for a moment and died. Meaulnes went back to his own room and closed the door. Despite the darkness, he recognized all the things that he had arranged a few hours earlier, in the fullness of daylight and of happiness. Item by item, he found all his shabby old clothes, old friends, from his worn boots to his coarse belt with its brass buckle. He got undressed and dressed again briskly, and put his borrowed clothes to one side on a chair, absent-mindedly taking the wrong waistcoat . . .

A commotion had arisen under the windows in the yard with the carriages. There was pulling, shouting, pushing, everyone trying to extricate his carriage from the impossible jam in which they were caught. From time to time, a man climbed on to the seat of a cart or the roof of a coach and swung round his lantern. The beam of this light would strike the window and for a moment the room around Meaulnes became familiar: the room in which everything had seemed so friendly to him throbbed and lived again . . . And so it was that, carefully closing the door behind him, he left that mysterious place, which he would surely never see again . . .

XVII

THE STRANGE FETE

(end)

Already a line of carriages was moving slowly through the night towards the gate on the forest side. At its head, a man wearing a goat's skin, with a lantern in his hand, was leading the first of the horses by its bridle.

Meaulnes was in a hurry to find someone willing to take him along. He was in a hurry to leave. Deep inside him, he was worried that he might find himself alone on the estate and his deception be revealed.

When he arrived in front of the main building, the drivers were balancing the loads on the final carriages. All the travellers were being asked to get up so that the seats could be put closer together or moved back, and the girls, wrapped in their shawls, were finding it awkward to stand: blankets were slipping to the ground and you could see the worried faces of those bending their heads on the side with the lamps.

Meaulnes recognized one of the drivers as the young peasant who had recently offered to take him.

'Can I get up?' he shouted.

'Where are you going, my lad?' the other boy asked, no longer recognizing him.

'Towards Sainte-Agathe.'

'Then you want to ask Maritain to take you.'

So now the schoolboy was having to look for this unknown Maritain among the last to leave. He was pointed out to him among the drinkers singing in the kitchen.

'He's a merrymaker,' Meaulnes was told. 'He'll still be there at three in the morning.'

For a moment, Meaulnes thought about the anxious young

woman, feverish and distressed, who would have to listen to these ebrious peasants singing in the château into the middle of the night. Which rooms was she in? Among these mysterious buildings, which was her window? But there was no sense in him waiting; he had to leave. Once he was back in Sainte-Agathe, everything would become clearer. He would no longer be a runaway schoolboy. He could once more think about the young lady of the manor.

One by one, the carriages set off, their wheels grating on the gravel in the main drive. And, through the dark, you could see them turn and vanish, laden with women wrapped against the cold and with children in shawls, already falling asleep. Another big wagon, then a charabanc in which the women were pressed shoulder to shoulder, went by, leaving Meaulnes disconcerted on the threshold of the house. Soon, all that would be left was an old berlin driven by a peasant in a smock.

'You can climb aboard,' he replied, when Augustin asked. 'We're going in that direction.'

Meaulnes struggled to open the door of the antique conveyance, its windows rattling and its hinges creaking. On the seat, in one corner of the carriage, were two quite small children, a boy and a girl, sleeping. They woke up with the noise and the cold air, stretched, looked vaguely around, then shuddered as they snuggled into their corner and went back to sleep.

The old vehicle was already on its way. Meaulnes shut the door quietly and cautiously took his place in the other corner, then, avidly, struggled to make out through the window the places that he was leaving and the route by which he had come. Despite the dark, he guessed that the carriage was crossing the courtyard and the garden, passing the stairway up to his room, going through the gate and leaving the estate to enter the wood. He could vaguely make out the trunks of the old fir trees as they flew past the window.

'Perhaps we shall meet Frantz de Galais,' he thought, with beating heart.

After a short while, in the narrow road, the carriage swung to one side to avoid an obstacle. As far as one could make out in the dark from its massive bulk, it was a caravan that had halted almost in the middle of the road and must have stayed there for the past few days, close to the festivities.

Once this obstacle was out of the way, the horses set off at a trot. Meaulnes was starting to get tired of looking through the glass and trying in vain to see through the surrounding gloom when suddenly, in the depths of the wood, there was a flash, followed by the sound of a detonation. The horses set off at a gallop, and at first Meaulnes did not know if the coachman in the smock was attempting to hold them back or, on the contrary, urging them on. He tried to open the door. As the handle was on the outside, he made vain efforts to lower the window, shaking it . . . The children, waking up in a fright, pressed closer to one another, saying nothing. And while he was shaking the window, with his face pressed to the pane, thanks to a bend in the road, he noticed a white shape running along. It was the tall pierrot from the party, haggard and distraught, the gypsy in his carnival dress, carrying in his arms a human body, which he was holding against his chest. Then they vanished.

In the carriage driving at full gallop through the night, the two children had gone back to sleep. There was no one to whom he could talk about the mysterious events of the previous two days. After going over in his mind for a long time all that he had seen and heard, the young man, too, tired and heavy of heart, abandoned himself to sleep, like a sad child . . .

It was not yet dawn when Meaulnes was awakened, the carriage having stopped on the road, by someone knocking on the window. The driver struggled to get the door open and shouted, while the icy night wind was freezing the boy to the marrow of his bones: 'You'll have to get out here. Day is breaking. We're going to turn off here. You're quite close to Sainte-Agathe.'

Only half awake, Meaulnes did as he was told, groping mechanically for his hat, which had fallen under the feet of the two children sleeping in the darkest corner of the carriage. Then he bent over and got down.

'Goodbye, then,' said the man, getting back on to his seat. 'You've only got six kilometres to walk. Look, there's the distance stone, by the side of the road.'

Meaulnes, who was not yet fully awake, walked over, stooping and stumbling, as far as the stone and sat down on it, his arms crossed and head bent forward, as though preparing to go back to sleep . . .

'No, no!' the driver shouted. 'You mustn't go back to sleep there. It's too cold. Come on, get up and walk a bit . . .'

Swaying like a drunken man, the tall boy, with his hands in his pockets and his shoulders hunched, set off slowly down the road to Sainte-Agathe. Meanwhile, the old berlin, a last link with the mysterious festivities, left the gravel road and silently jolted its way into the distance over the grass of the side road. All that could be seen was the driver's hat, bouncing up and down above the hedgerows . . .

PART TWO

I

THE GREAT GAME

High winds and cold, rain and snow, and finding ourselves, Meaulnes and I, unable to undertake any lengthy search, meant that we did not speak again about the lost land before winter was over. We couldn't start anything serious, in those short February days, those squally Thursdays[7] which would usually end at around five o'clock with dismal, icy rain.

Nothing reminded us of Meaulnes' adventure except the peculiar fact that since the afternoon of his return we had no longer had any friends. In breaks from lessons, they organized the same games as before, but Jasmin never again spoke to The Great Meaulnes. In the evenings, as soon as the classroom had been swept out, the yard emptied as it used to when I was alone, and I saw my friend wander from the garden to the shed and from the yard to the dining room.

On Thursday mornings, sitting on the desk in one of the classrooms, we would each read works by Rousseau and Paul-Louis Courier[8] which we had found in the cupboards between English primers and music books, carefully copied out. In the afternoon, some visitor or other would force us out of the flat and back into the school . . . Sometimes, we would hear groups of older boys stop for a moment, as though by chance, in front of the main gate, crash against it while playing some incomprehensible war game and then go off. This sad existence continued until the end of February. I was starting to think that Meaulnes had forgotten it all, when an adventure happened, stranger than the rest, which proved to me that I had been wrong, and that a violent outburst was gathering beneath the dreary surface of our winter life.

It was actually one Thursday evening, around the end of the
month, when the first news reached us of the Strange Estate,
the first ripple from an adventure that we no longer mentioned.
We had settled down for the evening. My grandparents had
left, so only Millie and my father were there; and they had no
idea of the secret feud that had divided the whole class into two
tribes.

At eight o'clock, Millie opened the door to throw some
crumbs from the table outside and said, 'Oh!' in such a loud
voice that we went over to take a look. There was a blanket of
snow on the doorstep . . . Since it was quite dark, I went a short
way into the yard to see how deep it was. I felt the light flakes
brushing against my face and melting as they did so. I was soon
called back inside, and Millie shut the door, shivering.

At nine we were getting ready to go up to bed. My mother
had already picked up the lamp, when we clearly heard two
heavy knocks struck with full force against the gate at the far
end of the yard. She put the lamp back on the table and we all
stood there, waiting and listening.

There was no question of going to see what was up. Before
we had crossed even half the yard, the lamp would have gone
out and the glass shattered in the cold. There was a brief silence,
and my father was starting to say, 'It must have been . . .', when,
right under the window of the dining room (which, as I have
said, overlooked the station road), there was a strident and very
long whistle; it must have been audible as far as the road to the
church. And, immediately outside the window, hardly muffled
by its panes and made by people who must have hauled themselves up using the outside ledge, there was a series of piercing
cries: 'Bring him out! Bring him out!'

This was echoed by the same shout from the far end of the
building. These were people who must have got through Old
Martin's field and climbed up on the low wall separating it
from our courtyard.

Then eight or ten unknown callers, disguising their voices,
yelled, 'Bring him out!' in succession: from the cellar roof,
which they must have reached by climbing on a pile of logs
standing against the outer wall; from a little wall linking the

shed to the gateway, with a rounded top that was convenient for sitting astride; from the iron fence along the station road that could easily be climbed ... And, finally, at the back, a band of late arrivals reached the garden, and made the same kind of racket, this time with yells of: 'Come on, board them!'

We could hear the echoes of their shouts ringing through the empty classrooms, where they had opened the windows.

Meaulnes and I were so well acquainted with the corners and corridors in the big building that we could envisage very clearly, as though on a map, all the points at which these unknown people were assaulting it.

In fact, it was only in the very first moment that we felt afraid. The whistling made all four of us think that we were being attacked by marauders and gypsies. Indeed, for the past fortnight, a tall ruffian and a young lad with a bandaged head had taken up residence on the square behind the church. There had also been workers, at the wheelwrights' and the blacksmiths', who were not from our part of the world.

But as soon as we heard the attackers shouting, we were convinced that they were people – probably young people – who belonged to the town. Moreover, in the party storming our house, like pirates boarding a ship, there were definitely some children: you could hear that from their high voices.

'Well, I never!' my father exclaimed.

And Millie asked quietly: 'What can it mean?'

Suddenly the voices at the gate and the fence, then those outside the window, fell silent. There were two blasts on a whistle beyond the casement. The shouts of the people who had climbed on the storehouse and the attackers in the garden faded steadily, then ceased, and, along the wall outside the dining room, we could hear the rustling sound of the whole army as it hurried away, its footsteps muffled by the snow.

Someone must have disturbed them. At that time, when everyone was asleep, they had thought they could carry out their attack on the house undisturbed, situated as it was alone on the edge of the town. But now their plan of campaign had been interrupted.

Scarcely had we had time to recover our wits – because the

attack had been as sudden as a well-organized boarding party
– and were getting ready to go outside, than we heard a voice
calling at the little gate, 'Monsieur Seurel! Monsieur Seurel!'

It was Monsieur Pasquier, the butcher. This plump little man
scraped his clogs on the threshold, shook the powdering of
snow off his short smock and came in. He had adopted the
knowing and startled manner of someone who has uncovered
the secret of a mysterious plot:

'I was in my yard, which looks out on the Place des Quatre-
Routes. I was on my way to shut the goats up in their stable.
All at once, what do I see standing up in the snow but two
great lads who appeared to be on guard or keeping watch for
something. They were over by the cross. I went forward. I took
a couple of steps – and hop! They'd set off at full speed towards
your house. Oh, I didn't stop to think. I got my lantern and
said, "I'll go and tell Monsieur Seurel about this . . ."'

Then he started his story all over again:

'I was in the yard behind my house . . .' At which he was
offered a drink, which he accepted, and they asked him for
details that he was unable to supply.

He hadn't seen anything when he got to our house. All the
attackers had been warned by the two sentries he had disturbed
and they immediately dispersed. As for telling us who the
sentries might have been . . .

'They could well have been gypsies,' he suggested. 'They've
been there on the square for nearly a month now waiting for
the weather to improve so they can put on their show, and they
must have thought up some trick or other.'

None of which got us very far, and we were left standing
there, quite puzzled, while the man was sipping his liqueur and
once more acting out his story, when Meaulnes, who had so
far been listening very attentively, picked up the butcher's
lantern and said firmly, 'We must go out and investigate.'

He opened the door, and we followed: Monsieur Seurel,
Monsieur Pasquier and I.

Millie, whose mind was now at rest, since the attackers had
left, and who, like all well-ordered and scrupulous people, was

not at all inquisitive by nature, declared, 'You go, if you want. But shut the door and take the key. I'm going to bed. I'll leave the lamp on.'

WE ARE CAUGHT IN
AN AMBUSH

We set out through the snow, in complete silence. Meaulnes was walking ahead, his covered lantern casting a fan of light ahead of us. We had only just left through the main gate when, from behind the municipal weighing scales which stood against the wall of our shed, two hooded figures shot off together like startled partridges. Whether in mockery, or from pleasure at the strange game they were playing, or from nervous excitement and the fear of being caught, they called out the odd word to us as they ran, laughing at the same time.

Meaulnes dropped the lantern in the snow and shouted to me, 'Come on, François!'

Leaving behind the two older men, who were incapable of running like that, we set off in pursuit of the two shadows, who, after briefly going round the lower part of the town, following the Chemin de la Vieille-Planche, pointedly headed towards the church. They were running steadily without too much haste and we had no trouble following them. They crossed the church road, where everything was quiet and still, and plunged into a maze of small streets and alleyways behind the graveyard.

This was a district of day labourers, dressmakers and weavers, known as the 'small corners' or *Petits-Coins*. We were not too familiar with it and had never been there after dark. The place was empty by day, with the labourers away at work and the weavers shut up indoors; and on this particularly silent night it seemed more abandoned and asleep than the other parts of the little town. So there was no chance of anyone appearing to help us.

I only knew one route through these little houses, which were set down haphazardly like cardboard boxes: this was the way leading to the dressmaker known as the Dumb Woman. First, you went down quite a steep slope, paved erratically, then, after turning two or three times through little weavers' yards and empty stables, you came to a wide street that ended as a cul-de-sac in a long-abandoned farmyard. When we went to see the Dumb Woman, while she was engaged in a silent conversation with my mother, wiggling her fingers, with no sound except for the little noises a deaf person makes, I could look out of the window and see the great yard of the farm, which was the last house on this side of the town, and the closed gate of the dry yard where there was no straw and nothing ever happened . . .

This was precisely the route that the two unknown figures were taking. At each corner we were afraid that we would lose them, but to my surprise, we always reached the turning into the next street before they had left it. I say, 'to my surprise', because this would not have been possible, given the short length of these sidestreets if, whenever we lost sight of them, they had not slowed down.

Finally, without hesitation, they started down the street leading to the Dumb Woman's house, and I shouted to Meaulnes, 'We've got them, it's a dead end!'

In fact, it was they who had got us. They had been leading us where they wanted. Once they reached the wall, they turned round on us with a determined air and one of them gave that same whistle which we had already heard twice that night.

Immediately, some ten or so boys emerged from the yard of the abandoned farm, where they seemed to have been stationed to wait for us. They were all wearing hoods and had their mufflers over their faces . . .

We knew already who they were, but we had resolved to say nothing to Monsieur Seurel: our affairs did not concern him. It was Delouche, Denis, Giraudat and all the rest. As we struggled, we could recognize their way of fighting and the snatches of their voices. But one thing was still disturbing and almost seemed to make Meaulnes afraid: there was someone there whom we did not know, who seemed to be their leader.

He did not touch Meaulnes. Instead, he watched his soldiers as they took him on, and had a hard time of it: dragged through the snow, with their clothes ripped from top to bottom, they struggled against the tall boy, who was panting as he fought. Two of them were looking after me and had immobilized me with some difficulty, because I was fighting like a devil. I was on the ground, my knees bent, sitting back on my heels, while they held me with my hands behind my back as I watched what was happening with intense curiosity and anxiety.

Meaulnes had disposed of four boys from the school, unfastening their grip on his smock by turning a smart circle and sending them flying into the snow ... Firmly planted to one side, the stranger was following the battle with interest, but very calmly, repeating from time to time in a clear voice, 'Go on ... Be brave ... Don't give up ...' then, in English, '*Go on, my boys ...*'

He was clearly in command. Where did he come from? Where and how had he trained them to fight? We had no idea. Like the rest of them, he had a scarf round his face, but when Meaulnes, having disposed of his adversaries, was advancing on him in a threatening way, he made a movement so that he could see better and defend himself, at the same time revealing a piece of white linen wrapped like a bandage around his head.

That's when I shouted to Meaulnes, 'Look out! There's another one behind you.'

He did not have time to turn round before a large fellow leapt out from the gate behind his back and adroitly flung his muffler around my friend's neck, pulling him over. At once the four others whom Meaulnes had tipped into the snow returned to the fight and pinned down his arms and legs, tied his arms with a rope and his feet with a muffler, while the young man with the bandaged head was looking through his pockets. The last to arrive, the man with the lasso, had lit a small candle, which he cupped in his hand; whenever he found a new piece of paper, the leader went across to this light to see what it said. Finally, he unfolded the rough map covered with annotations on which Meaulnes had been working ever since his return, and he shouted gleefully: 'This time, we've got it. Here is the plan! Here is the guide. We'll see if this gentleman really went where I think he did . . .'

His subordinate blew out the candle, and each of them picked up his cap or his belt. Then they all vanished silently, as they had come, leaving me free to hastily untie my friend.

'They won't go very far with that plan,' said Meaulnes, getting to his feet.

We set off slowly, because he was limping a little. On the church road we found Monsieur Seurel and Old Pasquier.

'So you didn't find anything?' they said. 'Nor did we . . .'

Because it was pitch black, they couldn't see anything. The butcher left us, and Monsieur Seurel hurried home to bed.

But the two of us, up in our room, by the light of the lamp that Millie had left us, stayed for a long time patching up our torn smocks and talking in low voices about what had happened to us, like two fellow soldiers on the evening of a lost battle . . .

III

THE GYPSY COMES
TO SCHOOL

It was hard to get up the next morning. At half-past eight, just as Monsieur Seurel was about to give the signal for the boys to go into school, we arrived panting for breath to take our places in line. As we were late, we slipped in where we could, but usually The Great Meaulnes was first in the long line of pupils waiting for Monsieur Seurel to inspect them as they stood elbow-to-elbow carrying their textbooks, exercise books and pencil cases.

I was surprised by the silent alacrity with which they made room for us near the centre of the line; and while Monsieur Seurel, momentarily delaying the move to the classroom, was inspecting Meaulnes, I leant forward and looked curiously along the line to right and left, to examine the faces of our enemies from the night before.

The first one I noticed was the very one about whom I had not ceased to think, but the last that I could have expected to see here. He was in Meaulnes' usual place, the first of all, with one foot on the stone step, and one shoulder and a corner of the satchel on his back resting against the doorpost. His fine, very pale face, slightly freckled, was bent forward and turned towards us with a sort of contemptuous and ironic curiosity. His head and one whole side of his face were wrapped in a white bandage. I recognized the head of the gang, the young gypsy who had robbed us the night before.

We were already going into the classroom, and everyone was taking his place. The new pupil sat down near the pillar on the left of the long bench on which Meaulnes occupied the first place, at the right. Giraudat, Delouche and the three others on the first bench had pressed together to make room for him, as though it had all been agreed in advance . . .

Often in winter odd pupils like this would spend time with us: bargees trapped in the ice in the canal, apprentices and snow-bound travellers. They would stay at school for two days, perhaps a month, seldom longer . . . Objects of curiosity to begin with, they would soon cease to attract attention and quickly blended into the mass of ordinary pupils.

But this one was not to be so soon forgotten. I can still remember this unusual being and all the strange treasures he brought along in the satchel that he wore on his back. At first, there were 'picture' penholders that he brought out to write dictation: if you closed one eye you could see a picture, through a peephole in the handle, blurred and magnified, of the Basilica at Lourdes, or some unknown monument. He chose one, and the others were quickly passed around. Then there was a Chinese pencil box, full of compasses and curious instruments, which travelled along the bench to the left, slipping silently and surreptitiously from hand to hand, under the exercise books, so that Monsieur Seurel wouldn't see.

Brand-new books also did the rounds, books the titles of which I had eagerly read on the spines of the few in our library: *La Teppe aux Merles*, *La Roche aux Mouettes*, *Mon ami Benoist* . . . Some of us were leafing through these volumes on our knees while writing our dictation with the other hand. We didn't know where they came from: they might have been stolen. Other pupils were turning the compasses round inside their desks, while still others, hastily, Monsieur Seurel's back being turned as he continued the dictation while walking from the desk to the window, had one eye shut and the other fixed on the blue-green, speckled view of Notre-Dame de Paris. Meanwhile, the new arrival, pen in hand, winking, with his fine profile outlined against the grey pillar, was enjoying all this furtive activity going on around him.

However, bit by bit the whole class began to get worried: the objects, which were being passed along in turn, one by one reached The Great Meaulnes who, carelessly, without looking at them, put them down next to him. Very soon there was a heap, geometrical and multicoloured like the pyramid at the feet of the woman representing Science in an allegorical painting. Monsieur Seurel was inevitably going to notice this unusual display and realize what was going on. In any case, it would occur to him to inquire into the events of the previous night – and the presence of the gypsy would make it that much easier for him . . .

Indeed, he very soon stopped in surprise in front of Meaulnes.

'Whose is all this?' he asked, pointing at 'all this' with the back of his book, which he had shut on his index finger.

'I don't know,' Meaulnes replied, gruffly, without looking up.

But the stranger interrupted. 'It's mine,' he said. And he immediately added, like a young lord, with an elegant, expansive gesture that the old schoolmaster was unable to resist, 'But it is entirely at your disposal, Monsieur, if you should wish to look at it.'

So, in a matter of seconds, noiselessly, as though to avoid disturbing the new state of affairs that had just arisen, the whole class gathered inquisitively around the teacher, who was bending his head, half bald, half curly-haired, over this treasure and the pale young man who was explaining everything as required with an air of calm triumph. Meanwhile, silent on his bench and completely abandoned, The Great Meaulnes had opened his rough-work book and, with a raised eyebrow, was absorbed in solving a difficult maths problem . . .

Time for the morning break arrived while we were still engaged in this. The dictation was not finished, and disorder reigned in the class. In reality, the break had lasted all morning.

So at ten o'clock, when the dark and muddy yard was invaded by the boys, it was soon easy to see that a new master was presiding over the games.

I can only recall the most bloodthirsty of all the new delights to which the gypsy, that morning, first introduced us: it was a kind of tournament in which the horses were the big boys, carrying the younger ones on their shoulders.

Divided into two groups and starting from opposite sides of the yard, they charged at one another, trying to throw off their opponents through the violence of the impact while the riders, using their scarves as lassos or their outstretched arms as lances, attempted to unseat their opposite numbers. Sometimes the opponent dodged a horse, which then lost its balance, falling into the mud with its rider underneath. There were boys who had been half unseated: the horses caught them by the legs and, still eager for the fray, hoisted them back on their shoulders. The slim rider with the bandaged head, mounted on Big Delage, with his overgrown limbs, his red hair and his protruding ears, urged on the two rival groups and steered his mount skilfully, roaring with laughter.

At first, standing at the classroom door, Augustin watched the setting-up of these games with irritation. I was standing beside him, not sure what to do.

'He's a sly one,' he snarled, his hands in his pockets. 'Coming here, this morning, was the only way for him not to attract suspicion. And Monsieur Seurel was taken in by it!'

He stayed there for a long while, his close-cropped head bare to the wind, cursing the mountebank who was going to have all these boys bludgeoned, when only recently Meaulnes had been their chief. And, as the peaceable lad I was, I could only agree with him.

As the teacher was not there, the battles continued every-where, in every corner. In the end the smallest boys were climbing on each other; they were running around and falling over before even clashing with their opponents . . . Very soon, all that was left standing, in the middle of the yard, was a determined, seething mass, out of which, from time to time, emerged the new leader's white bandage.

By now, The Great Meaulnes could stand it no longer. He bent down, put his hands on his thighs and shouted, 'Come on, François!'

I was surprised by this sudden decision, but still jumped without hesitation on his shoulders, and in an instant we were in the thick of the scrum, while most of the combatants ran away in fright, shouting, 'It's Meaulnes! The Great Meaulnes is here!'

In the midst of those who remained, he started to turn round in a circle, saying to me: 'Reach out your arms and grab them as I did last night.'

Intoxicated by the battle and sure of victory, I caught hold of the little ones as we went past; they struggled, wavered for a moment on the shoulders of the big boys, then fell into the mud. In no time, only the new arrival, mounted on Delage, was left; but the latter, not anxious to get into a fight with Augustin, suddenly straightened up, bent backwards and threw off the white knight.

With his hand on his mount's shoulder, like a captain holding his horse's bit, the boy stood there and looked at The Great Meaulnes with some astonishment and immense admiration.

'Well done!' he said.

But at that moment the bell rang, scattering the pupils who had gathered round us in the hope of some interesting scene. And Meaulnes, annoyed at not having overthrown his enemy, turned his back and said angrily, 'We'll settle this later!'

Until midday, lessons went on as they do when holidays are approaching, mingled with amusing interludes and conversations, this time centred on the schoolboy-mountebank.

He explained how he and his partner had been immobilized by the cold weather: they didn't consider putting on evening performances, since no one would come to them, so they decided that he would go to school to keep him occupied during the day, and his friend would look after the tropical birds and the performing goat. Then he described their journeys round the countryside: the rain falling against the leaky zinc roof, having to get out of the caravan to push it up the hills. The pupils at the back of the room left their desk to come forward and listen, the more practically minded taking advantage of this opportunity to get warm around the stove. But soon even they were overcome with curiosity and shifted over to the chattering group, straining their ears, while still touching the stove with one hand to keep their places.

'And what did you live on?' Monsieur Seurel asked, following everything with the rather childlike curiosity of a schoolmaster and asking lots of questions.

The boy paused for a moment, as though this was a detail that he had never considered.

'Well,' he answered, 'from what we had earned during the previous autumn, I think. Ganache looked after the accounts.'

No one asked who Ganache was. But I remembered the big fellow who had unsportingly attacked Meaulnes from behind on the previous evening and knocked him down . . .

IV

WE HEAR ABOUT THE MYSTERIOUS ESTATE

The afternoon brought the same amusements and, through the rest of the school day, the same disorder and the same underhand dealing. The gypsy had brought along other precious objects: sea shells, games, songs and even a little monkey which scratched faintly inside his gamekeeper's pouch. Monsieur Seurel had to pause constantly to look at what the sly rogue had pulled out of his bag . . . When four o'clock came, Meaulnes was the only one to have finished his school work.

Everyone left unhurriedly. It seemed as though the hard and fast line between lessons and playtime, which made school life simple and ordered like the succession of night to day, had been eliminated. We even forgot to nominate to Monsieur Seurel the two pupils who had to stay behind to sweep out the classroom, as we usually did at around ten to four. Yet this was something that we never forgot because it was a way of marking and hastening the end of the lesson.

As it turned out, on that day it was the turn of The Great Meaulnes. And in the morning I had chatted to the gypsy and warned him that newcomers were always chosen to make the second sweeper on the day that they joined the class.

Meaulnes came back to the room as soon as he had fetched the bread for his snack. As for the gypsy, he kept us waiting for a long time and came in last, running, just as night was falling . . .

'You stay in the room,' my friend had told me, 'and while I have him occupied, you take back the map he stole from me.'

So I sat on a little table near the window, reading by the last light of day, and saw both of them moving back the school benches, without a word: Meaulnes, sternly silent, his black smock fastened with three buttons at the back and with a belt round the waist, and the other boy, delicate, nervous, his head bandaged like a wounded soldier. He was wearing a shabby coat: I had not noticed earlier that there were tears in it. Driven by almost savage eagerness, he was picking the tables up and pushing them around at breakneck speed, with a smile hovering on his lips. It was as though he were playing some extraordinary game, the aim of which was known only to himself.

In that way, they reached the darkest corner of the room, to move the last table.

In that spot, Meaulnes could have thrown his enemy over in an instant without anyone outside having a chance of seeing or hearing them through the windows. I could not understand why he was letting such an opportunity slip. The other boy had gone back towards the door and would escape at any moment, claiming that the job was finished, and we would not see him again. The map and all the information that Meaulnes had taken so long to gather, to piece together and to assemble, would be lost to us . . .

At any moment, I was expecting a sign or a gesture from my friend that would signal the start of the battle, but the tall boy did not make a move. From time to time, he simply looked closely and questioningly at the gypsy's bandage which, in the half-dark, seemed to be extensively marked with black spots.

The last table was moved and nothing happened; but just as they were both returning to the end of the room where they would give a final brush to the doorway, Meaulnes lowered his head and, without looking at our enemy, said in an undertone, 'Your bandage is red with blood and your clothes are torn.'

The other boy looked at him for a moment, not surprised at what he was saying, but deeply moved at hearing him say it.

'They tried to take your map away from me,' he answered. 'Just now, on the square. When they found out that I wanted to come back here and sweep out the classroom, they realized that I was going to make peace with you, so they rebelled against me. But I did save it from them, even so,' he added, proudly, handing the precious folded sheet of paper to Meaulnes.

Meaulnes slowly turned towards me.

'Do you hear that?' he asked. 'He's just fought and been wounded for us, while we were setting a trap for him!'

Then, switching to the familiar *tu* from the formal *vous* (which he had been using even though it was not customary between pupils at Sainte-Agathe), he held out his hand and said, 'You're a true friend.'

The mountebank took Meaulnes' hand and stood there for a moment, speechless with emotion. After a short while, he continued, driven by curiosity:

'So you were setting a trap for me! That's a laugh! I guessed as much and told myself: they'll be really surprised when they get the map back off me and find out that I've completed it . . .'

'Completed?'

'Oh, hang on now! Not altogether . . .'

Then, in a change from this playful tone, he came closer to us and said, slowly and seriously: 'Meaulnes, I have to tell you something. I, too, went where you did. I was there for the extraordinary festivities. I thought, when the boys at the school told me about your mysterious adventure, that it must be the old lost estate. To make sure, I stole your map . . . But I am like you: I don't know the name of the château, or how to get back there. I'm not sure of the whole way from here to there.'

How eagerly and with what curiosity and friendly feeling we clustered round him! Meaulnes keenly asked him questions . . . Both of us felt that, if we pressed our new friend hard enough, we might even get him to tell us what he claimed not to know.

'You'll see, you'll see,' the boy replied, a little irritated and uncomfortable. 'I've just added a few details to the plan which you didn't have – that's all I could do.'

Then, seeing how full we were of admiration and enthusiasm, he said, with pride and sadness, 'Look, I might as well tell you. I'm not like other boys. Three months ago, I tried to put a bullet through my head: that explains why I have a bandage round my forehead, like the men mobilized from the Seine in 1870 . . .'[9]

'And this evening, while you were fighting, the wound reopened,' Meaulnes said, in a friendly tone.

But the other boy, without taking any notice, went on in a faintly grandiloquent way, 'I wanted to die. And since I didn't succeed, I shall only go on living in order to amuse myself, like a child or a gypsy. I've given everything up. I have no more father, or sister, or house, or love ... Nothing, except playfellows.'

'Those fellows have already betrayed you,' I said.

'Yes,' he replied sharply. 'It's the fault of someone called Delouche. He guessed I was going to join forces with you. He demoralized my troops, who were so well disciplined. You saw the assault on the house yesterday evening: how it was carried out, how well it worked! Never, since I was a child, have I set up anything that went off so well ...'

He paused and thought for a moment, then, to dispel any illusions we might have about him, added: 'If I came to see the pair of you this evening, it's because – as I realized this morning – there's more enjoyment to be had with you than with the whole gang. Delouche is the one I particularly don't like. What an idea: pretending to be a man, at seventeen! There's nothing I dislike more ... Do you think we can get even with him?'

'Definitely,' said Meaulnes. 'But will you be staying with us a long time?'

'I don't know. I'd like to very much. I'm dreadfully lonely. All I have is Ganache ...'

All at once the fire and the fun had gone out of him. For a moment, no doubt, he was sunk in the same despair as when, one day, the idea of suicide had crept up on him.

'Be my friends,' he said, suddenly. 'Look: I know your secret and I have defended it against everyone. I can put you on the track of what you have lost ...'

And he added, almost with solemnity: 'Be my friends, for the day when I am again on the brink of hell, as I was once before ... Promise me that you'll answer when I call – when I call you like this ...' (and he made a strange noise: *whoo, whoo!*). 'You, Meaulnes, swear first!'

And we swore because, children that we were, anything more solemn and serious than real life appealed to us.

'In return,' he said, 'this is all I can tell you: I'll let you know the name of the house in Paris where the girl from the château used to spend the holidays, Easter and Whitsun, June and sometimes part of the winter.'

Just then, an unknown voice called from the main gate, several times, through the dark. We guessed it must be Ganache, the gypsy who didn't dare or didn't know how to cross the courtyard. In an urgent, anxious voice he called, at times very loudly, at others very softly: 'Whoo! Whoo!'

'Tell us, quickly,' Meaulnes said to the young gypsy who had shivered and was getting ready to leave.

The boy quickly gave us an address in Paris, which we repeated in an undertone. Then he ran through the shadows to his friend at the iron gate, leaving us in an indescribable state of uneasiness.

V

THE MAN WITH THE
ROPE-SOLED SANDALS

That night, around three o'clock in the morning, Widow Delouche, the innkeeper who lived in the middle of the little town, got up to light her fire. Her brother-in-law Dumas, who lived with her, was due to leave at four o'clock, and the unfortunate old woman, whose right hand was crippled by an old burn, busied herself in the dark kitchen making coffee. It was cold. She put an old shawl over her nightdress, then, holding her lighted candle in one hand and shading the flame by holding up her apron with the other – the crippled one – she crossed the yard, which was cluttered with empty bottles and soapboxes, and opened the door of the woodshed (which also served as a henhouse) to get out some kindling. However, no sooner had she pushed open the door than someone burst out of the murky depths with such a forceful swing of his cap that it caused a draught which put out the candle; with the same blow, he knocked the old woman down, before escaping as fast as he could, while the terrified hens and cockerels set up the most infernal racket.

The man – as Widow Delouche would discover on recovering her wits a moment later – had carried off a dozen of her finest chickens in a sack.

Hearing his sister-in-law's shouts, Dumas ran down. He ascertained that the rogue must have got in using a skeleton key in the door of the yard and that he had fled by the same way without closing the door behind him. Being a man who was accustomed to poachers and pilferers, he lit the lantern on his cart and, with that in one hand and his loaded gun in the other, he tried to follow the thief's traces – though they were very vague, since the man must have been wearing rope-soled sandals – which led him along the station road then disappeared at a gate leading into a field. As he couldn't continue his search, he looked up, stopped . . . and heard the sound of a fleeing carriage being driven away at full tilt on the same road.

For his part, Jasmin Delouche, the widow's son, had got up and, quickly throwing a cape over his shoulders, went out in his slippers to inspect the town. Everyone was asleep, everything was plunged in darkness and that deep silence that precedes the first light of day. When he got to the Quatre-Routes, like his uncle, he heard far away in the distance on the Riaudes hill the sound of a vehicle drawn by a horse that must have been galloping at a furious rate. He was a cunning, boastful lad, who later told us in the ghastly, guttural accent of Montluçon that he had thought: 'Those ones have gone off towards the station, but that doesn't mean I may not "spring" some others on the other side of town.'

And he turned back towards the church, in the same silence of night.

On the town square, there was a light in the gypsy caravan. Probably someone ill. He was going to go up and ask what had happened when a silent shadow – a shadow wearing rope-soled sandals – emerged from the Petits-Coins and headed at full speed, without seeing him, towards the running board of the caravan . . .

Jasmin had recognized Ganache by his way of running. He suddenly stepped forward into the light and asked, quietly, 'Well? What's up?'

Wild-eyed, dishevelled and toothless, Ganache stopped and looked at him with a pitiful grin, brought on by fear and shortness of breath, and panted as he replied: 'It's my friend, he's ill . . . He got in a fight yesterday and his wound reopened . . . I've just been to fetch the nurse.'

And, sure enough, just as Jasmin Delouche, who was very intrigued, was on his way home to bed, he met a nun in the middle of town, hurrying along . . .

*

The next morning, several inhabitants of Sainte-Agathe came out on to their front doorsteps with the same eyes – bloodshot and puffy after a sleepless night. There was a cry of protest from all of them, which ran through the town like a trail of gunpowder.

At the Giraudats', around two o'clock in the morning, a two-wheeled cart had been heard drawing up, then being loaded with packages that made a dull sound as they landed. There were only two women in the house, and they had not dared to do anything. When daylight came, they opened up the farmyard and realized that the packages in question had been the rabbits and poultry . . . During the first school break, Millie found several half-burnt matches in front of the washhouse door. We came to the conclusion that they were unfamiliar with the layout of our house and had not been able to get in . . . At Perreux's, Boujardon's and Clément's, it was thought at first that they had stolen the pigs as well, but the animals turned up in the course of the morning, digging up the vegetables in various people's gardens, the whole herd having taken advantage of the open door to go on a little night walk . . . The poultry had been taken from almost everywhere, but the thieves had been content with that. Mme Pignot, the baker's wife, who did not keep any animals, did complain throughout the next day that her washboard and a pound of blue had gone, but this was never proved, and it did not appear in the police report . . .

A state of turmoil, anxiety and gossip lasted the whole morning. At school, Jasmin described the previous night's adventure.

'Oh, they're clever!' he said. 'But if my uncle had caught one, he told us straight, "I'd shoot him like a rabbit!"' And he added, with a look at us, 'It's a good thing he didn't meet Ganache, because he could easily have shot him. They're all the same, according to him, and Dessaigne says the same.'

Yet no one thought of bothering our new friends. It was only on the evening of the following day that Jasmin pointed out to his uncle that Ganache, like their thief, wore rope-soled sandals. They agreed that it was worth pointing this out to the gendarmes, so they decided, in the greatest secrecy, that as soon as they could they would go to the chief town in the canton and inform the police sergeant.

In the next few days, we saw nothing of the young gypsy, who was ill because his wound had reopened a little.

In the evening, we would prowl around the church square, just to see his lamp behind the red curtain in the caravan. Restless, nervous, we stayed there not daring to go up to the humble dwelling, which seemed to us like the mysterious entrance and antechamber to the Land to which we had lost the way.

VI

AN ARGUMENT BEHIND
THE SCENES

All these anxieties and different upheavals in recent days had
prevented us from taking account of the fact that March had
arrived and that the wind had softened. But on the morning of
the third day after this adventure, I went down into the yard
and suddenly realized that it was spring. A delicious breeze,
like warm water, was flowing over the wall, and during the
night a fall of rain had noiselessly dampened the leaves of the
peonies. There was a pungent smell to the freshly dug earth in
the garden and, in a tree beside the window, a bird was learning
to sing . . .

In our first break, Meaulnes suggested trying out at once the
itinerary given us by the gypsy schoolboy. I had great difficulty
in persuading him to wait until we had seen our friend again
and the weather was definitely warmer . . . that is, until all the
plum trees in Sainte-Agathe were in flower. We were leaning
against the low wall on the little street and talking, bareheaded
and with our hands in our pockets, while the wind alternately
made us shiver with cold and at other times, with gusts of warm
air, aroused some long-buried excitement in us. O, my brother,
my friend! O, wanderer! How certain we were, the two of us,
that happiness was close by and that we only had to start out
down the road to find it!

At half-past twelve, during lunch, we heard a drumroll on
the Place des Quatre-Routes. In an instant, we were by the iron
gate with our napkins in our hands. It was Ganache announcing
that in the evening at eight o'clock, 'in view of the fine weather',
there would be a great performance in front of the church. Just
in case, 'to protect against the eventuality of rain', a tent would

be put up. There followed a long list of attractions, which were carried away by the wind, though we did manage to make out 'pantomime . . . songs . . . equestrian acrobatics . . .', each item marked by a roll of the drum.

At dinner that evening, the big drum heralded the perform-ance with a thunderous noise under our windows which shook the panes. Shortly afterwards we heard a buzz of talking as the people from the outskirts of town came past in little groups, heading for the church. And there we were, the two of us, forced to remain seated at table while we fidgeted with impatience.

At last, at around nine o'clock, we heard the sounds of shuffling feet and stifled laughter at the little gate: the women teachers had come to fetch us. In total darkness our group set out towards the place where the performance would happen. From a distance, we could see the wall of the church lit up as though by a great fire. Two oil lamps hanging in front of the entrance to the tent were flickering in the wind.

Inside, there were tiers of seats, as in a circus. Monsieur Seurel, the women teachers, Meaulnes and I sat down in the lowest tier. I now imagine the place – which must have been very small – as the size of a real circus, with large murky patches through which the seats rose, and on them Madame Pignot, the baker's wife, and Fernande, the grocer's wife, as well as the girls of the town, the blacksmiths, ladies, children, peasants and others.

The show was more than halfway through. In the arena, a little performing nanny goat was obediently putting its hoofs first on four glasses, then two, then just one. Ganache was gently giving it orders with taps of his stick, looking anxiously towards us with open mouth and expressionless eyes.

Sitting on a stool near two further oil lamps, at the place where the passage from the arena went to the caravan, we recognized the ringmaster, in fine black tights and with his head bandaged. It was our friend.

We had scarcely sat down before a pony in full harness bounded into the ring, and the young man with the bandage got him to circle round it while performing tricks and always stopping in front of us when it was asked to point out the most likeable person or the bravest in the audience, and always in front of Madame Pignot when it had to show up the greatest liar, or the meanest, or the 'most amorous'. And around her there would be a burst of laughter, shouts and *cackle-cackle* like the noise of a flock of geese being chased by a spaniel!

During the interval, the ringmaster came over for a moment to talk to Monsieur Seurel, who could not have been prouder if he had been speaking to Talma or Léotard,[10] while we listened intently to everything that he said – about his wound, which had healed; about this performance, which had been many long winter days in preparation; about their departure, which would not be before the end of the month, because up to then they were planning new and different performances.

The show was to end with a big pantomime.

Near the end of the interval, our friend left us and, on his way to the door of the caravan, had to go through a group that had spilled out into the ring and in the middle of which we suddenly noticed Jasmin Delouche. The women and girls stepped aside: all had been captivated by the young man with his black costume and his injured air, strange and brave. As for Jasmin, he looked as though he had at that moment returned from far away. He was speaking in a low voice, but eagerly, to Madame Pignot, and it was clear that a sailor's piping, low collar and bell-bottomed trousers would have been more to his liking . . . He had hooked his thumbs under the lapels of his jacket in an attitude that was at once very smug and very self-conscious. As the gypsy went past, Jasmin, with a gesture of irritation, said something that I could not hear to Madame Pignot, but which must surely have been some kind of insult or provocative remark addressed to our friend. It must have been a serious, unexpected threat, because the young man could not restrain himself from turning round and looking at Jasmin, who, to avoid losing face, nudged those next to him with his elbow, as though to get them on his side . . . Actually, all this happened in a few seconds . . . I was certainly the only person on my bench to notice it.

The ringmaster joined his companion behind the curtain hiding the caravan door. Everyone went back to his or her seat, thinking that the second part of the show was going to start right away, and silence fell. Then, while the last whispered conversations were dying away, the sound of an argument came from behind the curtain. We could not hear every word that was being said, but we recognized the two voices: those of the big lad and the young man, the first explaining and justifying himself, the other rebuking him, with a mixture of sadness and indignation. 'But, you idiot,' he was saying, 'why didn't you tell me?'

The rest could not be made out, even though every ear was strained. Then suddenly all went quiet. The row continued in low voices and the kids on the upper rows started to shout, 'Lights! Curtain!' and stamp their feet.

VII

THE GYPSY TAKES OFF
HIS BANDAGE

At last, slowly, between the curtains slid the face – wrinkled, beaming now with merriment, now with anguish, and dotted with sealing wafers – of a tall pierrot in three badly jointed pieces, bent over as though suffering from colic and walking on tiptoe, as from exaggerated caution or fear, with his hands entangled in excessively long sleeves which dragged along the ground.

I'm at a loss today to reconstruct the story of his pantomime; all I remember is that, as soon as he arrived in the ring, after hopelessly, desperately trying to keep his balance, he fell over. He got up again, but it was no good: he fell over. He was constantly falling. He managed to get caught up in four chairs at once. As he fell, he took with him a huge table that they had brought into the arena. In the end, he fell right over the barrier round the ring and at the feet of the spectators. Two assistants, recruited with much difficulty from the audience, set him upright again after an unbelievable struggle. And every time, as he fell, he gave a little cry, different every time, an unbearable little cry, in which distress and satisfaction were equally mixed. At the climax of the act, climbing on a heap of chairs, he made a tremendous, very slow fall, and his shrill, agonized wail of triumph lasted as long as the fall did, accompanied by gasps of terror from the women in the audience.

In the second part of his pantomime, I remember (though I don't quite know why) seeing the 'poor falling clown' taking a little doll, stuffed with bran, out of one of his sleeves and miming a whole tragi-comic drama with her. In the end, he made all the bran that was inside her emerge from her mouth.

Then, with doleful little cries, he filled her up again with porridge and, at the moment of greatest concentration, when all the spectators were watching open-mouthed and all eyes were on the poor pierrot's slimy, tattered little doll, he suddenly grasped her in one hand and threw her with all his strength into the audience towards the face of Jasmin Delouche – she brushed damply past his ear and crashed into Madame Pignot, just below the chin. The baker's wife gave such a shout and flung herself back so hard that all the people around her did the same, breaking the bench, with the result that the baker's wife, Fernande, sad Widow Delouche and twenty or so others collapsed, with their legs in the air, amid a burst of laughter, shouts and clapping, while the tall clown, who had fallen face downwards on the ground, got up, bowed and said, 'Ladies and gentlemen, we have the honour to thank you!'

But at that very moment, in the midst of this huge uproar, The Great Meaulnes, who had not said a word since the start of the pantomime and seemed constantly more preoccupied as it went on, suddenly stood up, grasped my arm and, as though unable to contain himself, cried, 'Look at the gypsy! Look! At last, I know who he is!'

Without even a glance, as though the thought had long been hatching inside me, unconsciously, and had only been waiting for that moment to emerge from its shell, I guessed what he meant. Standing by a lantern at the door of the caravan, the young unknown person had undone his bandage and thrown a cloak over his shoulders. There he was, in the smoky light, as he had once been in the candlelight in the room at the château, with his fine, aquiline, clean-shaven face. He was pale, with half-open lips and hastily leafing through a sort of little, red-bound book that must have been a pocket atlas. Apart from a scar across his temple, disappearing under the mass of hair, he was just as The Great Meaulnes had minutely described him to me: the fiancé from the Strange Estate.

It was clear that he had taken off his bandage so that we would recognize him. But no sooner had The Great Meaulnes leapt up and let out that cry than the young man went back into the caravan, after giving us a complicit look and smiling, in his usual way, with a kind of melancholy.

'And the other one!' Meaulnes said urgently. 'Why didn't I recognize him straightaway! He was the pierrot from there, from the fête . . .'

He started to go down the rows towards him. But Ganache had already closed all the entrances to the ring. One by one, he was turning off the four circus lights, and we were forced to follow the crowd as it made its way out, very slowly, channelled between the parallel benches, while we were stamping our feet with impatience in the gloom.

As soon as he was outside, at last, The Great Meaulnes dashed towards the caravan, rushed up the steps and knocked on the door. But everything was already shut. No doubt, in the caravan with its curtains, as in the cart belonging to the pony, the goat and the performing birds, everyone was already gathered in and starting to sleep.

VIII
THE GENDARMES!

We had to join up with the crowd of men and women making their way back towards the school through the dark streets. Now we understood everything. The tall white figure that Meaulnes had seen on the last evening of the celebration running between the trees was Ganache, who had picked up the heartbroken fiancé and fled with him. Frantz de Galais had accepted this wild life full of risks, games and adventures. It was like going back to his childhood...

Up to now, he had kept his name from us and pretended not to know the way back to the estate, no doubt because he was afraid that he would be forced to return to his parents. But why had he suddenly seen fit that evening to make himself known to us and to let us guess the whole truth?

How many plans The Great Meaulnes was making as the crowd of spectators slowly dispersed around the town. He decided that he would go and look for Frantz the very next morning, which was a Thursday. Then the two of them would set off for *there*! What a journey it would be on the wet road. Frantz would explain everything, it would all be settled, and the wonderful adventure would start again at the point where it had been broken off...

For my part, I was walking through the darkness with a vague weight pressing on my heart. Everything was combining to make me happy, from the small pleasure that I gained from anticipating the Thursday holiday to the immense discovery that we had just made by some astonishing piece of luck. And I remember that, with this sudden feeling of generosity in my heart, I went over to the ugliest of the notary's daughters – the one to whom, as a punishment, I was sometimes required to offer my arm – and spontaneously took her hand.

Bitter memories! Vain hopes crushed!

The next day, at eight o'clock, as the two of us came into the church square, with our brightly shining shoes, our well-polished belt buckles and our new caps, Meaulnes – who up to then had been trying not to smile when he looked at me – gave a shout and started to run into the empty square ... In the place where the tent and the caravan had been, only a broken pot and some rags remained ... The gypsies had gone.

A little wind, which seemed icy to us, was blowing. I felt as though with every step we took we would trip up on the hard, stony ground of the square and fall over. Twice, Meaulnes made as though to run, firstly along the road to Le Vieux-Nançay, then along the road to Saint-Loup-des-Bois. He shaded his eyes with his hand, hoping for a moment that they had only just left. What could we do? There were the tracks of ten carts crisscrossing the square, then vanishing on the hard surface of the road. There was nothing for it but to stand there, helpless.

And while we were going back through the village, where Thursday morning was beginning, four mounted gendarmes, who had been alerted by Delouche the previous evening, galloped into the square and deployed themselves around it to seal off every entrance, like dragoons reconnoitring a village. But it was too late. Ganache, the chicken thief, had fled with his friend. The gendarmes found no one: neither Ganache nor the person who had loaded the wagons with the chickens that he had strangled. Informed by Jasmin's rash but timely remark, Frantz must have learnt suddenly how his friend and he managed to survive when the moneybox in the caravan was empty. Filled with shame and fury, he must have immediately drawn up an itinerary and decided to hurry away before the arrival of the gendarmes. But now, when his only fear was that they would try to take him back to his father's home, he wanted to show himself to us without his bandage before he vanished.

Only one thing remained unclear: how had Ganache managed to rob the farmyards and fetch a nursing sister to treat his

friend's high temperature? But wasn't that just typical of the
poor devil? A thief and vagrant on the one hand and a good
companion on the other . . .

IX

IN SEARCH OF
THE LOST PATH

On our way back, the sun was clearing the light mist of morning, the housewives on the porches of their homes were shaking carpets or chatting and, in the fields and woods on the outskirts of the little town, the most radiant spring morning I can remember in my life was just beginning.

All the older pupils in the school were to come in at around eight o'clock that Thursday, so that some could spend the morning preparing for the Certificat d'études supérieures and others the examination for the Ecole Normale.[11] When the two of us reached the school – Meaulnes so full of agitation and regret that he could not keep still and I feeling very downcast – the place was empty. A ray of fresh sunshine was glancing off the dust on a worm-holed bench and on the chipped varnish of a planisphere.

How could we stay there, poring over our books and thinking about our disappointment, when everything was calling us outside: the birds chasing one another through the branches by the window, the other pupils escaping to the woods and meadows, and most of all the urgent need as soon as possible to try out the partial itinerary that the gypsy had checked – the last item in our almost empty bag, the last key on the ring when all the rest had been tried? It was more than we could resist! Meaulnes strode up and down, went over to the windows, looked into the garden, then came back and looked towards the town as though waiting for someone who would surely not come.

'I've got an idea,' he said at last. 'It occurs to me that it may perhaps not be as far as we think . . . Frantz has cut out a whole part of the route that I showed on my plan. That suggests that the mare could have made a long detour while I was asleep . . .'

I was half seated on the corner of a large table with one foot on the ground and the other dangling, my head bent and with an air of listlessness and discouragement.

'But on the way back,' I pointed out, 'your journey in the berlin lasted all night.'

'We set out at midnight,' he said eagerly. 'He put me down at four in the morning, around six kilometres to the west of Sainte-Agathe – while I had started from the station road in the east. So we have to subtract those six kilometres between Sainte-Agathe and the Lost Land. Honestly, I think that once we're through the Bois des Communaux, then we can't be more than two leagues from the place we're looking for.'

'And those are precisely the two leagues missing from your map.'

'That's right. And the far end of the Bois is a good league and a half from here, but for a fast walker, it could be done in a morning.'

At that moment, Moucheboeuf arrived. He had an annoying habit of appearing to be a good pupil, not by working any harder than the rest, but by getting himself noticed at times like these.

'I knew it!' he said, triumphantly. 'I knew you'd be the only ones who'd be here. All the others have gone to the Bois des Communaux – with Jasmin Delouche leading, because he knows where to find the nests.'

And, in his holier-than-thou way, he started to tell us everything that they had said, making fun of the school, Monsieur Seurel and us, as they were planning the expedition.

'If they're in the woods, I expect I'll see them on my way,' said Meaulnes. 'Because I'm going there myself. I'll be back around half-past twelve.'

Moucheboeuf was speechless.

'Aren't you coming?' Augustin asked me, pausing for a moment at the half-open door, allowing a gust of air warm from the sun to sweep into the grey classroom accompanied by a medley of cries, shouts and birdsong, the sound of a bucket on the lip of a well and the distant crack of a whip.

'No,' I said, though I was sorely tempted. 'I can't, because of Monsieur Seurel. But hurry back, I'll be waiting for you.'

He made a vague gesture and left, hurriedly, full of hope.

When Monsieur Seurel arrived, at around ten o'clock, he had exchanged his black alpaca jacket for a fisherman's coat with huge buttoned pockets, a straw hat and short, shiny gaiters holding the bottom of his trousers. I think he was not at all surprised to find no one there and he paid no attention to Moucheboeuf, who told him three times what the boys had said: 'If he needs us, let him come and fetch us!'

Instead he ordered: 'Put away your things, get your caps and we'll comb the woods for them ourselves . . . will you be able to walk that far, François?'

I said I could, and we set off.

It was agreed that Moucheboeuf would guide Monsieur Seurel and act as decoy . . . That is, since he knew the woodland where the nest-hunters would be operating, he could shout out loudly from time to time, 'Hey! Hello! Giraudat! Delouche! Where are you? Are there any? Have you found some?'

As for me, much to my delight, I was given the task of following the eastern edge of the wood, in case any fleeting schoolboys tried to escape on that side.

Now, in the map amended by the gypsy, which I had many times studied with Meaulnes, it seemed that there was a single-lane track, a dirt road, leaving from this edge of the wood and heading towards the Estate. Suppose I should discover it that morning! I had started to convince myself that before midday I should be on the road towards the lost château . . .

What a wonderful walk. As soon as we had passed the Slope and gone round the Mill, I left my two companions, Monsieur Seurel, who looked as though he were going off to war – I truly think he had put an old pistol in his pocket – and the treacherous Moucheboeuf.

Following a transverse path, I soon reached the edge of the wood – alone in the countryside for the first time in my life, like an army patrol that has lost touch with its corporal.

This, I should think, is something close to that mysterious happiness that Meaulnes apprehended one day. The whole morning is mine, to explore the outskirts of the wood, the coolest, most hidden place thereabouts, while my big brother is also away on a journey of discovery. It is like a dried-up riverbed. I am walking beneath the low branches of trees that I do not know by name; they must be elms. Just now, I jumped over a stile at the end of the path and here I am, in this broad avenue of green grass flowing beneath the leaves, brushing through the nettles in places and knocking down the tall stalks of valerian.

Sometimes, for a few steps, my feet are resting on a bank of fine sand. And in the silence, I can hear a bird: I think it's a nightingale, but I must be wrong because they only sing in the evenings . . . This bird is relentlessly repeating the same phrase: voice of the morning, a recital in the shade, a delicious invitation to a journey between the elms. Invisible and obstinate, it seems to be accompanying me through the leaves.

For the first time, I too am on the road to adventure. No longer am I hunting for shells washed up by the sea under Monsieur Seurel's guidance, or wild orchids that even the schoolmaster does not recognize, or even, as often happened in Old Martin's field, the deeply sunk, dried-up spring covered by a grating and buried under so many weeds that every time we would take longer finding it . . . I am looking for something still more mysterious. I'm looking for the passage that they write about in books, the one with the entrance that the prince, weary with travelling, cannot find. This is the one you find at the remotest hour of morning, long after you have forgotten that eleven o'clock is coming, or midday. And suddenly, as you part the branches in the dense undergrowth, with that hesitant movement of the hands, held unevenly at face height, you see something like a long, dark avenue leading to a tiny circle of light . . .

But while I am intoxicating myself with these hopes and ideas, I suddenly come out into a kind of clearing which turns out to be nothing more than a field. Without expecting it, I have reached the end of the Bois des Communaux, which I had always imagined to be an infinite distance away. Now on my right, between piles of wood, buzzing in the shade, is the keeper's house. Two pairs of stockings are drying on the window ledge. In previous years, when we reached the entrance to the wood, we would always say, pointing to a patch of light far away at the end of the immense dark lane: 'Down there is the keeper's house, Baladier's house.' But never did we go that far. Sometimes we would hear people say, as if talking about some extraordinary expedition, 'He went as far as the keeper's house!'

This time, I've gone as far as Baladier's house – and found nothing . . .

My tired leg was starting to hurt, and I was suffering from the heat, which I had not felt up to then. I was afraid of undertaking the whole of the return trip by myself when I heard Monsieur Seurel's bird decoy near by and Moucheboeuf's voice, then others calling me . . .

There was a band of six big lads among whom only the treacherous Moucheboeuf seemed triumphant. They were Giraudat, Auberger, Delage and others . . . Thanks to the bird-call, some had been caught climbing a wild cherry tree in the middle of a clearing and the others as they were robbing a woodpecker's nest. Giraudat, the simpleton with the puffy eyes and dirty smock, had hidden the little birds on his belly between his shirt and his skin. Two of their friends had fled when Monsieur Seurel came up, probably Delouche and little Coffin. At first, they had laughed in answer to 'Mouchevache' (as they called him), and the wood threw their jokes as echoes back to them; while he, foolishly, thinking he had them in the bag, angrily replied: 'You might as well come down, you know! Monsieur Seurel is here . . .'

At that, everything suddenly went quiet: they were silently escaping through the woods. And since they knew every inch of the place, there was no sense in trying to catch them. No one knew, either, where The Great Meaulnes had gone. They had not heard his voice and decided to give up the search.

It was after midday when we started back towards Sainte-Agathe, slowly, our heads hanging, tired and grubby. As we came out of the wood and had shaken and rubbed the mud off our shoes on the dry road, the sun began to shine brightly. It was no longer that fresh, glowing spring morning. Afternoon sounds could be heard. Here and there, a cock crowed – a forlorn cry! – in one of the isolated farms beside the road. Coming down the Slope, we paused for a moment to chat with the farm hands who had resumed their work in the fields after lunch. They were leaning on the gate, and Monsieur Seurel told them, 'What a bunch of rascals! Why, just look at Giraudat: he put the fledglings in his shirt and they did just what you'd expect. A fine mess!'

I felt as though it was my disaster as well that the farmhands were laughing about, shaking their heads; but they did not entirely blame the boys, whom they knew well. They even told us, confidentially, when Monsieur Seurel had resumed his place at the head of the column: 'Another one came past, a tall one, you know him . . . On his way he must have met up with the cart from Les Granges, and they gave him a lift; he got down, covered in mud and his clothes all torn, just here, at the road to Les Granges! We told him we'd seen you go by this morning, but that you weren't back yet. And off he went, taking his time, towards Sainte-Agathe.'

In fact, The Great Meaulnes was waiting for us, sitting on a promontory of the Pont des Glacis, looking utterly exhausted. When Monsieur Seurel asked him, he said that he had also gone off looking for the truants, and when I questioned him he just whispered back, shaking his head in disappointment, 'No, nothing! Nothing like it!'

After lunch, in the closed classroom, which was dark and empty in the midst of a sunlit land, he sat down at one of the long tables and, with his head in his hands, he lapsed into a long, heavy and miserable sleep. Around evening, after thinking about it for a long time, as though he had just taken an impor- tant decision, he wrote a letter to his mother. And that is all I remember of that dreary end to a great day of disappointments.

X

THE WASHING

We had counted too soon on the arrival of spring.

On Monday evening, we wanted to get our homework done immediately after four o'clock, as in mid-summer, and so that we could see more clearly, we brought two large tables out into the courtyard. But all at once the weather clouded over, a drop of rain fell on an exercise book and we hurried back inside. And then, silently, from the great hall plunged in darkness, we watched through the wide windows as the clouds raced across the grey sky.

At that, Meaulnes, who was watching with us, one hand on a window catch, could not repress the remark (though he seemed annoyed at feeling so much regret inside him): 'Oh, the clouds were running differently from that when I was on the road in the cart from La Belle Etoile!'

'On what road?' Jasmin asked.

Meaulnes did not reply.

In order to change the subject, I said, 'Now, I'd like to have travelled like that in a cart under the driving rain with an umbrella to shelter me.'

'And be reading all the way, as though you were indoors,' said someone else.

'It wasn't raining and I didn't want to read,' said Meaulnes. 'All I thought about was watching the countryside go by.'

But when Giraudat again asked what countryside he was talking about, again Meaulnes said nothing. And Jasmin remarked: 'I know . . . It's that famous adventure again!'

He said this in a conciliatory, but self-important, tone of voice, as though he were himself somehow in the secret. He was wasting his time, though: his approach achieved nothing, and since night was falling, everyone hurried away, heads sheltering under smocks from the cold rain.

Until the following Thursday, the weather remained wet. And that Thursday was more dreary even than the one before. All the countryside was bathed in a kind of icy fog as in the worst days of winter.

Millie, taken in by the bright sunshine of the previous week, had got the washing done, but it was no use thinking of putting it out to dry on the garden hedges or even on lines in the loft, the air was so damp and cold.

Talking about this to Monsieur Seurel, she got the idea of hanging out the washing in the classrooms, since it was Thursday, and working the stove up to full heat. To save on the fires in the kitchen and dining room, we could cook our meals on the stove and spend the whole day in the main classroom.

At first – I was still so young – I thought of this novelty as a festive occasion.

Some festivity! All the heat from the stove was taken up by the washing, and it felt really cold. Outside, in the yard, a winter drizzle fell, weakly and endlessly; and yet it was there that, at nine in the morning, driven mad by boredom, I met The Great Meaulnes. Through the bars of the main gate, against which we were silently resting our heads, we watched a funeral procession arriving from the country to the high point of the town at the crossroads of Les Quatre-Routes. The coffin, which had come in an ox cart, was unloaded and placed on a stone slab at the foot of the great cross where the butcher had recently seen the gypsy sentries. Where was he now, the young captain who had so brilliantly led the attack? The curé and the choirboys halted in front of the coffin, according to custom, and we could hear the melancholy sound of singing in the distance. We knew that this would be the only event of the day and that otherwise it all would flow past like yellowed water in a gutter . . .

'And now,' Meaulnes said, suddenly, 'I'm going to do my packing. I've got to tell you, Seurel: I wrote to my mother last

Thursday to ask if I could complete my education in Paris. I'm leaving today.'

He went on looking towards the town, with his hands resting on the bars, level with his head. There was no point in asking if his mother, who was rich and granted his every wish, had also granted this one. Nor was there any point in asking why he suddenly wanted to go off to Paris!

But he certainly had some feelings of regret and fear about leaving the dear town of Sainte-Agathe, from which he had set out on his adventure. And I, for my part, felt a huge sense of desolation rise up inside me, unlike any that I had experienced before.

'Easter's coming!' he said, with a sigh, by way of explanation.

'As soon as you find her there, you'll write to me, won't you?' I asked.

'Of course, I promise. You're my friend and my brother, aren't you?'

And he put a hand on my shoulder.

Gradually, I came to realize that it was really over, since he wanted to finish his schooling in Paris. Never again would I have my tall friend with me.

There was only one hope that we would be reunited, and that was in the house in Paris where he might find the trail of the lost adventure ... But what a meagre hope it was for me, when I saw Meaulnes himself so sad!

My parents were informed. Monsieur Seurel appeared quite amazed, but soon accepted Augustin's reasons. Millie, a real housewife, was chiefly sorry at the thought that his mother would see our house in a state of unaccustomed disarray ... The trunk, alas, was quickly packed. We looked for his Sunday shoes in the cupboard under the stairs, some linen in the wardrobe and then his papers and schoolbooks – all that a young man of eighteen possesses in this world.

At midday, Madame Mcaulnes arrived in her carriage. She had lunch at the Café Daniel with Augustin and took him away almost without a word as soon as the horse was fed and harnessed. We said goodbye to them at the door ... and the

carriage vanished round the corner at the crossroads of Les
Quatre-Routes.

Millie scraped her shoes at the door and returned to the cold
dining room to put everything back in its place, while I, for the
first time for many months, found myself alone facing a long
Thursday evening – with the feeling that inside that old carriage
my adolescence had just vanished for evermore.

XI

BETRAYAL

What should I do? The weather was clearing a little, and it looked as though the sun might even come out.

A door closed in the school house. Then, again, silence. From time to time my father walked across the yard to fill the coal scuttle which he used to stoke up the stove. I could see the white clothes hanging from their lines and had no desire to go back to this sad place which had been transformed into a drying room, there to find myself confronted by the end-of-year exam, that competition for the Ecole Normale which should from now on be my sole concern.

An odd thing: mixed in with this sense of boredom and desolation, there was almost a feeling of freedom. Now that Meaulnes had gone, now that the whole adventure was over and a failure, I felt at least free of a strange preoccupation, of that mysterious obsession preventing me from behaving like everyone else. Now that Meaulnes had gone, I was no longer his companion in adventure, the brother of that pathfinder. I reverted to being a village boy like the rest. This was easy for me: I had only to follow my most natural impulse.

The youngest of the Roy brothers went past down the muddy street, swinging three conkers tied together on a piece of string, then launching them into the air, to fall into the school yard. So great was my boredom that I enjoyed throwing his conkers back to him two or three times over the wall.

Suddenly, I saw him abandon this childish game and run towards a cart coming down the Chemin de la Vieille-Planche. The cart did not even need to stop for him to clamber up behind. I recognized Delouche's little cart and horse. Jasmin was driving, with fat Boujardon standing behind. They were on their way back from the fields.

'Come and join us, François!' Jasmin shouted. He must already have known that Meaulnes had left.

Heavens! I told no one, but climbed aboard the shuddering cart and stood there with the others, steadying myself against one of the rails. He took us back to Widow Delouche's place . . .

Here we are now in the back of the shop with the good lady who is at the same time a grocer and an innkeeper. A ray of white sunshine is glancing through the low window on the tins of food and the casks of vinegar. Fat Boujardon is seated on the window ledge and turns towards us with the laugh of a podgy man; he is eating biscuits with a spoon, digging them out of an open box, standing within reach, on a barrel. Little Roy is producing small cries of pleasure. A sort of unwholesome intimacy has been established between us. From now on, I can see that Jasmin and Boujardon are to be my friends. The course of my life has suddenly changed. I have the feeling that Meaulnes left a very long time ago and that his adventure is an old, sad story, but over now.

Little Roy has found an open bottle of liqueur under the counter. Delouche offers a drop to each of us, but there is only one glass and we all drink out of it. I am the first to be served, with a hint of condescension, as though I were not accustomed to these hunters' and peasants' manners . . . I feel a bit awkward. And since they have just mentioned Meaulnes, I feel an urge to show that I know his story and to tell a little of it, so as to overcome my embarrassment and regain my self-confidence. How could it harm him, since all his adventures here are over now?

Was I telling the story badly? It didn't produce the effect that I expected.

The others, being good village lads, surprised by nothing, were not impressed by such a small thing.

'It was a wedding, then,' said Boujardon.

Delouche had seen one in Préveranges which was even odder.

The château? There were bound to be some people from round about who had heard of it.

The girl? Meaulnes would get married to her when he had finished his year's military service.

'He should have told us about it,' one of them remarked. 'He should have showed us his map instead of entrusting it to a gypsy!'

My failure makes me dig deeper. I try to take advantage of the moment to excite their curiosity and decide to explain who the gypsy was, where he came from and his strange destiny . . . Boujardon and Delouche are not interested: 'He's the one to blame for everything. He made Meaulnes unfriendly – Meaulnes who was such a good comrade! He's the one who arranged all those idiotic night-time attacks and raids, after marshalling us all together like a school battalion.'

'You know,' Jasmin said, looking at Boujardon and giving little shakes of his head, 'I did just the right thing reporting him to the police. That's someone who brought harm to the town and would do it again!'

I almost agree with them. No doubt everything would have turned out differently if we had not made such a mystery about the matter and seen it in such a tragic light. It was Frantz's influence that upset everything . . .

Then, suddenly, while I was taken up with these thoughts, there was a noise in the shop. Jasmin Delouche quickly hid his flask of liqueur behind a barrel, while fat Boujardon jumped off his window ledge, and landed on a dusty, empty bottle which rolled away under his foot and almost brought him down. Little Roy was pushing them from behind, to get them out more quickly, half suffocating with laughter.

Without entirely understanding what was going on, I fled with them. We crossed the yard and climbed up a ladder into a hayloft. I heard a woman's voice calling us good-for-nothings!

'I didn't think she'd be back so soon,' Jasmin whispered.

Only now do I see that we were doing something unlawful there, stealing cakes and liqueur. I'm as disappointed as the shipwrecked sailor who thought he was talking to a man and suddenly realizes that it's a monkey. I'm so fed up with all these adventures that I don't even want to leave the hayloft. Anyway, night is falling. They get me to go by the back way, across two gardens and round a pond. I end up in a wet, muddy street, with the lights of the Café Daniel shining on it.

I'm not proud of my evening's work. I'm at the crossroads of Les Quatre-Routes. Without wishing to, I can suddenly see, at the bend of the road, a hard, fraternal face smiling at me, a final wave of the hand . . . and the carriage vanishes.

A cold wind is making my smock flutter, reminding me of that winter that was so tragic and so beautiful. Already, everything seems to me to have got harder. In the large classroom where I am expected for dinner, there are brisk draughts of air cutting through the meagre heat given out by the stove. I shiver and I am told off for my afternoon's disappearance. I don't even have the consolation – in trying to recapture the routines of the past – of being able to take my usual place at table. It hasn't been laid that evening because each of us is going to eat off our knees, as best we can, in the dark classroom. In silence, I eat the griddle cake that should have been a reward for this Thursday spent at school; it has burnt on the ring of the stove, where it had cooked.

That evening, all alone in my room, I went to bed quickly to stifle the regret that I could feel rising up from the depths of my sadness. But twice in the night I woke up, the first time thinking I could hear the creaking of the nearby bed where Meaulnes used to turn over suddenly, in a single movement; and the second time, his light footsteps, like those of a hunter stalking some prey through the attics at the back of the house . . .

XII

THREE LETTERS FROM
MEAULNES

In all my life, I have only received three letters from Meaulnes.
They are still at home in a drawer. Every time I read them,
I feel the same sadness as before.

The first arrived as early as two days after he left.

My dear François,

Today, as soon as I got to Paris, I went to look at the house.
I saw nothing. There was no one. There will never be anyone.

The address that Frantz gave is that of a little, two-storey
private house. Mademoiselle de Galais' room must be on the first
floor. The upper windows are the ones most hidden by trees, but
looking up from the pavement you can see them very clearly.
All the curtains are drawn, and you would have to be mad to
hope that, one day, the face of Yvonne de Galais might appear,
looking through one of these curtains.

It's on a boulevard. The rain was falling a little on the already
verdant trees. You could hear the clear bells of the trams that
kept passing by.

For almost two hours, I walked backward and forwards under
the windows. There's a wine merchant's where I stopped to
drink, so that I would not be mistaken for a burglar planning a
robbery. Then I returned to my hopeless watching.

Night fell. The windows lit up all around, but not in that
house. There is definitely no one there; and yet Easter is coming.

Just as I was about to leave, a girl or young woman, I couldn't
tell, came and sat down on one of the benches that were damp
with rain. She was dressed in black with a little white collar.
When I left, she was still there, not moving despite the evening

chill and waiting for something or someone unknown. You see: Paris is full of mad people like myself.

                                                                    Augustin

Time passed. I waited in vain for a word from him on Easter Monday and all the days following – days that are so calm after the great excitement of Easter that it seems nothing is left except to wait for the coming of summer. June arrived, bringing examinations and dreadful heat, which settled in a stifling haze over the countryside, with not a breath of wind to dispel it. The nights were no cooler and so gave no respite from this torment. It was during this unbearable month of June that I received a second letter from The Great Meaulnes.

                                                           June 189–
     My dear friend,
     Now all hope is lost. I have known that since yesterday evening. The pain, which I hardly felt at first, has been getting more intense since then.
     Every evening I went to sit on the bench, waiting, thinking and, in spite of all, hoping.
     Yesterday, after dinner, the night was dark and stifling. Some people were chatting on the pavement under the trees. Above the black leaves, turning to green where lit by the street lamps, the apartments on the second and third floors were lit up. Here and there was a window that the summer heat had opened wide . . . You could see the lamp on the table, alight but barely able to dispel the warm darkness of June around it; you could see almost to the back of the room . . . Ah, if only Yvonne de Galais' black window had been lit as well, I think I should have dared to go up the stairs, knock on the door, go in . . .
     The girl I mentioned before was there again, waiting as I was. I thought that she must know the house and I asked her about it.
     'I know that at one time,' she said, 'a brother and sister came to spend their holidays in that house. But I heard that the brother ran away from his parents' home and that they never managed

to find him. And the girl got married. That explains why the rooms are empty.'

I left. I had only taken ten steps when my feet stumbled against the pavement and I nearly fell. That night – it was last night – when the women and children had finally ceased their noise in the courtyards, and it was quiet enough for me to sleep, I began to hear the cabs passing in the streets. Only occasionally did they go by, but when one had gone past, try as I might to avoid it, I would hear the next: the bell, the horses' hooves clicking on the roadway . . . and the sounds repeated: the forsaken city, your lost love, endless night, summer, fever . . .

Seurel, my friend, I am in great distress.

Augustin

Letters that confided much less in me than might appear! Meaulnes did not tell me why he had gone so long without writing, nor what he intended to do now. I had the impression that he was breaking off our friendship, because his adventure was over, just as he was breaking off from his past. And, indeed, even though I wrote to him, there was no answer – just a word of congratulations when I passed my Brevet simple.[12] In September, I learnt from a school mate that he had come to stay with his mother at La Ferté-Angillon on holiday. But that year, as we had been invited to Vieux-Nançay by my Uncle Florentin, that's where we had to spend the holidays. And Meaulnes went back to Paris without my being able to see him.

After school resumed – to be exact, towards the end of November, while I had settled in, with grim determination, to study for the Brevet supérieur, in the hope of qualifying as a schoolteacher the following year without having to go through the Ecole Normale in Bourges – I received the last of the only three letters that I ever had from Augustin:

I still go past that window. I am still waiting, without the slightest hope, out of pure madness. At the end of these cold autumn Sundays, just as night is falling, I cannot bear to go back home and close the shutters on my windows, without returning there, to that icy street.

I am like the madwoman in Sainte-Agathe who would come out of her front door all the time and, shading her eyes, look towards the station to see if her dead son was coming home.

Sitting on the bench, shivering, miserable, I like to imagine that someone will gently take my arm . . . I should look round and she would be there. 'I'm a bit late,' she would say, simply. And all the sorrow and the madness fade away. We go into our house. Her furs are icy cold and her veil is damp. She brings in the taste of the mist with her from outside, and while she is going over to the fire, I can see her frosty blonde hair and her fine profile with its sweet lines bending over the flames . . .

Alas, the window pane is whitened only by the curtain behind it. And even if the girl from the Lost Domain were to open it, I now have nothing left to tell her.

Our adventure is over. Last winter is as dead as a tomb. Perhaps when we die, death alone will give us the key, and the continuation, and the end of this failed adventure.

Seurel, the other day I asked you to think about me. Now, on the contrary, it is better for you to forget me. Better to forget everything.

A.M.

And it was a new winter, as dead as the last had been alive with some mysterious life: no gypsies on the church square, the school yard empty of children at four o'clock . . . the classroom where I studied alone, without enthusiasm . . . In February, for the first time that winter, the snow fell, finally and forever burying our romantic adventure from the previous year, covering the last traces of it. And I tried, as Meaulnes had asked me in his letter, to forget it all.

PART THREE

I

BATHING

Smoking cigarettes, putting sugar water on your hair to make it curl, kissing the girls from the Cours complémentaire[13] in the lanes and shouting 'magpies!' from behind a hedge to tease a nun as she goes by in her winged cornet – these were the delights of every hooligan in the village. At the age of twenty, by the way, young tearaways of that kind can very well reform and even become thoroughly considerate young men. It's more serious when the lad in question has a face that is already old-looking and battered, when he peddles dubious stories about the women of the locality and when he says a load of silly things about Gilberte Poquelin to make his friends laugh. But even then the cause is not entirely lost . . .

This is how it was with Jasmin Delouche. He stayed on at school – I don't know why, though it was certainly without any wish to take exams – in the Cours supérieur, though everyone would like to have seen him give up. Meanwhile, he was learning the trade of plasterer with his Uncle Dumas. And soon this same Jasmin Delouche, with Boujardon and another very gentle boy, the son of the deputy mayor, called Denis, were the only older boys I liked to be with, because they dated from 'Meaulnes' time'.

In any case, Delouche had a quite sincere desire to be friends with me. The truth was that, having been the enemy of The Great Meaulnes, he would have liked to be the Meaulnes of the school himself: at the least, he may have regretted not being his second-in-command. He was less thick than Boujardon and I think he had realized all the extraordinary things that Meaulnes had brought to our lives. Often I would hear him saying, 'The

Great Meaulnes used to say . . .' or else, 'Ah, that's what The
Great Meaulnes said . . .'

Apart from the fact that Jasmin was more grown-up than we
were, the little chap had a store of curiosities that established
his superiority over us: a mongrel dog with long white hair who
answered to the annoying name of Bécali and brought back
stones when you threw them for him, though he had no distinct
aptitude for any sport; an old second-hand bicycle on which
Jasmin would sometimes let us ride in the evening after school,
but on which he preferred to exercise the village girls; and
finally – and most of all – a blind white donkey that could be
harnessed to any vehicle.

The donkey belonged to Dumas, but he lent it to Jasmin in
summer, when we went to bathe in the Cher. On such occasions,
his mother would give us a bottle of lemonade, which we put
under the seat among the dry bathing trunks. And off we
would go, eight or ten big boys from the school, together with
Monsieur Seurel, some on foot, the rest clambering into the
donkey cart, which we would then leave on the farm of
Grand'Fons at the point where the path to the Cher became
too steep.

I have reason to recall one excursion of this kind in minute
detail. Jasmin's donkey carried our bathing trunks, our clutter,
the lemonade and Monsieur Seurel down to the Cher while we
followed behind on foot. It was August, and we had just taken
our exams. Now that we no longer had them hanging over us,
we felt that the whole summer and all its happiness belonged
to us and walked along the road singing whatever came into
our heads at the start of a fine Thursday afternoon.

This innocent picture was clouded on the outward journey
by just one thing: we saw Gilberte Poquelin walking ahead of
us. She had a tightly belted waist, a mid-length skirt and the
sweet, impudent look of a young girl on the way to becoming
a young woman. She left the road and took a side-path, probably to fetch milk. Little Coffin immediately suggested to Jasmin
that they follow her.

'It wouldn't be the first time I've kissed her,' said Jasmin.

And he started to tell various salacious stories about her and

her friends, while the whole band of us, out of bravado, set off
down the path, leaving Monsieur Seurel to carry on along the
road in the donkey cart. However, once we were there, the
band started to split up, and even Delouche seemed rather
uninclined to accost the girl in front of us and did not approach
her closer than fifty metres. There were some cock crows, hen
clucks and wolf whistles, then we headed back, slightly embarrassed, giving up the chase. On the road, we had to run, under
the bright sunshine. We were not singing any more.

We got changed among the dry reedbeds beside the Cher,
the reeds shielding us from prying eyes, but not from the sun.
With our feet in the sand and the dried mud, we could think of
nothing except the bottle of Widow Delouche's lemonade
which was keeping cool in the spring of Grand'Fons, which
forms a pool in the bank of the river. At the bottom of it you
could always see some blue-green water weeds and two or
three creatures like woodlice, but the water was so clear and
transparent that fishermen would readily come there and kneel
down, with a hand on each bank, to drink from it.

Alas, it was the same that day as on previous occasions!
When we had got dressed and were sitting in a circle on the
ground with our legs crossed so that we could share the cooled
lemonade in two large tumblers, all that was left for each of us
after Monsieur Seurel had been invited to take his share was a
little froth which tickled the back of your throat and only served
to make you more thirsty. So one after another we went to the
pool (which we had originally scorned) and slowly brought our
faces close to the surface of the pure water. But not everyone
was used to these peasant manners. Several of us, including
myself, did not manage to get a drink, some because they did
not like water, others because their throats were too clenched
through fear of swallowing a woodlouse, and still others who,
deceived by the great transparency of the still water, were not
able to judge precisely where the surface was and bathed half
their faces at the same time as their mouths, and as a result
breathed in what seemed like burning water through their noses,
and some, finally, for all these reasons at once . . . No matter!
To us, on these dried-out banks of the Cher, it seemed that all

the coolness of the earth was contained in that place. And even
now, whenever and wherever I hear the word 'spring', that is
the one that lingers in my mind.

We returned at dusk, at first with the same carefree spirits as
when we had set out. The Chemin de Grand'Fons, which led
up to the road, was a stream in winter and, in summer, a
near-impassable gully broken up with holes and large roots,
overshadowed as it made its way upward by tall rows of trees.
One group of bathers went up it, just to show they could. The
rest of us, with Monsieur Seurel, Jasmin and several of our
friends, chose a gentler, sandy path, parallel to the other, alongside a neighbouring field. We could hear the other boys talking
and laughing near by, below us and invisible in the darkness,
while Delouche told his grown-up stories . . . At the top of the
tall row of trees, evening insects were humming: we could see
them, against the clear light of the sky, flying all around the
lacy foliage. Sometimes one of them would suddenly drop and
its hum would become a harsh buzz. A fine, calm summer
evening! And our return – without hope, but without longing
– from an unremarkable country outing . . . It was Jasmin,
again, who unwittingly managed to upset this tranquillity . . .

Just as we arrived at the top of the hill, at the place where
there are two massive old stones which are said to be the
remains of a castle, he started to talk about estates he had
visited, and particularly about a half-abandoned estate near Le
Vieux-Nançay, called Le Domaine des Sablonnières. In his
Allier accent, which boastfully rounds out some words, while
affectedly clipping short others, he told how a few years before
he had seen in the ruined chapel of this old country estate a
tombstone on which the following words were carved:

> Here lies the knight Galois
> Faithful to his God, his King and his Lady

'Ah, why! Huh!' said Monsieur Seurel, shrugging his shoulders a little, and feeling slightly embarrassed at the direction
the conversation was taking, while still wanting to let us talk
like men.

So Jasmin went on to describe the château, as though he had spent his whole life there.

Several times on the way back from Le Vieux-Nançay, Dumas and he had been intrigued by the sight of an old grey turret rising above the fir trees. There was a whole maze of ruined buildings there in the middle of the woods which you could go round since no one lived in them. One day, the guardian of the place, to whom they had given a lift in their cart, had taken them to this strange estate. But since then, everything had been pulled down and, apparently, all that was left was the farm and a little summerhouse. The same people still lived there: an old, retired officer, now impoverished, and his daughter.

He talked on and on . . . I listened attentively, with the feeling at the back of my mind that this was something that I knew well, when suddenly, quite simply – such is the way that extraordinary things happen – Jasmin turned to me and touched my arm, struck by a novel idea.

'Why, do you know what? I've just thought,' he said. 'That must be where Meaulnes went – you know. The Great Meaulnes?'

'Yes, yes,' he went on, when I didn't answer. 'And I remember that the guardian mentioned the son of the family, an eccentric lad who had some extraordinary notions . . .'

I was no longer listening, convinced at once that he had guessed correctly and that before me – far from Meaulnes, far from all hope – had just opened, as clearly and simply as a familiar path, the road to the Estate Without a Name.

II

AT FLORENTIN'S

Now that I felt the outcome of this grave matter depended on me, I became as much a resolute and – as we say – 'decided' young man as I had previously been an unhappy, dreamy and withdrawn child. I do believe that it was from that very evening that my knee finally stopped hurting me.

All Monsieur Seurel's family, in particular Uncle Florentin, a shopkeeper with whom we would sometimes spend the end of September, lived in the *commune* of Le Vieux-Nançay, which was the one where Le Domaine des Sablonnières lay. Since I did not have any more exams, I said that I did not want to wait for late September, and got permission to go straightaway to see my uncle. But I decided not to tell Meaulnes anything until I was certain that I could give him some good news – for what was the sense in lifting him out of his despair, only afterwards perhaps to plunge him even deeper into it?

Le Vieux-Nançay had long been the place that I loved most in the world: the scene of summer endings where we only went on very rare occasions, when there happened to be a carriage for hire that would take us there. There had previously been some quarrel with the branch of the family that lived there, and this may have been why Millie always took such urging before she would get into the carriage. What did I care, though, for all their disputes? And as soon as we arrived I would be absorbed into the life of my uncles and cousins and revel in its many amusing diversions and delights. We would stay with Uncle Florentin and Aunt Julie, who had a boy of my age, Cousin Firmin, and eight daughters, the eldest of whom, Marie-Louise and Charlotte, might have been seventeen and fifteen respectively. They had a very big shop in front of the church at one of the gates of this little town, a general store which served all the landowners and hunters of this part of the Sologne, alone in the empty countryside, thirty kilometres from the nearest railway station.

The shop, with its grocery and dry-goods counters, had several windows overlooking the road and, on the side of the church square, a large glazed door. The odd thing, however, was that throughout the shop there was a dirt floor instead of a wooden one (though this was quite common in this poor region of the country).

At the back, there were six rooms, each containing one single kind of merchandise: the hat room, the gardening room, the lamp room, and so on ... When I was a child walking through this maze of objects for sale, I thought I would never exhaust the wonder of looking at it. And in those days, too, I felt that this was the only place where there were any real holidays.

The family lived in a large kitchen, the door of which opened into the shop, a kitchen in which at the end of September great fires always blazed in the chimney, and hunters and poachers who sold game to Florentin came early in the morning to get a drink, while the girls, already up, would run around and shout and put 'smells-good' lotion on one another's shining hair. On the wall were old photographs – with old school group photographs showing my father among his fellow students at the Ecole Normale (though it was hard to recognize him in his uniform).

This is where we spent the mornings, or else in the yard where Florentin grew dahlias and raised guineafowl, and where they roasted the coffee, sitting on soapboxes, and where we would unpack crates full of different objects meticulously wrapped – objects to which we could not always put a name ...

All day long the shop was invaded by countryfolk or the coachmen from the large houses of the district. Vehicles, up from the depths of the country, would stop, dripping in the late September fog in front of the glazed door. And from the kitchen we could hear what the farm women said, full of curiosity about all their tables.

But the evening, after eight o'clock, as by lantern light we took hay to the horses steaming in the stable, was when the whole shop belonged to us!

Marie-Louise, the eldest of my girl cousins, but one of the smallest, would be folding and stowing away the lengths of cloth on the shelves and would encourage us to come and amuse her. So Firmin and I, with all the girls, would burst into the big shop under its inn lamps, winding the coffee grinders and performing acrobatics on the counters; and sometimes, because the dirt floor invited one to dance on it, Firmin would go to the attic and fetch an old trombone, covered in verdigris.

I still blush to think that, in earlier years, Mademoiselle de Galais could have arrived at such a moment and surprised us in the midst of all this childish activity ... But it was a little before nightfall, one evening in that month of August, while I was quietly chatting with Marie-Louise and Firmin, that I saw her for the first time ...

On the first evening after my arrival at Le Vieux-Nançay, I asked Uncle Florentin about Le Domaine des Sablonnières.

'It's not a proper estate any more,' he said. 'They sold everything, and the purchasers, who are hunters, had the old buildings pulled down to increase their hunting ground. The main courtyard is just a waste of heather and gorse. The former owners just kept a little, one-storey house and the farm. You'll surely get a chance to see Mademoiselle de Galais here because she comes herself to buy groceries, either on horseback or in a trap, but always with the same horse, old Bélisaire ... It's an odd kind of set-up.'

I was so disturbed that I did not know what question to ask to find out more.

'Weren't they rich, though?'

'Yes. Monsieur de Galais threw parties to amuse his son, an odd boy, full of extraordinary ideas. He did whatever he could to entertain him, bringing women down from Paris ... and boys from Paris and elsewhere ...

'All of Les Sablonnières was in ruins, and Madame de Galais near the end of her life, but they still tried to entertain him

and humoured his every whim. It was last winter ... no, the
winter before that, when they held their biggest fancy dress
party. They had invited some people from Paris and some from
the country, and bought or hired lots of wonderful costumes,
games, horses and boats. Just to amuse Frantz de Galais. They
said that he was going to get married and that he was celebrating
his engagement, but he was much too young. And suddenly it
all fell to pieces. He ran off and hasn't been seen since ... When
the mistress died, Mademoiselle de Galais was suddenly left all
alone with her father, the old sea captain.'

'She's not married?' I asked, finally.

'No,' he said. 'I haven't heard it mentioned. Might you be a
suitor?'

Somewhat put out, I admitted as briefly and as discreetly as
possible that my best friend, Augustin Meaulnes, could perhaps
be one.

'Ah!' Florentin said with a smile. 'If he's not concerned about
money, she'd be a good match. Should I talk about it to Monsieur de Galais? He still comes here sometimes to look for some
buckshot for hunting. I always get him to try my old brandy.'

I hastily begged him not to do anything, but to wait. I, too,
was not in a hurry to inform Meaulnes. All these lucky accidents, one after another, made me rather uneasy, and this
anxiety told me to say nothing to Meaulnes until I had at least
seen the girl.

I did not have long to wait. The next day, a little before dinner,
night was just falling and a cold mist, more appropriate to
September than August, came down with the darkness. Firmin
and I, guessing that the shop would shortly be empty of customers, had come in to see Marie-Louise and Charlotte. I had
entrusted both of them with the secret that had brought me at
such an early date to Le Vieux-Nançay. Leaning on the counter
or sitting with both hands flat on the waxed wooden surface,
we were telling each other all that we knew about the mysterious young woman – which amounted to very little – when the
sound of wheels outside made our heads turn.

'Here you are,' they said quietly. 'It's her.'

A few moments later, the strange rig stopped in front of the glass door. An old farm wagon with rounded panels and little moulded cornices, of a kind that we had never seen thereabouts, an old white horse carrying his head so low as he walked that he seemed constantly to be trying to graze on some grass along the road, and on the seat – I say this with all the simplicity of my heart, fully aware of what I say – perhaps the most beautiful young woman that ever there was in this world.

Never have I seen such charm combined with such dignity. Her clothes made her waist so slender than she seemed fragile. A great brown cloak, which she took off as she came in, was thrown around her shoulders: she was the most solemn of girls, the most delicate of women. A heavy mass of hair hung across her forehead and over her delicately featured, finely moulded face. The summer had left two freckles on her pure white skin . . . I could see only one flaw in so much beauty: when she was sad, upset or simply deep in thought, her clear complexion became faintly mottled with red, like that of certain people who are very ill without knowing it. At such times, the admiration of the person looking at her would give way to a kind of pity that was all the more heartrending for being unexpected.

At least, that is what I learnt while she was slowly getting out of the cart and Marie-Louise at last introduced me to the young woman, quite unselfconsciously, inviting me to talk to her.

They brought over a waxed chair for her and she sat with her back to the counter while we remained standing. She seemed to know the shop well and to like it. My Aunt Julie was informed at once and arrived, so the time that she spent talking, demurely, with her hands crossed in front of her, gently nodding her peasant head in its white cap, put off the moment that I was slightly dreading, when I should have to speak to her.

It proved very simple.

'So,' Mademoiselle de Galais said, 'you'll soon be a teacher?'

My aunt lit the porcelain lamp above our heads, which cast its pale light across the shop. I saw the girl's soft, childlike face, her blue eyes, which had such innocence; and I was at first surprised by her voice, so firm and grave. When she finished speaking, her eyes would settle on something else and stay there, not moving, while she waited for an answer, and she bit her lip a little.

'I should teach, myself,' she said, 'if Monsieur de Galais wanted me to. I should teach little boys, as your mother does . . .'

And she smiled, showing that my cousins had spoken to her about me.

'The reason is,' she went on, 'that with me the village people are always polite, kind and helpful. And I am very fond of them. But I claim no credit for that.

'On the other hand, with the schoolmistress, they are quarrelsome and miserly, aren't they? There are endless arguments over lost pencil cases, exercise books being too dear or children who don't learn . . . Well, I should stick up to them and they would like me in spite of that. It would be much harder . . .'

At that, without smiling, she resumed her thoughtful, childlike pose, and her blue eyes were still.

All three of us were embarrassed at the ease with which she spoke of delicate matters, of things that are secret and subtle, and not usually well expressed outside books. There was a moment's silence, then slowly a discussion began . . .

However, with a kind of regret and animosity about something mysterious in her life, the young lady continued:

'And then I'd teach the boys to be sensible and wise and well behaved, as only I know how. I wouldn't give them an urge to go travelling all around the place as I expect you will, Monsieur Seurel, when you're a junior master. I'd teach them how to find the happiness that is right beside them, but which they don't see . . .'

Marie-Louise and Firmin were as speechless as I was. We stood there without a word. She realized we were embarrassed and stopped, biting her lip and lowering her gaze. Then she smiled, as though making fun of us, and said, 'So, there may be some tall, crazy young man looking for me at the furthest corner of the world, while I am here in Madame Florentin's shop under this lamp, with my old horse waiting for me at the door. If that young man could see me, I expect he wouldn't believe his eyes.'

Seeing her smile emboldened me, and I felt that it was the moment for me to say, also with a laugh, 'And perhaps I know that tall, crazy young man?'

She gave me a keen look.

At that moment, the bell on the door rang and two country women came in carrying baskets.

'Come into the "dining room", you won't be disturbed there,' my aunt said, opening the kitchen door. And, as Mademoiselle de Galais was refusing and wanted to leave at once, she added, 'Monsieur de Galais is here, talking to Florentin over the fire.'

Even in August, there was always a crackling fire of fir branches in the big kitchen. Here, too, there was a porcelain lamp lit, while an old man with a gentle face, lined and clean-shaven, almost always silent like someone weighed down with age and memories, was sitting next to Florentin in front of two glasses of *marc*.

Florentin welcomed us.

'François!' he shouted, in his loud, hawker's voice, as though a river and several hectares of land lay between us. 'I've just organized an outing beside the Cher for next Thursday. Some of us will go hunting, others will fish; some will dance and others bathe! You come on horseback, Mademoiselle. Monsieur de Galais and I are agreed, it's all settled . . .'

'And you, François!' he added, as though just thinking of this. 'You can bring your friend, Monsieur Meaulnes . . . That's his name, isn't it? Meaulnes?'

Mademoiselle de Galais stood up, the colour suddenly draining from her face. And at that very moment, I remembered that Meaulnes, once, in the mysterious domain, near the lake, had told her his name . . .

When she held out her hand to say goodbye, there was a secret understanding between us, clearer than if many words had passed – an understanding that only death would break and a friendship more poignant than a great love.

Next morning, at four o'clock, Firmin was knocking on the door of the little room that I occupied in the yard for the guineafowl. It was still dark, and I had a good deal of trouble finding my things on the table, which was cluttered with copper candlesticks and little, brand-new statues of saints that had been brought from the shop on the day before my arrival, to furnish my room. I could hear Firmin in the yard, pumping up the tyres of my bicycle, and my aunt in the kitchen blowing on the fire. The sun was barely up when I left. But I had a long day ahead of me: first I would go and have lunch at Sainte-Agathe to explain why I had been away so long, and then, carrying on, I was due to arrive before evening at La Ferté-d'Angillon, at the home of my friend, Augustin Meaulnes.

III

AN APPARITION

I had never before been on a long cycle ride: this was the first. But, despite my bad knee, Jasmin had for some time been teaching me to ride. And if for an ordinary young man a bicycle is a very enjoyable conveyance, just imagine what it would have seemed to a poor boy like myself, who until recently had had to limp along, bathed in sweat, after less than four kilometres! Plunging down from the top of a hill in the depths of the countryside, discovering the distant road ahead like a bird on the wing and watching it open and blossom around you, dashing through a village and taking it in with a single glance . . . So far only in dreams had I experienced such delightful, airy motion; even climbing the hills I felt full of energy, because, I have to admit, it was the road to Meaulnes' place that was flying beneath my wheels . . .

'A little before the entrance to the town,' Meaulnes had told me earlier when he was describing it to me, 'you can see a large wheel with vanes that turn in the wind.' He did not know the purpose of it, or perhaps was pretending not to, in order to fire my curiosity.

It was only towards the end of that late August day that, in a vast field, I saw the great wheel, which probably pumped up water for a nearby farm. Behind the poplars in the meadow you could already see the first outlying buildings of the little town. As I followed the wide bend that the road took to avoid crossing the stream, the countryside opened up until, reaching the bridge, I finally came upon the main street of the village.

Cows were grazing, hidden among the reeds in the meadow,

and I could hear their bells as I looked at the place to which I was about to bring such a serious piece of news. I had got down from my cycle and was holding the handlebar in both hands. The houses were all lined up along a ditch running the length of the street, and you entered them by crossing over a little wooden bridge: they were like so many boats, with their sails furled, moored in the evening calm. It was the moment when a fire was being lit in every kitchen.

At this, fear and some vague regret at coming to disturb such peace started to sap my courage. Just then, too, intensifying this sudden feeling of weakness, I remembered that Aunt Moinel lived there, on a little square of La Ferté-Angillon.

She was one of my great aunts. All her children were dead, and I had been well acquainted with Ernest, the last to go, a tall lad who was to be a schoolmaster. My great uncle Moinel, a former clerk of the court, had followed close after, and my aunt was left all alone in her odd little house where the carpets were made of samples sewn together and the tables covered with paper cockerels, hens and cats, but where the walls were lined with old diplomas, portraits of the dead and medallions formed of dead hair.

Despite so many sadnesses and so much mourning, she was the personification of eccentricity and good humour. When I had found the little square where she lived, I called her loudly through the half-open door and heard her from the very last of the three adjoining rooms give a little high-pitched shout: 'Oh, oh! My goodness!'

She threw her coffee on the fire – how could she be making coffee at this time of day? – and made her appearance . . . Very upright and wearing a sort of hat-hood-bonnet on the crown of her head, above her vast, protuding forehead, she had something of a Mongolian or Hottentot woman about her; and she gave little laughs, showing what was left of her very small teeth.

But while I was kissing her, she quickly and awkwardly took the hand that I was holding behind my back; and, with a quite unnecessary air of concealment, she slipped a small coin into it that I didn't dare look at, though it must have been a one-franc piece. Then, as I appeared to want an explanation, or to thank her, she gave me a dig in the ribs, shouting, 'Go on with you! I know what it's like!'

She had always been poor, always borrowing and always spending. 'I've always been stupid and always unhappy,' she would say, without bitterness, in her high-pitched voice.

Certain that I thought about money as much as she did, this good woman would not wait for me to draw breath before slipping her day's meagre savings into my hand. And from then on, this was how she would always greet me.

Dinner was as strange – both eccentric and sad – as her welcome had been. She always had a candle within reach and would sometimes take it, leaving me in the shadows, and sometimes put it down on the little table, covered in dishes and vases that were chipped or cracked.

'Now that one,' she would say, 'lost its handles when the Prussians broke them off in seventy,[14] because they couldn't take it away.'

Only then, seeing this vase with its tragic history, did I remember that we had eaten and slept there in the past. My father used to bring me to the Yonne to see a specialist who was meant to heal my knee. We had to take a big express train that came past before daylight . . . I recalled the sad dinners we used to have and all the old court clerk's stories as he sat leaning on the table in front of his bottle of pink liquid.

I also recalled my terrors . . . After dinner, sitting in front of the fire, my great aunt had taken my father to one side to tell him a story about ghosts: 'I looked round . . . Ah! My poor Louis! What did I see? A little grey woman.' She was said to have her head stuffed with this terrifying rubbish.

And now that evening, when dinner was over and, tired out by my cycle ride, I was lying in the big bedroom in a checked nightshirt that had belonged to Uncle Moinel, she came and sat by the bed and started to say, in her most mysterious and shrill voice, 'My poor François, I have to tell you something that I have never told anyone before . . .'

I thought, 'That's it! Now I'll be scared stiff the whole night, as I was ten years ago.'

I listened. She shook her head, staring directly ahead as though telling the story to herself:

'I was coming back from a wedding with Moinel. It was the first that we had been to together since our poor Ernest died, and among the guests was my sister Adèle, whom I hadn't seen for four years. An old friend of Moinel's who was very rich had invited her to his son's wedding at Le Domaine des Sablonnières. We had hired a carriage: it cost us a lot. At around seven in the morning we were driving back along the road, in mid-winter. The sun was rising, and there was absolutely no one around. Then suddenly what did I see on the road ahead? A little man, a little young man standing there, very good-looking, not moving, just watching us drive towards him. As we got nearer, we made out his pretty face, which was so white and so pretty that it scared you!

'I took Moinel's arm – I was shaking like a leaf . . . I thought it was the Good Lord himself! I said: "Look! An apparition!"

'He answered me angrily, under his breath, "I've seen him! Shut up, you old chatterbox!"

'He didn't know what to do; then the horse stopped . . . Close up, the thing had a pale face, the forehead beaded with sweat, and it was wearing a dirty beret and long trousers. We heard a soft voice saying, "I'm not a man, I'm a girl. I've run away and I can't go on. Please could you take me in your carriage, Monsieur and Madame?"

'At once, we told her to get in. No sooner was she sitting down than she fainted. And just guess who it was? The fiancée of the young man from Les Sablonnières, Frantz de Galais, to whose wedding we had been invited!'

'But there was no wedding,' I said, 'because the bride ran away.'

'Why, that's right,' she said, looking at me sheepishly. 'There was no wedding, because the poor foolish girl had got a thousand silly ideas into her head, as she told us. She was one of the daughters of a poor weaver. She was sure that so much

happiness was not possible, that the young man was too young
for her, and that all the wonderful things that he had told her
about were imaginary, so when Frantz finally came to get her,
Valentine took fright. He was walking with her and her sister
in the garden of the archbishop's palace in Bourges, even though
it was cold and very windy. The young man, surely being
considerate and because he was in love with the younger sister,
paid a lot of attention to the elder one. So my silly girl got I
don't know what ideas into her head. She said she was going
to fetch a scarf from the house and there, to make sure she was
not followed, she dressed in men's clothes and ran away down
the Paris road.

'Her fiancé received a letter in which she told him that she
was going to be with a young man that she loved. It wasn't
true . . .

'"I'm happier because of my sacrifice," she told me, "than
I would be as his wife." Yes, little idiot, but meanwhile he had
no intention of marrying her sister. He shot himself with a
pistol – they saw the blood in the woods, but never found his
body.'

'What did you do with this unfortunate girl?'

'We gave her a sip of brandy, first of all, then something to
eat, and she fell asleep in front of the fire when we got home.
She spent a good part of the winter here with us.'

'All day long, while it was light, she cut out and sewed
dresses, decorated hats and furiously cleaned the house. She
was the one who stuck back all the wallpaper that you can see
there. And since that time, the swallows have been nesting
outside. But in the evening, when night fell and her work was
done, she always found an excuse to go out into the yard, into
the garden or on the porch, even when it was icy cold. And
we'd find her standing there, crying her heart out.

'"Come now, what's wrong? Tell me."

'"Nothing, Madame Moinel."

'And she would come back inside.

'The neighbours used to say, "You've found a pretty little
maid there, Madame Moinel."

'Even though we begged her not to, she wanted to carry on

towards Paris when March came. I gave her some dresses that she altered to her size and Moinel bought her ticket at the station and gave her a little money.

'She didn't forget us. She's a dressmaker in Paris near Notre-Dame. She still writes to us to ask whether we have any news from Les Sablonnières. To put that idea out of her head, I told her once and for all that the estate had been sold and pulled down, and that the young man had vanished for ever and that the girl was married. I think all that must be true. Since then my Valentine has been writing to us much less often.'

It was not a ghost story that Aunt Moinel had told me in her shrill little voice that was so well suited to telling them. Even so, I was as uneasy as could be. The reason was that we had sworn to Frantz the gypsy to serve him like brothers, and now I had the opportunity to do so . . . But was this the moment to spoil the joy that I was going to bring Meaulnes the next morning by telling him what I had learnt? What was the sense of launching him on an utterly impossible quest? Certainly, we had the girl's address, but where to start looking for the gypsy who was wandering the world? Let the mad look after their mad, I thought. Delouche and Boujardon had been right. What a lot of harm that romanticizing Frantz had done us! I decided to say nothing until I had seen Augustin Meaulnes married to Mademoiselle de Galais.

Even when I had made up my mind, I still had a painful sense of foreboding – though I was quick to dispel this ridiculous idea.

The candle had almost burnt down, and a mosquito was humming, but Aunt Moinel, leaning with her elbows on her knees and her head bowed under the velvet hood that she did not take off even to sleep, started her story again . . . From time to time, she looked up and examined me to see what I was thinking (and perhaps to make sure that I was not dropping off to sleep). Eventually, with my head on the pillow, I slyly closed my eyes, pretending to doze off . . .

'What's this? You're sleeping,' she said, in a lower voice, slightly disappointed.

I felt sorry for her and protested, 'No, aunt, I promise . . .'

'Yes, you are!' she said. 'Anyway, I can understand if it doesn't interest you very much. It's all about people you don't know . . .'

Coward that I am, that time I didn't reply.

IV

THE GREAT NEWS

When I reached the main street the next morning, it was such lovely holiday weather, so tranquil and with such gentle, familiar sounds throughout the town, that I regained all the joyful confidence of a bringer of good news.

Augustin and his mother lived in the old schoolhouse. His father had inherited a lot of money and retired early; after his death, Meaulnes wanted them to buy the school where the old master had taught for twenty years and where he himself had learnt to read. Not that it was a particularly prepossessing building: it was a large, square house, like the town hall that it had also been, and the ground-floor windows facing the street were so high up that no one ever looked out of them. As for the yard at the back, there was not a single tree in it, and a high shed blocked the view over the countryside: it was far and away the most barren and desolate school yard that I have ever seen . . .

There was a complicated passage with four doors leading off it where I came on Meaulnes' mother bringing a large bundle of washing in from the garden: she must have put it out to dry at dawn on that long holiday morning. Her grey hair was half undone, with wisps hanging across her face, and her features were puffy and tired under her old-fashioned cap, as though she had not slept. She had a thoughtful look and downcast eyes.

But, suddenly noticing me, she recognized me and smiled.

'You've come just at the right moment,' she said. 'You see, I'm just bringing in the clothes that I was drying for when Augustin goes away. I spent the night settling his accounts and getting his things ready. The train goes at five, but we will manage to prepare everything.'

You would have thought, seeing her so definite, that she had taken the decision herself. In fact, she certainly had no idea where Meaulnes was going.

'Go on up,' she said. 'You'll find him in the town hall, writing.'

I hastily climbed the stairs, opened the door on the right, which still bore a sign saying *Town Hall*, and went into a large room with four windows, two on the town, two on the country side, its walls decorated with yellowing portraits of Presidents Grévy and Carnot.[15] On a long dais that extended the whole length of the room you could still see the seats of the town councillors in front of a table with a green baize cloth. In the middle, sitting on an old armchair that had belonged to the mayor, Meaulnes was writing, dipping his pen deep into an old-fashioned porcelain inkwell in the shape of a heart. It was here, to this place that seemed to have been made for some well-to-do villager, that Meaulnes would retire in the holidays, when he was not roaming the countryside . . .

He got up when he recognized me, but not with the eagerness I had expected, just saying 'Seurel!' with an air of profound amazement.

He was the same boy with his bony face and close-cropped head; an unkempt moustache was starting to grow on his upper lip. He still had the same frank and honest look . . . but it was as though a mist had settled over the enthusiasm of earlier times, a mist that was only momentarily parted by glimpses of his former ardour.

He seemed very disturbed at seeing me. I had bounded up on to the dais but, strangely, he didn't even think to offer me his hand. He turned towards me with his hands behind him, leaning back against the table with a deeply embarrassed air. He was looking at me without seeing me, already absorbed in thinking about what he would say. As ever and always, he was slow in beginning to speak, like all solitary people and hunters and adventurers: he had taken a decision without considering the words needed to explain it. And only now that I was there in front of him did he start painfully to mull over how to say it.

Meanwhile, I was merrily describing my journey, where I spent the night and how surprised I had been to see Madame Meaulnes getting ready for her son's departure.

'Ah! She told you?' he asked.

'Yes, but I don't suppose it's for a long journey, is it?'

'On the contrary, for a very long journey.'

For a moment I was at a loss, not daring to say anything, sensing that very soon, with a word, I would abolish his decision, though I had no idea why he had taken it, and not knowing where to begin.

But at length he started to speak, like someone trying to justify himself.

'Seurel,' he said, 'you know how important that strange adventure at Sainte-Agathe was for me . . . It was my reason to live and hope . . . Once I had lost that hope, what would become of me? How could I live like other people? Well, I tried to live in Paris, when I saw that it was all over and that it was not even worthwhile trying to find the Lost Domain . . . But once a man has taken a step in Paradise, how can he afterwards get used to living like everyone else? The things that make up the happiness of other people seemed ludicrous to me. And when, one day, quite sincerely and deliberately, I decided to behave as others do, that day I stored up enough remorse to last a long time . . .'

Sitting on a chair on the dais with my head lowered, listening to him without looking at him, I did not know what to think of these vague explanations.

'Meaulnes,' I said, 'can you be a bit clearer? Why the long journey? Do you have to make amends for something? Or do you have a promise to keep?'

'In fact, yes,' he replied. 'Do you remember the promise I made to Frantz?'

'Ah!' I said, with relief. 'Is that it?'

'That's it. And perhaps something to make amends for. Both at the same time . . .'

There followed a moment's silence in which I made up my mind to start speaking and prepared my words.

'There's only one explanation that I believe in,' he went on. 'Certainly, I would have liked to see Mademoiselle de Galais once more, just to see her . . . But now I'm sure that when I discovered the Estate Without a Name, I reached a height, a degree of perfection and purity that I shall never achieve again. In death alone, as I once wrote to you, I may perhaps recapture the beauty of that time . . .'

His tone changed and he continued, coming closer to me and with a strange intensity in his manner:

'But, listen, Seurel: this new development and this great journey, the sin that I committed and for which I have to atone, all this, in a sense, is the continuation of my old adventure . . .'

There was a pause while he tried painfully to recapture his memories. I had missed the last opportunity and I was absolutely determined not to let this one pass, so this time I was the one to speak – but too soon: later I bitterly regretted not having waited for his confession.

Anyway, I spoke my piece, which had been prepared for an earlier moment, and was no longer appropriate. Without a gesture and merely raising my head a little, I said, 'Suppose I were to tell you that all hope is not lost?'

He looked at me, then, quickly looking away, blushed as I have never seen anyone blush: a rush of blood that must have been beating great hammer blows in his temples.

'What do you mean?' he asked at last, in a barely audible voice.

So, without pausing, I told him what I knew, what I had done and how, with the turn that matters had taken, it almost seemed that it was Yvonne de Galais who had sent me to him.

By now, he was horribly pale.

During my story, which he heard in silence, his head bowed a little, with the attitude of someone who has been taken by surprise and does not know how to defend himself, whether to hide or run away, I remember that he only interrupted me once. I was telling him, incidentally, that all of Les Sablonnières had been demolished and that the old estate no longer existed.

'There!' he said. 'You see . . .' (as though he had been waiting for an opportunity to justify his behaviour and the despair into which he had fallen). 'You see: there is nothing left . . .'

At the end, convinced that my assurance of how easy it would now be would dispel the remains of his misery, I told him that a picnic had been organized by my Uncle Florentin, that Mademoiselle de Galais was to come on horseback and that he, too, was invited . . . But he appeared completely bewildered and didn't say anything.

'You must put off your journey at once,' I said, impatiently. 'Let's go and tell your mother . . .'

And as we were both going down together, he asked, hesitantly, 'Do I really have to go on this picnic?'

'Come, now,' I replied. 'How can you ask such a question?'

He looked like someone being pushed along by his shoulders.

Downstairs, Augustin informed Madame Meaulnes that I would be having lunch with them, then dinner, that I would spend the night there and the next day that he would hire a bicycle and cycle with me to Le Vieux-Nançay.

'Oh! Very good,' she said, nodding her head, as though this news had confirmed all her suspicions.

I sat down in the little dining room, under the illustrated calendars, the ornamented daggers and the Sudanese leather bottles that one of Monsieur Meaulnes' brothers, a former soldier in the marines, had brought back from his distant travels.

Augustin left me there for a moment before the meal and, in the adjoining room, where his mother had been packing his suitcases, I heard him tell her, in a quiet voice, not to unpack his trunk because his journey might only be temporarily adjourned . . .

V

THE OUTING

I had a hard time keeping up with Augustin on the road to Le Vieux-Nançay. He rode like a racing cyclist. He didn't get off for hills. His inexplicable uncertainty of the previous day had been replaced by a fever, a nervousness, an urge to get there as soon as possible, which even scared me a little. He showed the same impatience at my uncle's, seeming unable to take an interest in anything until we were settled in the trap around ten o'clock the next morning, ready to set out for the river bank.

It was the end of August, in the last days of summer. The empty burrs of the yellow chestnuts were starting to litter the white roads. It was not a long journey. The farm of Les Aubiers, near the Cher, where we were going, was only two kilometres from Les Sablonnières. From time to time, we met other guests driving to the spot and even young men on horseback whom Florentin had boldly invited in Monsieur de Galais' name. As in the past, an effort had been made to mix rich and poor, landowners and peasants. So it was that we saw Jasmin Delouche arrive on a bicycle: he had earlier made the acquaintance of my uncle through the forester, Baladier.

'Now,' said Meaulnes when he saw him, 'there is the one who had the key to everything while we went looking as far away as Paris. It's enough to drive you to despair!'

Every time he looked at him, this bitterness increased. The other boy, who by contrast imagined that he was fully entitled to our gratitude, closely escorted our trap right to the end of the journey. You could see that he had made a pitiful effort to make himself presentable, to no great effect, and the tails of his worn coat were flapping against his cycle mudguard...

Much as he tried to be agreeable, he could not make his old man's face pleasant to look at; if anything, I felt sorry for him. But, then, for whom would I not feel sorry before that day was done?

I can never recall that outing without a vague and, as it were, stifling feeling of regret. I had been so looking forward to that day! Everything seemed perfectly coordinated for happiness, yet there was so little happiness to be had . . .

Yet how lovely the Cher looked! On the bank where we stopped, the hillside levelled out into a gentle slope which was divided into little green fields, willow groves with fences between them, like so many minute gardens. On the far side of the river, the banks were made up of steep, rocky, grey hills, and on the furthest of these you could make out, among the fir trees, romantic little châteaux with single turrets. Occasionally, in the distance, we could hear the barking of the hounds from the château of Préveranges.

We had got here through a maze of little paths, some covered with white stones, others with sand, which water springs transformed into streams as we got closer to the river. As we went past, the branches of wild gooseberries clutched at our sleeves, and we were sometimes plunged into the cool darkness at the bottom of gullies, and sometimes, by contrast, when there were gaps in the hedges, bathed in the clear sunlight that spread across the valley. In the distance, on the far bank, there was a man perched among the rocks, casting a fishing line with a slow gesture. Oh, God, what a lovely day it was!

We settled down on a patch of lawn in the clearing formed by a copse of birch trees. It was a broad expanse of short grass that seemed to have been put there for endless games.

The horses were unharnessed and taken to the farm of Les Aubiers. We started to unpack the food in the woods and to set up on the grass little folding tables which my uncle had brought.

Now, volunteers were needed to go back to the fork on the main road and look out for latecomers to show them where we were. I immediately put up my hand, and Meaulnes did the same, so we went to take up our post near the suspension bridge where several roads joined the one coming from Les Sablonnières.

As we walked up and down, talking about the past and trying as best we could to make the time go by, we waited. Another carriage came from Le Vieux-Nançay, with some unknown countryfolk and a big daughter with ribbons in her hair. Then, nothing – oh, except for three children in a donkey cart, the children of the former gardener at Les Sablonnières.

'I think I recognize them,' Meaulnes said. 'They were the ones, I feel sure, who took my hand, that time, on the first evening in the château, and led me into dinner.'

But just then the donkey stopped, and the children got down to goad him, pull him and hit him as hard as they could and Meaulnes, disappointed, said that he must have been mistaken . . .

I asked them if they had met Monsieur and Mademoiselle de Galais along the road. One said, no, he hadn't, while the other said, 'I think so, Monsieur.' So that got us nowhere. Finally they started off towards the river bank, some pulling the donkey by its bridle, the rest pushing the cart from behind. We resumed our watch. Meaulnes was staring hard at the bend in the road from Les Sablonnières, awaiting the arrival of the young woman whom he had looked for so eagerly before, but now awaited with a kind of terror. An odd, almost comic, nervous state had seized him, and he took it out on Jasmin. From the top of the little mound up which we had climbed to see further down the road, we could see a group of guests on the grass below us, with Delouche in the middle trying to impress them.

'Look at him, speechifying, the idiot,' Meaulnes said.

'Let him be,' I answered. 'He's doing his best, poor boy.'

Augustin would not let go. A hare or a squirrel must have broken cover and run across the grass. Jasmin was showing off by pretending to pursue it.

'Just look at that! Now he's running . . .' Meaulnes said, as though this exploit were the worst of all.

I couldn't help laughing. Meaulnes, too – but only for an instant.

After a further quarter of an hour, he said, 'Suppose she doesn't come?'

I answered: 'But she promised – so just be patient!'

He resumed his watch over the road. But eventually, unable to bear this intolerable wait any longer, he said, 'Listen, I'm going back to the others. I don't know what's up with me at the moment, but I feel sure that if I wait here, she won't ever come . . . that it's impossible that she should appear sometime soon at the end of that road . . .'

He went back down towards the river bank, leaving me all alone. I marched back and forth once or twice on the side road, to waste time. And at the first bend I saw Yvonne de Galais, riding sidesaddle on her old white horse, though he was so frisky that morning that she had to pull on the reins to stop him from trotting. In front of the horse, in strained silence, walked Monsieur de Galais. They had probably been taking turns as they came, each getting a ride on the old animal.

When she saw me by myself, the girl smiled, lightly dismounted, handed the reins to her father and headed to meet me as I ran towards her.

'I'm so happy to find you alone,' she said. 'I don't want anyone but you to see old Belisarius or to put him with the other horses. For a start, he's too old and ugly, and then I'm always scared that one of the others will hurt him. Yet he's the only horse I dare ride, and when he dies, I won't go on horseback again.'

Under this charming vivacity and apparently so tranquil grace, in Mademoiselle de Galais as in Meaulnes, I sensed impatience and something close to anxiety. She spoke faster than usual and, despite the pinkness of her cheeks, there was an intense pallor in places around her eyes and on her forehead, in which you could detect the extent of her unease . . .

We agreed to tie Belisarius up to a tree in a little wood near the road. Old Monsieur de Galais, without a word as always, removed the halter from the saddlebag and tied the creature up – a little low down, I thought. I promised shortly to send hay, oats and straw from the farm . . .

And Mademoiselle de Galais went down to the river bank as

she had once approached the shore of the lake, on the day when Meaulnes saw her for the first time . . .

Giving her arm to her father and holding aside the flap of the loose white cloak that was wrapped around her, she made her way towards the guests, with that look of hers, at once so serious and so innocent. I was walking beside her. All the guests, scattered around the grassy space or playing some way off had got up and gathered to receive her. There was a brief moment of silence while each of them watched her approach.

Meaulnes had joined the group of young men, and only his height distinguished him from the rest; and even then, there were some young men almost as tall as he was. He did nothing that could draw attention to himself: not a movement, not a step forward. I could see him, dressed in grey, motionless, staring like all the others at this beautiful young woman coming towards them. Yet, at the end, with an awkward, instinctive movement, he put a hand to his bare head as though he wanted, amid the well-combed hair of his companions, to hide his rough, close-cropped peasant's head.

Then the group surrounded Mademoiselle de Galais, and she was introduced to the young men and women whom she did not know. It was about to be my friend's turn, and I felt as anxious as he must have been. I was getting ready to do the introduction myself. But before I could say anything, the girl went over to him with surprising gravity and firmness.

'I recognize you, Augustin Meaulnes,' she said. And she held out her hand.

VI

THE OUTING

(end)

New arrivals came almost at once to greet Yvonne de Galais, so the two young people were separated. By ill luck they were not put together at the same little table for lunch. But Meaulnes seemed to have regained strength and confidence. Several times, as I was cut off between Delouche and Monsieur de Galais, I saw him giving me a friendly wave from a distance.

It was only towards the end of the afternoon, when most people had been organized into playing games, bathing, conversational groups and the boating trips on the nearby pond, that Meaulnes found himself once more in the young woman's company. We were chatting with Delouche, sitting on some garden chairs that we had brought with us, when, deliberately leaving a group of young people who seemed to be boring her, Mademoiselle de Galais came over to us. I remember that she asked why we were not boating with the others on the Lac des Aubiers.

'We did go out a few times this afternoon,' I said. 'But it's a bit tedious and we soon got tired of it.'

'So why not go on the river?' she asked.

'The current is too strong; we could be carried away.'

'What we need,' said Meaulnes, 'is a motor boat or a steam boat, like the one you used to have.'

'We don't have it any longer,' she said, almost whispering. 'We sold it.'

There was an embarrassed silence. Jasmin took advantage of it to announce that he was going to join Monsieur de Galais.

'I'll find him,' he said.

By a quirk of fate these two, quite dissimilar individuals had taken a liking to one another and had been together since the morning. Monsieur de Galais had led me to one side for a moment earlier in the afternoon and congratulated me on having a friend who was so full of tact, so respectful and possessed of so many other fine qualities. He might even have gone so far as to tell him about the existence of Belisarius and confide the secret of where he was hidden.

I was also thinking of leaving, but I felt the two of them to be so ill at ease and so nervous with one another that I decided it would be wiser not to do so.

Little was achieved by all Jasmin's discretion and all my own solicitude. They talked; but invariably, with a persistence of which he was surely not aware, Meaulnes kept returning to all the wonders of the past, and each time, the girl, miserably, had to repeat that it had all vanished: the old mansion, which was so strange and so convoluted, had been pulled down; the great lake had been dried up and filled in; the children, with their delightful costumes, had gone their own ways . . .

'Ah!' was all that Meaulnes said, despairingly, as though each of these disappearances proved him right, while either she or I was in the wrong.

We were walking along, side by side. I tried in vain to offer some distraction from the sadness that affected all three of us. Once again, Meaulnes gave in to his obsession, asking for information about everything that he had seen there: the little girls, the driver of the old berlin, the racing ponies . . . 'Have the ponies been sold, too? Aren't there any more horses at the château?'

She said that there were none; she didn't mention Belisarius.

Then he began to list the objects in his room: the candelabra, the large mirror, the old broken lute . . . He was inquiring about all this with extraordinary eagerness as though trying to persuade himself that there was nothing remaining of his great adventure and that the young woman would not have anything to bring him, not a single piece of wreckage that would prove that they had not both dreamt it all, like a diver lifting a stone and some seaweed from the ocean depths.

Mademoiselle de Galais and I could not help smiling sadly, and she made up her mind to explain everything:

'You'll never see again the fine château that Monsieur de Galais and I got ready for poor Frantz. We spent our lives doing what he asked. He was such a strange and charming creature! But everything vanished with him on the evening of his failed betrothal. Monsieur de Galais was already ruined without us knowing. Frantz had run up debts, and his former friends, when they found out that he had gone, immediately turned to us for payment. We became poor. Madame de Galais died and we lost all our friends in a matter of days.

'Should Frantz come back, if he is not dead, and should he return to his friends and his fiancée, so that the interrupted wedding can take place, then everything might go back to what it was before. But can one return to the past?'

'Who knows?' said Meaulnes, thoughtfully. And he asked no further questions.

All three of us were walking on the short grass, which was already turning a little yellow. Near him, to Augustin's right, was the girl whom he had thought lost for ever. When he asked one of his hard questions, she turned slowly towards him to answer, with an anxious look on her charming face. And once, as she spoke, she gently put a hand on his arm, with a movement full of trust in his greater strength. Why was The Great Meaulnes behaving like a stranger, like a person who had not found what he was looking for and who could not be interested in anything besides? Three years earlier, he could not have borne this happiness without panic, perhaps without madness. So where had he found this emptiness, this distance, this inability to experience happiness which was in him now?

We were coming to the little wood where, that morning, Monsieur de Galais had tied up Belisarius. The setting sun was lengthening the shadows on the grass. At the far end of the glade, deadened by distance, we could hear a happy buzzing, the sound of people playing games and of young girls, and we remained silent in this admirable calm, when we heard singing from the other side of the wood, towards Les Aubiers, the farm at the water's edge. It was the distant, young voice of someone taking cattle to water, a melody as rhythmical as a dance tune, but which the young man was drawing out and making as languorous as a plaintive old ballad:

> My shoes are red . . .
> Farewell, my loves . . .
> My shoes are red . . .
> Farewell, for ever . . .

Meaulnes had looked up and was listening. It was just one of those songs that the peasants were singing as they lingered on their way, at the Estate Without a Name, on the last evening of the festivities, when everything had already fallen through . . . Just a memory – and the saddest – of those lovely days that would never return.

'Can you hear him?' Meaulnes said quietly. 'Oh, I'm going to see who it is!' And at once he set off through the little wood. Almost immediately, the singing stopped. For a moment after that we heard the man whistling to his animals as he went away, then nothing more . . .

I looked at the young woman. She was thoughtful and dejected, staring at the thicket into which Meaulnes had just vanished. How often, later, would she stare in that way, pensively, at the place where The Great Meaulnes had vanished for ever!

She turned back towards me. 'He is not happy,' she said, sorrowfully. And she added, 'And perhaps there is nothing that I can do for him . . .'

I was reluctant to answer because I was afraid that Meaulnes, who must have quickly got to the farm and would by now be coming back through the wood, might overhear our conversation. Even so, I was going to say something encouraging: to tell her not to worry about offending the tall young man; that he must surely have some secret that was troubling him and that he would never entrust it of his own accord, either to her or to anyone else – when suddenly there was a shout from the far side of the wood. Then we heard what sounded like the stamping and snorting of a horse and the intermittent sound of a quarrel. I guessed at once that old Belisarius had had an

accident and ran towards the spot from which the noise was
coming. Mademoiselle de Galais followed me at a distance.
Our movement must have been observed from the far end of
the meadow, because, just as I was going into the thicket, I
heard the shouts of people running towards us.

Old Belisarius, who was tied too low down, had got one of his
forelegs caught in the tether. He had not moved until Monsieur
de Galais and Delouche had approached him on their walk.
Then, startled and over-excited by the oats that he had been
given, which he was not used to, he had struggled furiously.
The two men tried to release him but so clumsily that they only
managed to entangle him further, at the same time risking a
dangerous kick from his hooves. It was at that moment that
Meaulnes, who happened to be returning from Les Aubiers,
had come across the group. Angry at their ineptitude, he had
pushed the two men aside, almost sending them tumbling into
the bushes. Cautiously, but deftly, he freed Belisarius – too late,
because the harm was already done. The horse must have a
pulled tendon or perhaps even have broken something, because
he was in a pitiful state, with his head hanging, his saddle half
slipping from his back, one leg drawn up under his body and
trembling all over. Meaulnes bent over, felt his leg and examined him in silence.

When he stood upright, almost everyone had gathered
around, but he saw nobody. He was red with fury.

'I wonder who on earth could have tied him up like that!' he
shouted. 'And left his saddle on all day? Besides, who dared
put a saddle on this old horse who is hardly fit to pull a cart!'

Delouche tried to speak and take the blame on himself.

'Quiet, you! It's your fault again. I saw you stupidly pulling
his tether to get him free.'

And, bending down again, he started to rub the horse's hock
with the flat of his hand.

Monsieur de Galais, who had said nothing up to now, made
the mistake of trying to join the conversation. He stammered:
'Naval officers are in the habit . . . My horse . . .'

'So! It's your horse?' Meaulnes said, calming down a little,
though still very flushed, turning towards the old man.

I thought that he would change his tone and make some excuse. For a moment, he breathed heavily, and I noticed that he was taking a bitter, despairing pleasure in aggravating the situation, in destroying it all for ever, as he said, insolently, 'Well, I can't congratulate you.'

Someone suggested, 'Perhaps some cold water . . . We could bathe him in the ford . . .'

Meaulnes didn't reply. 'What has to be done is to take this old horse away while he can still walk,' he said. 'And there's no time to lose! Then put him in a stable and never take him out again.'

Several young people volunteered their services at once. But Mademoiselle de Galais politely refused them all. Her face blazing, on the brink of tears, she said goodbye to everyone, even to Meaulnes, who was quite abashed and did not dare to look her in the face. She took the animal by the reins, as though giving someone a hand, to draw him towards her rather than to lead him . . . The late-summer wind was so warm on the road to Les Sablonnières that it felt like May, and the leaves on the hedges were shivering in the southern breeze. We watched her leave, her arm half out of her coat, holding the thick leather rein in her slender hand. Her father walked painfully beside her . . .

What a sad ending to the day! Little by little, everyone collected the bits and pieces, and the blankets. The chairs were folded and the tables taken down. One by one, the carts set off, loaded with luggage and people, with hats raised and handkerchiefs waving. We stayed until we were the last on the spot with Uncle Florentin, who like us was silently mulling over his regrets and disappointment.

Then we, too, left, carried quickly away in our well-sprung carriage by our fine chestnut horse. The wheel screeched in the sand as it took the corner, and soon Meaulnes and I, who were on the back seat, were looking at the track that old Belisarius and his master had taken as it vanished down the little side road.

But then my friend, who was the person of all I knew least

likely to give in to tears, suddenly turned towards me with his face twisted by an irresistible urge to weep.

'Stop, please stop,' he said, putting his hand on Florentin's shoulder. 'Don't worry about me. I'll come back on my own, on foot.'

With a single bound, holding on to the mudguard, he leapt down and, to our amazement, started to run back the way we had come, running as far as the little track that we had just passed, the track leading to Les Sablonnières. He must have come to the Estate along the avenue of fir trees that he had taken in that former time, and where, a vagabond hiding among the low branches, he had overheard the mysterious conversation of the pretty, unknown children . . .

And that evening, sobbing, he asked Mademoiselle de Galais for her hand in marriage.

VII

THE WEDDING DAY

It is a Thursday, early in February, a fine, icy Thursday evening, with a high wind blowing, between three-thirty and four. Since midday, in the villages, the washing has been hanging out on the hedges and drying in the gusts. In every house, the dining-room fire casts its light on a whole votive altar of polished toys. Tired of playing, the child has gone to sit beside his mother and is getting her to tell him about her wedding day . . .

Anyone who does not wish to be happy has only to go up into the attic and there, until nightfall, he can listen to the whistling and creaking of foundering ships; or else he can go outside on the road, and the wind will throw his scarf back against his mouth like a sudden, warm kiss that will bring tears to his eyes. But for anyone who loves happiness, there is the house of Les Sablonnières, beside a muddy road, where my friend Meaulnes came back with Yvonne de Galais, who had been his wife since noon.

The engagement lasted five months. It was a tranquil time, as tranquil as that first meeting had been troubled. Meaulnes went frequently to Les Sablonnières, by bicycle or in the trap. More than twice a week, as she sat sewing or knitting by the large window, Mademoiselle de Galais would suddenly see his tall shadow quickly going past behind the curtain – because he always came along the side path that he had taken that very first time. But this is the only (and tacit) allusion that he would make to the past. Happiness seems to have quieted his strange anguish.

Small incidents have marked those five calm months. I have been appointed teacher in the hamlet of Saint-Benoist-des-

Champs. Saint-Benoist is not a village, but a number of farms scattered across the countryside, and the schoolhouse stands completely by itself on a hill beside the road. Mine is a very solitary existence, but if I walk through the fields, I can be at Les Sablonnières in three-quarters of an hour. Delouche is now with his uncle, a builders' merchant in Le Vieux-Nançay. He will soon be boss himself. He often comes to see me. Meaulnes, at Mademoiselle de Galais' request, is now very friendly towards him. And that explains why the two of us are walking along at around four in the afternoon, when all the wedding guests have already left.

The wedding took place at noon, as quietly as possible, in the old chapel of Les Sablonnières, which has not been pulled down, but is half hidden by the fir trees on the slope of the opposite hill. After a brief wedding breakfast, Meaulnes' mother, Monsieur Seurel, Millie, Florentin and the others drove off. Only Jasmin and I were left.

We are wandering along the edge of the wood behind the house of Les Sablonnières, on the edge of the large expanse of wasteland which was the site of the now demolished mansion. Without admitting it and without knowing why, we are both full of unease. We try to distract our thoughts and calm our fears by pointing out the burrows of hares as we wander along or the little tracks of sand where rabbits have recently been digging ... or a snare ... the sign of a poacher ... But we return constantly to the edge of the woods, from where we can see the house, silent and closed.

Below the big window overlooking the fir trees there is a wooden balcony, invaded by weeds that bend in the wind. A light, like that of an open fire, shines on the window panes. From time to time, a shadow passes behind the curtains. All around, in the fields, in the vegetable garden and in the only farm that remains of those on the estate, there is silence and solitude. The tenants have gone to the village to celebrate their masters' joy.

From time to time, the wind, laden with a mist that is almost rain, dampens our faces and brings us the faint sound of a piano which someone is playing in the closed house. At first it

is like a trembling voice, far, far away, scarcely daring to express
its happiness. It's like the laughter of a little girl in her room
who has gone to fetch all her toys and is displaying them to a
friend. I am reminded, too, of the still timorous joy of a woman
who has left to put on a lovely dress and returns to show it off
without being sure of the effect it will have . . . This unknown
tune is also a prayer, an entreaty to happiness not to be too
cruel, like a greeting and a genuflection to happiness . . .

I think, 'At last they are happy. Meaulnes is there with
her . . .'

And knowing this, being sure of it, is enough to bring content
to the innocent child that I am.

At that moment, lost in thought and with my face wet from
the wind of the plain as though from the spray of the sea, I feel
a hand on my shoulder.

'Listen!' Jasmin whispers.

I look at him. He signals to me not to move; and he listens,
with his head on one side and one eyebrow raised . . .

VIII

FRANTZ CALLS

'Whoo, whoo!'

This time, I did hear it. It was a signal, a two-note call, high then low, which I had heard once before ... Ah, I remember: it was the cry of the tall actor hailing his young friend from the school gate. It was the cry to which Frantz had made us promise to respond, anywhere and at any time. But what did he want of us here, today?

'It's coming from the large fir grove to the left,' I said in an undertone. 'It must be a poacher.'

Jasmin shook his head. 'You know very well that it isn't,' he said.

Then, lower: 'They're both here, in the village, they've been here since this morning. I caught Ganache at eleven o'clock keeping watch in a field near the chapel. He took off as soon as he saw me. They may have come a long way by bicycle, because he was covered in mud halfway up his back.'

'But what do they want?'

'I don't know. One thing's sure; we've got to chase them off. They can't be allowed to loiter around here. Or else all the madness will start again.'

I agreed, though I didn't say so.

'I think the best would be to go and find them,' I said. 'To see what they want and get them to see sense ...'

So we bent down and, slowly, silently, we crept through the undergrowth as far as the large fir grove from which, at regular intervals, the long call was coming. In itself, it was no sadder than anything else, but to both of us it seemed to bode nothing but ill.

In this part of the fir wood, where the trees are planted in regular rows and the eye has a straight line between the trunks, it is hard to take anyone by surprise or to go forward without being seen. We did not even try. I stationed myself at one corner of the wood, and Jasmin went to the diagonally opposite one, so that together we could each see two sides of the rectangle from outside and no gypsy could leave the wood without us calling to him. Once we had taken up our posts, I started to play my part as a peaceful negotiator and shouted, 'Frantz! . . . Frantz! Don't worry. It's me, Seurel. I want to talk to you . . .'

There was a moment's silence. I was about to shout again when, from the very heart of the wood, just beyond where I could see clearly, a voice ordered, 'Stay where you are. He's coming out to you.'

Bit by bit, through the tall fir trees, which from a distance seemed bunched together, I could make out the form of the young man coming towards me. He seemed to be badly dressed and covered in mud. He had bicycle clips around the bottom of his trousers and an old yachting cap planted on his long hair. Now, I could see his face. It was thinner, and he seemed to have been crying . . .

Striding boldly across to me, he asked: 'What do you want?' in an insolent tone of voice.

'What about you, Frantz? What are you doing here? Why have you come to disturb people who are happy? Tell me: what is it that you want?'

He blushed at this direct question, stammered, then replied simply, 'I'm unhappy, I'm so unhappy . . .'

After that, with his head in his hands and leaning against the trunk of a tree, he started to sob bitterly. We took a few steps into the wood. The place was absolutely quiet, without even the sound of the wind, which was blocked by the tall firs at the edge. The muffled sound of the young man's sobs echoed and faded through the regularly spaced trunks of the trees. I waited for the crisis to pass, then put my hand on his shoulder and said, 'Frantz, come with me. I'll take you to them. They will welcome you like a child that has been lost and found, and it will all be over.'

But he did not want to listen. In a voice deadened by crying, miserable, obstinate and angry, he went on, 'So Meaulnes doesn't care about me any more? Why doesn't he answer when I call him? Why hasn't he kept his promise?'

'Come on, Frantz,' I said. 'The time for childish make-believe is over. Don't let some folly spoil the happiness of those you love, your sister and Augustin Meaulnes.'

'But he alone can save me, as well you know. Only he is able to find the trail I've lost. For almost three years, Ganache and I have been hunting all over France, to no avail. Your friend was the only one I still trusted. And now he's not answering any more. He has found his love. So why doesn't he think of me, now? He has to get started on his way: Yvonne will let him go. She has never refused me anything.'

He turned towards me a face on which his tears had drawn dirty furrows through the dust and mud, the face of an exhausted, defeated old child. There were freckles around his eyes, his chin was badly shaved and his overgrown hair was hanging down on to his dirty collar. He was shivering, with his hands in his pockets. This was no longer the princely child in rags of former times. In heart, no doubt, he was more a child than ever: imperious, capricious and easily discouraged. But such childishness was painful in a boy who was already showing signs of age. At one time, he possessed such arrogant youth that it seemed he could get away with any folly that he liked. Now, you were more likely to feel sorry for him, because he had failed in life, and then to resent the fact that he evidently persisted in playing this ridiculous part of the young romantic hero. And finally, despite myself, it occurred to me that our fine Frantz, with his exalted loves, must have been reduced to stealing to survive, just like his friend Ganache . . . All that pride had come to this!

'Suppose I promise,' I said at last, after thinking about it, 'that in a few days Meaulnes will join your quest, just for you?'

'He will succeed, won't he? You're sure?' he asked, his teeth chattering.

'I think he will. Everything is possible with him!'

'How will I know? Who will tell me?'

'Come back here exactly a year from now, at the same time. You will find the girl that you love.'

As I said this, I was not thinking of bothering the newly wed couple, but of making inquiries from Aunt Moinel and doing my best to find the girl myself.

The gypsy was looking me directly in the eye with a truly admirable urge to believe. Fifteen! After all, he was still only fifteen – the age that we all had been in Sainte-Agathe on the evening when they swept the classroom out and the three of us swore that terrible, childish oath.

He found himself obliged to say, 'Very well, we'll leave', and a wave of despair flooded over him again.

It must have been with great sorrow that he gazed at all the woods around us, having to leave them behind once more.

'In three days,' he said, 'we'll be on the road to Germany. We left our vehicles some way off; we have been walking constantly for the past thirty hours. We thought that we would arrive in time before the wedding to take Meaulnes and look for my fiancée, as he looked for the Estate of Les Sablonnières.'

Then, giving way once more to his dreadful childishness, he said, 'Call your Delouche, because there would be trouble if I met him.'

Slowly I saw his grey form vanish among the trees. I called Jasmin and we went back to our watch. But almost at once, we saw Augustin in the house, closing the shutters, and we were struck by how odd he looked.

IX

THE HAPPY PEOPLE

Later, I would learn in the minutest detail what had happened there.

From early afternoon, in the drawing room at Les Sablonnières, Meaulnes and his wife, whom I still call Mademoiselle de Galais, were left completely alone. Once the guests had gone, Monsieur de Galais opened the door and, for a second, allowed the high wind, howling, to come into the house; then he set out towards Le Vieux-Nançay, not to return until dinner time, when he would lock everything up and give orders to the workers on the farm. From then on, no noise reached the young people from outside. There was just one leafless branch of a rosebush brushing against the window pane facing the moors. Like two passengers in a drifting boat, in the strong winter wind, the two lovers were enclosed with their happiness.

'The fire looks as if it's going out,' said Mademoiselle de Galais, getting up to take a log from the chest. But Meaulnes hurried forward and put the wood on the fire himself.

Then he took the girl's outstretched hand and they stood there opposite one another, as though choked by some great, unutterable piece of news.

The wind was blowing past with the sound of a flooding river, and from time to time a drop of water would streak across the window, diagonally, like rain on the window of a railway carriage.

Then the girl ran off. She opened the door to the corridor and vanished with a mysterious smile. For a moment, Augustin was left alone in the half-dark . . . The ticking of a small clock recalled the dining room at Sainte-Agathe . . . He must have thought, 'So this is the house I have been looking for, for so long, the corridor that was once so full of whispers and strange comings and goings . . .'

It was at that moment that he must have heard – Mademoiselle de Galais would later tell me that she heard it too – Frantz's first call, close to the house.

After that, though the young woman showed him all the wonderful things she had brought – her childhood toys and all the photographs of her as a child: dressed up in a uniform, herself and Frantz on their mother's knee (their mother who was so pretty . . .), and then all the remaining prim little dresses that she used to wear, 'right down to the one that I was wearing, you see, around the time when you were soon about to meet me, when you were just coming to the school at Sainte-Agathe, I think . . .' – Meaulnes neither saw nor heard anything.

Yet for a moment he seemed to have reverted to the idea of his extraordinary, unimaginable good fortune: 'You are there,' he said, in an expressionless voice, as though just to say it made him dizzy. 'You really are just passing by the table and your hand rests on it for a moment . . .'

And again: 'My mother, when she was young, used to lean forward slightly like that to speak to me . . . And when she sat down at the piano . . .'

At this, Yvonne de Galais suggested that she should play something before nightfall. But it was dark in that corner of the drawing room, and they had to light a candle. The pink shade, reflecting on the young woman's face, heightened the redness on her cheeks, the sign of deep anxiety.

Over at the edge of the wood, I started to hear the tremulous music carried on the wind, soon interrupted by a second shout from the two madmen who had come towards us through the trees.

Meaulnes stayed for a long time listening to the young woman play and silently staring through a window. He turned several times to look at the gentle face, so vulnerable and full of unease. Then he went over to Yvonne and very softly put his hand on her shoulder. She felt the soft weight of the hand on her neck and felt sure she ought to know how to respond to its caress.

'It's getting dark,' he said, at length. 'I'm going to close the shutters. But don't stop playing . . .'

What was going on in the mysterious wildness of his heart? I have often wondered and only understood when it was too late. Some buried remorse? Some inexplicable regret? Or was it the fear of seeing this unexpected happiness that he was holding so tightly soon slip between his fingers? And in that case was there some dreadful urge to cast away this marvel that he had gained, at once and for ever?

He went out slowly, silently, after looking one more time at his young wife. From the wood's edge we saw him firstly close one shutter, hesitantly, then look vaguely in our direction, close another, then suddenly run as fast as he could towards us. He came near before it occurred to us to make ourselves less conspicuous. He saw us as he was about to cross a low, recently planted hedge marking the edge of a field. He swerved. I remember his crazed manner and how he looked – like a hunted animal. He seemed to be turning back to cross the hedge near to the little stream.

I called out to him, 'Meaulnes! Augustin!'

But he did not even turn round. Then, convinced that this was the only way to hold him back, I shouted, 'Frantz is here! Stop!'

And at last he did stop. Panting, not giving me a chance to think what I was going to say, he said, 'He's there? What does he want of me?'

'He's unhappy,' I answered. 'He came to ask for your help in his quest for what he has lost.'

'Ah!' he said, lowering his head. 'I guessed as much. I tried as hard as I could to forget that idea . . . But where is he? Tell me quickly.'

I said that Frantz had just left, and that we would surely not be able to catch up with him now. This was a great disappointment for Meaulnes. He hesitated, took a step or two, then stopped. He appeared to be in the depths of uncertainty and woe. I told him what I had promised the young man in his name. I said that I had made an appointment with him in the same place a year from then.

Augustin, usually so calm, was now in a state of extraordinary nervousness and impatience.

'Ah, why did you do that?' he said. 'Yes, yes, no doubt I can save him. But it has to be at once. I have to see him, to speak to him, so that he can forgive me and I can make it up to him . . . Otherwise, I shall not be able to go back there . . .'

And he turned towards Les Sablonnières.

'In other words,' I said, 'for the sake of some childish promise that you made to him, you are destroying your happiness.'

'Oh, if that promise were the only thing,' he said.

And thus is was that I learnt that there was some other bond between the two young men, though I could not guess what it was.

'In any case,' I said, 'it's too late to run. They're now on their way to Germany.'

He was about to reply, when a dishevelled, wild-eyed figure appeared between us. It was Mademoiselle de Galais. She must have been running because her face was bathed in sweat. She must have fallen and hurt herself, because her forehead was scratched above the right eye, and there was dried blood in her hair.

In some of the poor districts of Paris, I have sometimes seen a couple bursting out into the street and kept apart by some police who have intervened in their quarrel – a couple who were thought up to then to be happy, united and decent. The outburst came suddenly, at no particular moment, when they were sitting down to eat, one Sunday before going out or just as they were celebrating their little son's birthday . . . And now everything is forgotten and broken apart. The man and woman in the midst of this chaos are now just two pitiful demons, and the tearful children cling to them, hugging them tightly and begging them to be quiet and to stop fighting.

When Mademoiselle de Galais came up to Meaulnes, she reminded me of those children, of one of those poor frightened children. I think that if all her friends, a whole village, a whole world had been looking at her, she would have run up even so and fallen down in the same way, dishevelled, weeping and mud-stained.

But when she realized that Meaulnes was there and that this time, at least, he would not abandon her, she put her arm in his and then could not help laughing through her tears like a little child. Neither one of them said a word. But since she had taken out her handkerchief, Meaulnes gently took it from her hands and, carefully and methodically, wiped the blood from the young girl's hair.

'We must go back now,' he said.

And I let them both go back, with the fine high wind of the winter evening lashing their faces – he reaching out his hand to help her over the rough ground, and she smiling and hastening with him towards the home that they had momentarily abandoned.

X

'FRANTZ'S HOUSE'

Full of misgivings and vague anxieties that the fortunate outcome of the previous day's turmoil was unable to dispel, I had
to stay inside at school throughout the following day. As soon
as the study period following the evening lesson arrived, I set
out for Les Sablonnières. Night was falling when I reached the
line of fir trees leading to the house. All the shutters were
already closed. I was afraid that I would not be welcome at this
late hour, on the day after a wedding. I stayed for a long time,
wandering up and down on the outskirts of the garden and the
surrounding fields, always hoping that I would see someone
come out of the closed house. But my hopes were not realized.
Even in the adjoining farm, nothing moved; so I had to go back
home, with the darkest fears haunting my imagination.

There were the same worries on the following day, a Saturday. In the evening, I hastily took my cloak and stick, with a
piece of bread to eat on my way, and I reached Les Sablonnières
when night was already falling to find everything as it had been
on the previous day. There was a glimmer of light on the first
floor, but no sound or movement . . . However, this time, from
the courtyard of the farm, I could see the farmhouse door open,
with a fire lit in the great kitchen, and I could hear the sound
of voices and footsteps that one might expect at supper time.
I was reassured by this, but not better informed. I couldn't say
or ask anything of these people. So back I went again to watch
and wait, in vain, still hoping that I would see the door open
and Augustin's tall figure emerge at last.

It was only on Sunday, in the afternoon, that I resolved to
ring the doorbell of Les Sablonnières. While I was climbing the

bare hillsides, I could hear the bells ringing in the distance for winter Vespers. I felt lonely and abandoned. A sad but indefinable foreboding overcame me. I was only half surprised when, after I had rung the bell, Monsieur de Galais came to the door by himself, to whisper to me that Yvonne de Galais was in bed, with a high temperature, and that Meaulnes had had to leave that Friday morning on a long journey. They did not know when he would return . . .

Since the old man was very awkward and sad, and did not invite me inside, I left straightaway. As the door closed, I stood for a moment on the steps, with a heavy heart, utterly confused, watching – I don't know why – a melancholy, dry wisteria branch swaying in a ray of sunlight.

So the secret regret that Meaulnes had been harbouring since his trip to Paris had proved too strong, and eventually my friend had fled the tight embrace of happiness . . .

Every Thursday and Sunday, I came to ask for news of Yvonne de Galais, until the evening when, finally convalescing, she asked for me to be invited in. I found her sitting by the fire in the drawing room with its large window overlooking the fields and woods. She was not pale, as I had imagined she would be, but on the contrary feverish, with bright red patches under her eyes and in an extremely nervous state. Although she still appeared very weak, she was dressed as though to go out. She said little, but enunciated every sentence with extraordinary emphasis, as though trying to persuade herself that her happiness had not yet faded . . . I can't remember what we said, only that I eventually got round to asking, hesitantly, when Meaulnes would return.

'I don't know when he'll come back,' she said, quickly.

Her eyes were begging, and I was careful not to allude to it again.

I often went back to see her. I would often talk with her beside the fire in that low-ceilinged room, where night arrived sooner than elsewhere. She never talked about herself or her hidden sorrow, but also she never tired of hearing from me about the details of our life as schoolboys at Sainte-Agathe.

She listened gravely, tenderly, with almost maternal interest,

as I told her about our youthful trials and tribulations. She
never seemed surprised, even at our most childish and most
dangerous exploits. She had this attentive tenderness from
Monsieur de Galais, and it had not been exhausted by the
deplorable adventures of her brother. Her only regret about the
past, I think, was that she had not been enough of a close friend
for her brother to confide in, since he had not dared to say
anything to her or to anyone else at the time of his great disaster,
and had felt himself to be irretrievably lost. And, when I think
about it, this was a heavy burden that the young woman had
taken on – a perilous enterprise, supporting someone like her
brother whose mind was full of extravagant fantasies, and an
overwhelming one, when she was throwing in her lot with an
adventurous heart like that of my friend Meaulnes . . .

One day, she gave me the most touching, I might even say the
most mysterious, proof of the faith that she had in her brother's
childish dreams and the effort that she put into him keeping at
least some traces of the dream that he had inhabited until he
was twenty.

It was an April evening as desolate as one in late autumn.
For nearly a month we had been enjoying a gentle, premature
spring, and the young woman had gone back to taking the long
walks that she loved, in the company of Monsieur de Galais.
But on that day, as the old man felt tired and I was free, she
asked me to go with her, despite the threat of rain. More than
half a league from Les Sablonnières, as we were walking beside
the pond, we were caught by a storm of rain and hail. We took
refuge against the unending rainfall in a shelter where the wind
chilled us as we stood next to one another, staring in silence at
the dark landscape. I can see her, in her sweet, austerely simple
dress, pale and anguished.

'We must go back,' she said. 'We have been gone such a long
time. Who knows what might have happened?'

But to my surprise, when we were finally able to leave our
shelter, instead of going back towards Les Sablonnières, she
continued to go forward and asked me to follow. After walking
for a long time, we reached a house that I did not know,

standing alone beside a sunken lane that must have led towards Préveranges. It was a commonplace little house, with a slate roof, just like so many other ordinary houses in the region, except for its remoteness and isolation.

Seeing Yvonne de Galais, you would have thought that the house belonged to us and that we had left it while we were away on a long journey. Leaning forward, she opened a little gate, and anxiously hurried to look over the lonely place. A large, grass-covered yard, where children must have come to play in the long, slow evenings of late winter, had been ravaged by the storm. There was a hoop lying in a puddle. In the little plots where the children had sown flowers and peas, the heavy rain had left only trails of white gravel. And finally, huddled against the step of one damp door, we found a whole brood of rain-soaked chicks. Most of them had died beneath the stiffened wings and ruffled feathers of the mother hen.

The young woman stifled a cry at this piteous scene. She leant over and, without heeding the water or the mud, sorted the living chicks from the dead and put them in a fold of her coat. Then she unlocked the door, and we went into the house. Four doors opened on a narrow corridor, along which the wind howled. Yvonne de Galais opened the first one on our right and led me into a dark room in which, as my eyes adjusted to it, I managed to make out a large mirror and a little bed covered, in country style, with a red silk eiderdown. As for Yvonne, after briefly looking around the rest of the house, she came back with the ailing brood in a basket filled with down, which she cautiously pushed under the quilt. And while a lingering ray of sunlight, the first and last of the day, made our faces paler and made darker the coming of night, we stood there, chilled and uneasy in our minds, in that strange house!

From time to time, she went to look in the feverish nest and took out another dead chick to prevent it from killing the others. And each time, we felt that something like a great wind through the broken windows of the loft, like the mysterious sorrow of unknown children, was silently mourning.

'This was Frantz's house,' my companion told me at last, 'when he was small. He wanted a house all to himself, far from everyone, where he could go and play, enjoy himself and live in when he felt like it. My father thought this such a funny and unusual whim that he did not refuse. And when he wanted to, on a Thursday or a Sunday, or whenever, Frantz would go off and live in his own house, like a grown-up. The children from the farms around came to play with him or help him with the housework or the gardening. What a wonderful game it was! And when evening came, he was not afraid to sleep here all alone. As for us, we admired him so much that we didn't even think of worrying.

'Now, for a long time, the house has been empty,' she went on, sighing. 'Monsieur de Galais, weighed down by age and grief, has never done anything to find Frantz or bring him back. What could he do, for that matter?

'I come here quite often. The little peasants from hereabouts come and play in the courtyard as they would in the old days. I like to imagine that they are Frantz's old friends, that he is still a child himself and that he will soon return with the fiancée he has chosen for himself.

'The children know me well. I play with them. This brood of little chickens was ours . . .'

It had taken the shower and this small-scale disaster for her to confide in me all that great, unspoken sorrow and her regret at losing her brother – so crazy, so charming and so much admired. I heard her without saying anything, my heart full of tears . . .

When the doors and gate were shut, and the chicks put back in the wooden hutch behind the house, she sadly took my arm, and I led her home . . .

Weeks and months went by. Time past! Lost happiness! She had been the fairy, the princess and the mysterious love of all our adolescence, and it fell to me, my friend having left us, to take her arm and say the words that would assuage her grief. Those days, those conversations in the evening after the class that I took in the hillside school of Saint-Benoist-des-Champs, those walks when the only thing that we needed to discuss was the one thing about which we had both decided to say nothing

– what can I say now about all this? I remember nothing but the memory, already half erased, of a lovely face, grown thin, and of two eyes with lids slowly lowered as they looked at me, as if already wishing to see no world except the one inside.

I remained her faithful friend – her companion in an unspoken vigil – for a whole spring and summer, the like of which will never come again. We went back many times, in the afternoons, to Frantz's house. She opened the doors to air it, so that there would be no mould when the young couple returned. She took care of the semi-wild poultry in the farm-yard. And on Thursdays or Sundays, we joined in the games of the little country children from the farms around, their cries and laughter in that isolated place adding to the solitude and emptiness of the little abandoned house.

XI

CONVERSATION IN THE RAIN

August, holiday time, took me away from Les Sablonnières and Yvonne de Galais. I had to spend my two months' holiday at Sainte-Agathe. I saw again the great dry yard, the shelter and the empty classroom . . . Meaulnes was everywhere, everything was filled with memories of our adolescence, now ended. In those long, yellowed days, I would shut myself up as I used to, before Meaulnes came, in the Archive Room or in the empty classrooms. I read, wrote and remembered . . . My father was away fishing, and Millie in the drawing room, sewing or playing the piano, as in the old days . . . And in the utter silence of the classroom where everything – the torn, green paper crowns,[16] the wrappings from prize books, the blackboards sponged clean – told you that the school year was over, the awards had been handed out, everything was turned towards autumn, the start of classes in October and renewed effort, the thought came to me that in the same way our youth was ended and happiness had passed us by, as I too was waiting for the start of term at Les Sablonnières and the return of Augustin . . . who perhaps might never return at all . . .

However, there was one piece of good news that I gave Millie when she began to question me about the new bride. I was not expecting her questions: she had a way that was at once very innocent and very sly of suddenly plunging you into confusion by putting a finger on your most secret thoughts. I called a halt to it all by announcing that my friend Meaulnes' young wife would become a mother in October.

Inside myself, I recalled the day when Yvonne de Galais had intimated this great piece of news to me. There was a silence: a young man's slight embarrassment on my part. And then, to dispel it, I blurted out (thinking too late of all the tragic events that I was stirring up with this remark), 'You must be very happy.'

But without any reservation, regret, remorse or bitterness, she gave a fine, contented smile and answered, 'Yes, very happy.'

During that last week of the holidays, which is generally the finest and most romantic, a week of great rainstorms, a week when you start to light the fires and that I would usually spend hunting among the black damp fir trees of Le Vieux-Nançay, I got ready to return directly to Saint-Benoist-des-Champs. Firmin, my Aunt Julie and my cousins at Le Vieux-Nançay would have asked me too many questions that I did not want to answer. This time, I abandoned the idea of spending a week living the intoxicating life of a hunter and returned to my schoolhouse four days before the new term began.

I arrived before nightfall, crossing a courtyard that was already carpeted in yellow leaves. Once the carter had left, I sadly unpacked in the echoing, musty dining room the parcel of foodstuffs that my mother had packed for me. After snatching a hasty meal, impatiently, anxiously, I put on my cape and set off on a feverish walk that brought me right to the outskirts of Les Sablonnières.

I did not want to intrude on the first evening after I arrived. But, bolder than I had been in February, after walking all round the house, where only the young woman's bedroom window was lit, I went in through the garden gate at the back and sat down on a bench against the hedge in the gathering gloom, happy at simply being there, close to what absorbed and preoccupied me most of anything in the world.

Night was coming. A light drizzle was starting to fall. With head bowed, lost in thought, I was watching my shoes shining as they gradually got wetter. The darkness was slowly enfolding me, and the chill of evening was overtaking me without disturbing my revery. I dreamed, tenderly and sadly, of the muddy paths of Sainte-Agathe on that same late September evening; I imagined the square full of mist, the butcher's boy whistling

on his way to the pump, the café lit up, the merry carriage full
of people with its shell of open umbrellas arriving before the
end of the holidays at Uncle Florentin's . . . And I thought sadly,
'What does all that happiness amount to, if Meaulnes, my
friend, cannot be there, or his young wife?'

It was then that, looking up, I saw her a few yards away from
me. Her shoes were making a little noise in the sand, which
I had mistaken for the drops of water dripping from the hedgerow. She had a large black woollen scarf over her head and
shoulders, and her hair was flattened against her forehead and
spattered with fine drops of rain. She must have seen me from
her bedroom window, the one that overlooked the garden, and
she came out to me. So, in the old days, my mother would get
worried and come out to tell me, 'It's time to come indoors';
but she would take a liking to this walk through the rain and
the night, and just say gently, 'You'll catch cold!' then stay with
me, talking for a long time.

Yvonne de Galais offered me a burning hand and, giving up
hope of getting me to go into Les Sablonnières, sat down on
the bench, covered in moss and verdigris, while I stood, my
knee resting on the same bench and leaning towards her to hear
what she said.

First of all, she scolded me in a friendly way for cutting short
my holidays.

'I had to come,' I told her, 'as soon as possible, to keep you
company.'

'It's true, I'm still alone,' she said, almost in a whisper, sighing. 'Augustin is not back.'

Taking the sigh for one of regret and a stifled reproach, I
started to say, slowly, 'So much folly in such a noble head.
Perhaps the yearning for adventure, stronger than any other . . .'

But she interrupted me. And it was there, that evening, for
the first and last time, that she spoke to me of Meaulnes.

'Don't say that, François Seurel, my friend,' she told me,
gently. 'Only we . . . Only I am at fault. Think what we did . . .
We said to him, "Here's happiness, this is what you have been
searching for throughout your youth and here is the girl who
was at the end of all your dreams!"'

'What else could he do, when we were pushing him by the shoulders in that way, except be seized with uncertainty, then dread, then terror? How could he do otherwise than give in to the temptation to escape?'

'Yvonne,' I said quietly. 'You know very well that you were his happiness. You were that girl.'

'Oh!' she sighed. 'How could I for a moment have had such an arrogant thought? That thought was the whole trouble.

'I told you, "Perhaps I can't do anything for him." But in my deepest self, I was thinking, "Since he searched so long for me and since I love him, I must make him happy." But when I saw him next to me, with all his feverish unease and his mysterious sense of remorse, I realized that I was just a poor woman like the rest . . .

'"I am not worthy of you," he kept saying as day broke at the end of our wedding night. I tried to console him, to reassure him, but nothing would calm his anxiety. So I said, "If you must go, if I have come to you at the moment when nothing could make you happy, if you have to abandon me for a while so that afterwards you can come back to me at peace, then I am the one asking you to go . . ."'

In the dark, I saw that she was looking up at me. This was like a confession, and she was anxiously waiting for me to approve or condemn. But what could I say? Of course, in my mind, I saw The Great Meaulnes of earlier times, gauche and wild, who always preferred to be punished rather than to say he was sorry or to ask for permission, even when it would certainly have been granted. Of course, what Yvonne de Galais should have done was to attack him directly, to take his head in her hands and say, 'Do I care what you have done? I love you. Aren't all men sinners?' Of course, she had been quite wrong – out of generosity, in a spirit of self-sacrifice – to send him off along the road to adventure . . . But how could I disapprove of so much goodness and love!

There was a long silence, during which, deeply troubled, we heard the cold rain pouring off the hedges and under the branches of the trees.

'So he left in the morning,' she continued. 'By then, there was nothing any more that separated us. He kissed me, simply, like a husband leaving his young wife before a long journey . . .'

She stood up. I took her feverish hand in mine, then her arm, and we went back up the avenue in the dark of night.

'And has he never even written to you?' I asked.

'Never,' she replied.

At that, the same thought came to both of us, about the adventurous life that he was leading at that very moment on the roads of France or Germany, and we started to speak about him as we had never done before. Forgotten details and old impressions came back to our minds as we slowly made our way back to the house, with long pauses at every step while we exchanged memories. For a long time, right up to the garden fence, I could hear her precious voice, sounding low in the darkness. And, seized by my old enthusiasm, I spoke continually to her, with deep affection, of the one who had abandoned us . . .

XII

THE BURDEN

School was due to resume on a Monday. On the Saturday evening, at around five o'clock, a woman from the Estate came to the school yard, where I was sawing some wood for the winter. She wanted to announce that a little girl had been born at Les Sablonnières. It had been a difficult birth, and at nine in the evening, the midwife had to be called from Préveranges. At midnight, the trap was sent again to call the doctor from Vierzon. He had to use forceps. The child's head was hurt, and she was crying a lot, but she seemed healthy enough. Yvonne de Galais was now very weak but she had suffered and fought with extraordinary courage.

I dropped my work and hurried to put on another jacket; pleased enough with the news, I went with the woman back to Les Sablonnières. Cautiously, for fear that one of the two patients might be sleeping, I climbed the narrow wooden staircase to the first floor. There, Monsieur de Galais, looking tired but happy, led me into the room where they had temporarily installed the cradle, surrounded by curtains.

I had never before been into a house on the very day when a child was born there. How strange and mysterious and good it seemed to me! It was such a lovely evening – a real summer evening – that Monsieur de Galais had not hesitated to open the window overlooking the yard. Leaning beside me on the window ledge, exhausted but joyful, he described the drama of the night before; and as I listened to him I felt vaguely that some stranger was now in the room with us . . .

Behind the curtains, she started to cry, a sharp, long, little cry; and Monsieur de Galais said softly to me, 'It's the wound on her head that makes her cry.'

Mechanically – you could tell that he had been doing this since that morning and was now used to it – he began to rock the crib.

'She can already laugh,' he said. 'And she holds your finger. Haven't you seen her?'

He opened the curtains, and I saw a puffy little red face and a little head that had been lengthened and deformed by the forceps.

'It's nothing to worry about,' said Monsieur de Galais. 'The doctor said that it will all put itself right. Give her your finger and she'll grasp it.'

I was discovering a world here that I did not know and felt my heart full of a strange joy that I had not previously experienced . . .

Monsieur de Galais carefully half opened the door to the young woman's bedroom. She was not asleep.

'You can come in,' he said.

She was lying there, her face flushed and her blonde hair spread around it. She offered me her hand, smiling, with a weary look. I complimented her on her daughter. In a rather hoarse voice and with unaccustomed roughness – the curt manner of someone returning from combat – she said, with a smile, 'Yes, but they damaged her for me!'

I soon had to leave so as not to tire her.

The next day, Sunday, in the afternoon, I hurried round to Les Sablonnières in an almost joyful mood. A notice pinned to the door stopped my hand in mid-air: 'Please do not ring'.

I did not guess what it meant. I knocked quite loudly and heard muffled footsteps running inside. Someone I did not know, the doctor from Vierzon, opened the door.

'Well, what is it?' I asked.

'Hush! Hush!' he said softly, with an air of irritation. 'The little girl almost died last night, and the mother is very ill.'

Completely taken aback, I followed him on tiptoe to the first floor. The baby asleep in her cot was very pale, quite white,

like a dead child. The doctor thought he could save her. As for
the mother, he could not guarantee anything . . . He explained
it to me at length, as the only friend of the family, talking
about pulmonary congestion and embolism. He was hesitant,
uncertain . . . Monsieur de Galais came in, grown horribly old
in two days, haggard and shaking.

He took me into the bedroom without quite knowing what
he was doing.

'You mustn't frighten her,' he whispered. 'The doctor's order
is that we must persuade her that it will be all right.'

Yvonne de Galais was lying with her face congested and her
head back as she had been on the day before. Her cheeks and
her forehead were dark red and her eyes rolled intermittently
as though she were suffocating, as she fought against death
with indescribable courage and patience.

She could not speak, but she held out her burning hand to
me with so much affection that I almost burst into tears.

'Well, well, now,' Monsieur de Galais said, very loudly, with
a frightful jollity that seemed close to madness. 'You can see
that for someone ill she doesn't look so bad!'

I did not know how to reply, but held the young, dying
woman's burning hand in mine.

She was trying to say something to me, to ask me a question.
She looked towards me, then at the window, as if telling me to
go outside and look for someone . . . But then she was seized
by a terrible fit of breathlessness. Her lovely blue eyes, which
had for a moment made such a tragic appeal to me, rolled
upwards; her cheeks and her brow darkened, and she struggled
gently, seeking to the last to control her terror and her despair.
They rushed forward – the doctor and the nurses – with an
oxygen flask, with towels and bottles, while the old man, leaning over her, was shouting – shouting as though she were
already far away from him – in his rough, quavering voice,
'Don't be afraid, Yvonne. It's nothing. There's nothing to be
afraid of.'

Then the crisis passed. She was able to breathe a little, but
she was still half suffocating, her eyes white, her head thrown
back, still struggling, but unable, even for a moment, to pull

herself out of the abyss into which she had already sunk, in
order to look at me and speak to me. And, since I was unable
to do anything, I had to bring myself to leave. Of course, I
could have stayed a moment longer – and at the thought I feel
seized by terrible remorse. But what can I say? I still had hope.
I convinced myself that the end was not so near.

When I reached the edge of the wood behind the house,
remembering the young woman's eyes turning towards the
window, I scrutinized like a sentry or a manhunter the depth
of this wood through which Augustin had once come and
through which he had left the previous winter. Alas, nothing
stirred; not an unusual shadow, not a branch moving . . . But
eventually, in the distance, towards the avenue that led from
Préveranges, I heard the faint sound of a bell, and soon at the
corner of the path a child in a red skullcap and a schoolboy's
smock appeared, walking behind a priest . . . And I left, fighting
back my tears.

The next day was the first day of term. By seven o'clock, there
were already two or three boys in the courtyard. I waited some
time before going down and showing myself. When at last I
did appear, turning the key in the door of the musty classroom which had been closed for two months, the thing that
I most feared in the world happened: the biggest of the boys
left the group playing under the shelter and came over to me.
He wanted to let me know that 'the young lady from Les
Sablonnières died yesterday at nightfall'.

Everything now is muddled for me, everything confused in
grief. It seems to me that I shall never again have the strength
to teach.

Just walking across the desolate school yard is a knee-
breaking effort. Everything is painful, everything bitter, now
that she is dead. The world is empty, the holidays are over.
Those long carriage rides are over, the mysterious fête is over
. . . Everything has reverted to the misery it was before . . .

I have told the children that there would be no class that
morning. They leave in small groups to pass the news on to
others in the country around. As for me, I take my black hat

and a braided coat that I have, and make my miserable way towards Les Sablonnières.

Here I am in front of the house that we searched for so long, three years ago. It was in this house that Yvonne de Galais, wife of Augustin Meaulnes, died yesterday evening. A stranger would think it was a chapel, so deep is the silence that has fallen since yesterday on this desolate place.

So this is what that fine morning at the start of term had in store for us, the treacherous autumn sunlight shining through the branches. How am I to fight against this bitter feeling of outrage, those tears choking in my throat? We had found the beautiful girl; we had conquered her. She was the wife of my friend and I loved her with that deep, secret love that is never spoken. When I looked at her, I was happy as a little child. One day, perhaps, I should have married another girl, and Yvonne would have been the first in whom I would have confided that great secret . . .

Yesterday's notice is still there, near the bell, in the corner of the door. They have already brought the coffin into the hall, downstairs. In the room on the first floor, it is the child's nurse who greets me, who tells me about her end and gently opens the door . . . There she is. No more fever, no more struggle. No more flushed face, no more waiting . . . Only silence and, wrapped in cotton wool, a hard face, white and unfeeling, and a dead brow beneath stiff, hard hair.

Monsieur de Galais, crouching in a corner with his back to us, is in stockinged feet, without shoes, and searches with dreadful obstinacy in some muddled drawers taken out of a wardrobe. From time to time, with a burst of sobbing that makes his shoulders heave like a burst of laughter, he takes out an already yellowing old photograph of his daughter.

The burial is to take place at noon. The doctor is afraid of the rapid decomposition that sometimes accompanies an embolism. This is why the face, and, indeed, the rest of the body, is surrounded by cotton wool steeped in phenol.

When the body was dressed – they put her in her splendid dark-blue velvet dress, spangled with little silver stars, though they had to flatten and rumple the leg-of-mutton sleeves which were by then out of fashion – as the coffin was being brought upstairs, they realized that it would not go round the corner in the narrow corridor. It had to be taken up with a rope through the window and afterwards lowered down in the same way. But Monsieur de Galais, who was still bending over some old things, looking for heaven knows what lost memories in them, refused with dreadful vehemence.

'Rather than allow such an awful thing,' he said, in a voice stifled with tears and anger, 'I will take her myself and bring her down in my arms . . .' And he would have done so, at the risk of weakening halfway and crashing down the stairs with her!

At this, I came forward and did the only thing I could: with the help of the doctor and one of his women assistants, I put one arm under the back of the outstretched corpse and the other under her legs, and held her against my chest. Lying against my left arm, her shoulders resting against my right one, and her head lolling under my chin, she weighed dreadfully on my heart. Slowly, step by step, I went down the long, steep staircase, while they prepared everything downstairs.

Very soon, both arms feel as if they are dropping with weariness. Every step with this weight against my chest makes me more breathless. Clasping the dead weight of the lifeless body, I bend my head over that of the woman I am carrying; I am breathing heavily and her blonde hair is sucked into my mouth – dead hair with a taste of earth. This taste of earth and of death and this weight on my heart are all that remain for me of the great adventure, and of you, Yvonne de Galais, a woman so long sought and so much loved . . .

XIII

THE MONTHLY COMPOSITION BOOK

In that house full of sad memories, where all day long women were cradling and comforting a sick infant, old Monsieur de Galais soon had to take to his bed. He died peacefully in the first great cold spell of the winter, and I could not help weeping beside the bed of this delightful old man whose indulgence and whimsy, joined to that of his son, had been the cause of our whole adventure. Fortunately, he died without ever really understanding what had happened and moreover in almost absolute silence. As it was a long time since he had had any relatives or friends in this part of France, his will made me his sole heir until the return of Meaulnes, to whom I had to account for everything if he ever should come back ... And from then on I lived at Les Sablonnières. I only went to Saint-Benoist to teach, leaving early in the morning, lunching at noon from a meal that had been prepared at the house, which I had heated up on a stove, and returning home in the evening after prep. In this way, I was able to keep the child with me, and the servants on the estate looked after her. Most of all, I increased my chances of seeing Augustin, if he ever returned to Les Sablonnières.

In any case, I still hoped that eventually, in some piece of furniture or drawer in the house, I would uncover a sheet of paper or some other clue that would tell me how he had spent his time during the long silence of the preceding years – and so, perhaps, understand the reasons for his departure or at least find some trace of him ... I had already searched in vain through I don't know how many cupboards and wardrobes, and opened a large number of boxes of every kind in storerooms which turned out either to be full of packets of old letters and yellowing photographs of the Galais family, or else crammed with artificial flowers, feathers, plumes and old-fashioned stuffed birds. These boxes gave off an indefinable musty smell, a faded perfume that would suddenly awaken memories and regrets in me and put an end to my search for the rest of the day.

Finally, on one school holiday, I found a little old trunk in the attic: long and low, covered in worn pigskin, I recognized it as Augustin's school trunk. I blamed myself for not having started my search there. I had no difficulty in breaking the rusted lock. The trunk was chock full of exercise books and school books from Sainte-Agathe: arithmetic, literature, workbooks, and goodness knows what . . . More from nostalgia than curiosity, I started to leaf through them, rereading dictations that I still knew by heart because we had copied them out so many times – Rousseau's 'Aqueduct', P.-L. Courier's 'An Adventure in Calabria', and the letter from George Sand to her son . . .[17]

There was also a 'Monthly Composition Book'. I was surprised to find it because these books stayed at the school and pupils never took them away. It was a green exercise book, yellowing at the edge. The pupil's name, *Augustin Meaulnes*, was written on the cover in splendid copperplate. I opened it. From the date of the exercises, April 189–, I realized that Meaulnes had started it only a few days before leaving Sainte-Agathe. The first pages had been kept with the meticulous care that was obligatory when one was working on these composition books, but only three pages had been written on: the rest was blank, and this explained why Meaulnes had taken it away.

Crouching on the floor and reflecting on these childish forms and rules that had played such a large role in our adolescence, I was turning the edge of the unused pages of the book with my thumb. And so it was that I discovered the writing on the later pages: after leaving four pages blank, someone had started to use the book again.

It was still Meaulnes' writing, but fast, careless and barely readable: little paragraphs of unequal width, separated by blank

lines. Sometimes there was just one unfinished sentence, sometimes a date. As soon as I started reading, I guessed that there
might be some information here on Meaulnes' past life in Paris,
some clues to what I was seeking, so I went down into the
dining room to read through the strange document at my leisure
and in daylight. The light was that of a clear, breezy winter's
day. At times, the bright sunlight projected the cross of the
window frames on to the white curtains, at others a sharp wind
dashed an icy shower against the panes. And it was in front of
that window, by the fire, that I read the lines that explained so
much to me and which I now set down here exactly as I found
them . . .

XIV

THE SECRET

I have passed once more beneath her window. The pane is still dusty and whitened by the double curtain behind it. Were Yvonne de Galais to open it, I should have nothing to say to her, because she is already married ... What can I do now? How shall I live?

Saturday, 13 February. On the embankment, I met the young woman who told me about the closed house in June and who had been waiting, as I was, in front of it. I spoke to her. As she was walking along, I looked sideways at the slight defects of her face: a little line at the corner of the lips, a little sagging of the cheeks, some powder visible by her nose. She turned round suddenly and stared me straight in the face – perhaps because she is prettier full face than in profile – saying curtly, 'I find you very amusing. You remind me of a young man who once paid court to me in Bourges. We were even engaged ...'

And saying this, after dusk, on the damp, deserted pavement shining in the light of a gaslamp, she suddenly came close to me and asked me to take her to the theatre that evening with her sister. For the first time, I notice that she is dressed in mourning, with a lady's hat too old for her young face and a long, slender umbrella, like a walking stick. As I am right next to her, when I make a gesture my finger nails scratch the crêpe on her bodice ... I try to refuse. She is annoyed and wants to leave at once. Now I'm the one holding her back, begging. And then a workman walking past in the dark mutters, jesting, 'Don't go, girl, he'll do you harm!'

The two of us stayed there, reduced to silence.

In the theatre: the two girls, my friend, who is called Valentine Blondeau, and her sister, arrived with cheap scarves.

Valentine is sitting in front of me. She turns round constantly, uneasily, as though wondering what I want. And, close to her, I feel almost happy: I reply each time with a smile.

All around us there were women showing too much bosom. And we joked. She smiled first, then she said, 'I mustn't laugh: my dress is cut too low as well.' She wrapped her scarf around her. Under the square of black lace you could see that, in her haste to change her clothes, she had turned down the top of her simple, high-necked chemise.

There is something indefinably poor and naive about her. In her look, there is an intangible air of suffering and audacity that attracts me. Near her, the only creature in the world who could tell me about the people of the Estate, I think constantly of the strange adventure I once had ... I would like to have questioned her again about the little mansion on the boulevard, but she, in her turn, put such awkward questions to me that I was unable to say anything in reply. I feel that from now on we shall both of us stay silent on the subject. Yet, I know, too, that I shall see her again. Why? And for what? Am I now condemned to follow the trail of any being who has the vaguest and remotest connection with my failed adventure?

At midnight, alone, in the empty street, I wonder what this new, odd story is going to lead me to. I am walking along beside houses like rows of cardboard boxes in which a whole tribe is sleeping. Suddenly I remember a decision that I took a month or so ago: I would go there in the middle of the night, around one o'clock in the morning, open the garden door at the back of the house, enter like a thief and look for some clue that would allow me to find the Lost Estate, to see her again, just to see her ... But I'm tired and hungry. I too was in a hurry to change my clothes before the theatre and I didn't have dinner ... And yet, anxious, worried, I sit on my bed for a long time before going to sleep, feeling a vague sense of regret. Why?

Another thing: they did not want to be taken home or to tell me where they are staying. But I followed them as long as I could. I know that they live in a little winding street near Notre-Dame. But which number? I guess that they are seamstresses or milliners.

Without letting her sister know, Valentine arranged to meet me on Thursday at four o'clock in front of the same theatre where we had been.

'If I should happen not to be there on Thursday,' she said, 'come back on Friday at the same time, then Saturday, and so on, every day.'

Thursday, 18 February. I left to meet her in a gusting wind, damp with rain – the kind that makes you feel constantly that rain is coming.

I am walking through the half-dark streets, with a weight on my heart. A drop of water falls: I am afraid that it will start to rain: a shower might stop her from coming. But the wind starts to blow again and, once more, the rain does not fall. Up in the grey afternoon of the sky – now grey, now radiant – a large cloud has had to succumb to the wind. And I am here, earthbound, miserably waiting.

In front of the theatre. After quarter of an hour, I am sure that she will not come. From the embankment where I am standing, I am watching the lines of people walking across the bridge that she would have to take. My eyes follow all the young women in mourning that I see coming this way and I feel almost grateful to those who, for the longest time and closest to me, resemble her and keep my hopes alive ...

An hour of waiting. I am weary. At nightfall, a police officer drags a young tearaway off to the nearby police station while the lad is cursing him in a strangled voice with all the insults and filth that he can muster . . . The policeman is furious, pale and silent . . . As soon as he gets him inside, he starts to hit him, then closes the door on them so that he can beat him at his leisure . . . The dreadful thought occurs to me that I have given up paradise and am now standing at the gates of hell.

Tired of waiting, I leave the place and go to the low, narrow street between the Seine and Notre-Dame which I know is roughly the place where she lives. All alone, I walk up and down. From time to time, a maid or a housewife comes out under the drizzling rain to do her shopping before nightfall. There is nothing here for me, and I leave. Once again, I go past the square where we were due to meet, under the clear rain that is holding back the dark. There are more people than earlier – a black crowd . . .

Suppositions. Despair. Weariness. I cling to the idea of tomorrow. Tomorrow at the same time at this same spot I will come back and wait. And I am in a hurry to get to tomorrow. I imagine the boredom of this evening, then tomorrow morning, which I have to spend in idleness. But is today not almost over? Back home, beside the fire, I can hear them selling the evening papers. No doubt in her house, lost somewhere in the city, near Notre-Dame, she can hear them too.

She . . . I mean: Valentine.

This evening, which I have tried to spirit away, is a strange burden to me. While time moves on, while the day will soon end and I already wish it gone, there are men who have entrusted all their hopes to it, all their love and their last efforts. There are dying men or others who are waiting for a debt to come due, who wish that tomorrow would never come. There are others for whom the day will break like a pang of remorse; and others who are tired, for whom the night will never be long enough to give them the rest that they need. And I – who have lost my day – what right do I have to wish that tomorrow comes?

Friday evening. I thought I would write after that: 'I did not see her again'. And it would all be over.

But this evening at four o'clock, when I get to the corner by the theatre, there she is. Delicate and solemn, dressed in black, but with a powdered face and a collar that made her look like a guilty Pierrot – at the same time sad and mischievous.

She has come to tell me that she wants to leave me at once and will not come again.

Yet when night falls, here we are still, the two of us, walking slowly beside one another on the gravelled paths of the Tuileries Gardens. She is telling me her story, but in such a convoluted way that I cannot fully understand it. She says 'my love', talking about the fiancé whom she never married. She does it deliberately, I think, to shock me and so that I will not become attached to her.

There are some things that she says that I am reluctant to put down:

'Don't trust me,' she says. 'I've always done silly things.

'I roamed the highways, all alone.

'I drove my fiancé to desperation. I abandoned him because he admired me too much. He could only see me in his imagination and not as I was. And I am full of faults. We should have been very unhappy.'

I am constantly catching her out at making herself seem worse than she is. I think that she wants to prove to herself that she was right before in doing the silly thing that she mentions, that she has no cause for regret and that she was not worthy of the happiness that she might have enjoyed.

'What I like about you,' she said another time, staring hard at me. 'What I like about you, I don't know why, are my memories . . .'

'I still love him,' she told me, yet another time. 'More than you think.'

Then, suddenly, brusquely, brutally, sadly: 'What do you want, in the end? Do you love me, too? Are you, too, going to ask for my hand?'

I stammered something. I don't know what I replied. I may have said, 'Yes.'

*

This rough diary was interrupted at this point. What followed were rough copies of unreadable, shapeless letters, with many crossings out. What a precarious engagement! At Meaulnes' request, the girl had left her job, while he took charge of the preparations for the wedding. But he was constantly haunted by the desire to look further, to set out again on the trail of his lost love, and several times he must surely have disappeared. In the letters, with tragic chagrin, he tries to justify himself to Valentine.

XV

THE SECRET

(continued)

Then the diary resumed.

He had put down his memories of a stay that the two of them made in the country, I don't know where. The odd thing is that from here on, perhaps because of some secret feeling of embarrassment, the diary was written in such a disconnected and formless way, and scribbled so hastily, that I have had to go over and reconstitute this part of his story myself.

14 June. When he woke up early in the room in the inn, the sun was lighting the red pattern on the black curtain. Some farm workers in the room below were talking loudly as they took their morning coffee, with rough, but unimpassioned complaints about one of their bosses. Meaulnes must have been hearing this steady noise in his sleep for a long time, because at first he was not aware of it. The curtain, dappled with red clusters by the sunlight, these morning voices rising up into the silent room, everything mingled to give a feeling of waking up in the country at the start of some delightful summer holidays.

He got up and gently knocked on the room next door. There was no reply, so he silently opened it. This was when he saw Valentine and understood where her tranquil contentment came from. She was sleeping, quite motionless and silent, so that you couldn't hear the sound of her breathing, as birds must sleep. He stared for a long time at this child's face with its closed eyes, this face so calm that one would have wished never to wake or disturb it.

The only movement that she made to show that she was no longer asleep was to open her eyes and look.

As soon as she was dressed, Meaulnes came over to the girl.

'We're late,' she said.

At once, she was like a housewife in her home.

She tidied the rooms and brushed the clothes that Meaulnes had worn on the previous day; when she got to the trousers, she was in despair. The bottoms of the legs were coated in thick mud. She paused, then, carefully, before brushing them, began by scraping off the first layer of earth with a knife.

'That's how the kids at Sainte-Agathe did it,' Meaulnes said, 'when they'd fallen in the mud.'

'My mother taught me,' said Valentine.

This was the companion that Meaulnes, the hunter and peasant, must have wished for before his mysterious adventure.

15 June. At dinner in the farm where, thanks to some friends who had introduced them as husband and wife, they had been invited – much to their annoyance – they behaved as shyly as a newly married couple.

The candles had been lit in two candelabra, one at each end of the table covered in a white cloth, as for a quiet country wedding. As soon as anyone leant forward under this dim light, their face was plunged into shadow.

To the right of Patrice, the farmer's son, there was Valentine, then Meaulnes, who stayed taciturn throughout the meal, though he was almost always the one addressed. Since he had decided in this remote village to pass Valentine off as his wife, in order to avoid gossip, he had been riven by regret and remorse. And while Patrice, in the manner of a country gentleman, was playing host, Meaulnes was thinking, 'I am the one who should this evening, in a low room like this one, a fine room that I know well, be presiding over my wedding feast.'

Valentine, beside him, shyly refused whatever she was offered. She was like a young peasant girl. At each new offer, she looked at her friend and seemed to want him to shelter her. For a long time, Patrice had been urging her in vain to empty her glass, when finally Meaulnes leant towards her and said softly, 'You must drink, my little Valentine.'

So, docilely, she drank. And Patrice smiled and congratulated the young man on having such an obedient wife.

But both of them, Valentine and Meaulnes, stayed silent and thoughtful. They were tired, first of all. Their feet, soaked by the mud of their walk, felt chilled against the washed tiles of the kitchen floor. And then, from time to time, the young man had to say, 'My wife, Valentine. My wife . . .'

And each time, as he quietly said that word in front of these unknown country people, in this dark dining room, he had the impression that he was committing a sin.

17 June. The afternoon of the last day started badly.

Patrice and his wife accompanied them on their walk. Little by little, on the uneven hillside covered with heather, the two couples became separated. Meaulnes and Valentine sat down among the juniper trees in a small thicket.

Drops of rain were carried on the wind and the sky was low. The evening had a bitter taste, it seemed, the taste of such boredom that even love could not dispel it.

For a long time they stayed there, in their hiding place, sheltered by the branches and saying very little. Then the weather improved, and the sun came out. They felt that from now on, all would be well.

They started to speak about love, and Valentine talked on and on . . .

'There,' she said. 'That's what my fiancé promised me, like the child that he was: straightaway we should have had a house, like a cottage, far away in the country. It was all ready for us, he said. We should have come there as though we were returning from a long journey, on the evening of our marriage, around the time that is close to nightfall. And along the roads, in the courtyard, hidden in the bushes, strange children would have cheered us on, shouting, "Long live the bride!" What madness, isn't it?'

Meaulnes listened to her uneasily, saying nothing. In all this, he felt something like the echo of a voice already heard. And, also, as the young woman told this story, there was something like a faint note of regret in her voice.

But she was afraid she had upset him. She turned round towards him, gently, impulsively, saying, 'I want to give you everything I have, something that is more precious than anything else to me – and you can burn it!'

Then, staring at him anxiously, she took a small packet of letters out of her pocket and held them out to him: her fiancé's letters.

Oh, he recognized the fine writing at once. Why hadn't he realized it earlier? It was the writing of Frantz, the gypsy, which he had seen previously on the desperate note left behind in the room at the château . . .

By now, they were walking along a little narrow road past fields of daisies and hay lit obliquely by the rays of the five o'clock sun. So great was his amazement that Meaulnes did not yet understand what a disaster all this meant for him. He read the letters because she asked him to read them: childish, sentimental, pathetic phrases . . . This, in the final letter:

Ah, so you have lost the little heart, my unforgiveable little Valentine! What will become of us? Although, after all, I am not superstitious . . .

Meaulnes read, half blinded by regret and anger, his face unmoving, but quite pale, twitching slightly under the eyes. Valentine, troubled at seeing him like that, looked to see where he had got to and what was annoying him so much . . .

'It's a piece of jewellery,' she explained hastily. 'He gave it to me and made me swear to keep it always. That was one of his crazy ideas.'

But this only made Meaulnes more exasperated.

'Crazy!' he said, putting the letters in his pocket. 'Why keep repeating that word? Why did you never want to believe in him? I knew him: he was the most wonderful boy in the world!'

'You knew him?' she said, completely overcome. 'You knew Frantz de Galais?'

'He was my best friend, my brother in adventures – and now I've taken his fiancée from him!

'Oh, how you harmed us,' he continued, furiously. 'You, who never believed in anything. You are the cause of it all. You are the one who ruined everything – ruined it!'

She tried to speak, to take his hand, but he pushed her away roughly.

'Go away. Leave me.'

'Very well,' she said, her face burning, stammering and half weeping, 'if that's how it is, I shall leave. I'll go back to Bourges, go home, with my sister. And if you don't come to look for me, you realize, don't you, that my father is too poor to keep me. Well, I'll come back to Paris, I'll walk the roads as I did once before and certainly become a lost woman, since I don't have a trade.'

She went off to get her parcels and take the train, while Meaulnes, without even looking at her as she left, continued to walk along aimlessly.

The diary was once again interrupted at this point.

After that there were more rough copies of letters – the letters of a man who was lost and undecided. Returning to La Ferté-d'Angillon, Meaulnes wrote to Valentine, apparently to confirm that he had resolved not to see her again and to tell her exactly why, but perhaps in reality so that she would reply to him. In one of these letters, he asked her something that, in the confusion of the moment, it had not at first occurred to him to ask her: did she know where the long-lost Estate was to be found? In another, he begged her to be reconciled with Frantz de Galais. He would make it his business to find him for her . . . None of the letters that I saw in this rough form had been sent, but he must have written twice or three times without getting a reply. For him, this had been a period of conflict, frightful and miserable, in total solitude. The hope of ever seeing Yvonne de Galais again had completely faded, and he must have felt his great resolve weaken bit by bit. And, judging by the pages that follow – the last in his diary – I guess that he must one fine morning at the start of the holidays have hired a bicycle to go to Bourges and visit the cathedral.

He had left at first light, down the beautiful, straight road through the woods, on the way inventing a thousand excuses for presenting himself in a dignified manner, without asking for a reconciliation, to the woman whom he had rejected.

The last four pages, that I have managed to reconstruct, describe this journey and his final error.

XVI

THE SECRET

(end)

25 August. On the other side of Bourges, at the edge of the new suburbs, he found Valentine Blondeau's house, after a long search. A woman, Valentine's mother, seemed to be waiting for him on the doorstep. She was a good, housewifely figure, heavy, worn, but still attractive. She watched him curiously as he approached, and when he asked if the Mademoiselles Blondeau were there, she gently explained to him, in a considerate tone, that they had returned to Paris on 15 August.

'They told me not to say where they were going,' she added. 'But if you write to their old address, the letters will be sent on to them.'

Retracing his steps, wheeling his bicycle beside him through the little front garden, he thought, 'She has left . . . Everything turned out as I willed it . . . I forced her to do this . . . "I shall certainly become a fallen woman," she said. And I drove her to that! I'm the one who ruined Frantz's fiancée!'

And under his breath he repeated, insanely, 'All the better, all the better!' – but with the certainty that, on the contrary, it was really 'all the worse' and that, with this woman watching, he would trip up before he got to the gate and fall on his knees.

He did not think of having lunch and stopped in a café where he wrote a long letter to Valentine, just to cry out – to release the desperate cry that was stifling him. His letter said over and over: 'How could you? How could you? How could you do that? How could you ruin yourself?'

There were some officers drinking close by. One of them was noisily telling a story about a woman, snatches of which you could hear: 'I told her ... You ought to know me ... I play cards with your husband every evening!' The others laughed, turning their heads and spitting behind the benches. Haggard and covered in dust, Meaulnes watched them like a beggar; he could imagine them with Valentine on their knees.

For a long time he rode his bicycle around the cathedral, vaguely thinking, 'After all, it was to see the cathedral that I came.' At the end of every street, on its deserted square, it rose up, vast and indifferent. The streets were narrow and dirty like the streets around a village church. Here and there, he saw the sign of a brothel, a red lantern ... Meaulnes felt that his grief was lost in the dirt and vice of this district which had gathered, as in former times, under the flying buttresses of the cathedral. He felt a peasant's fear, a revulsion at this town church in which the secret corners have the sculpted images of every vice, a church built among brothels and offering no cure for the purest pains of love.

Two street women went past, holding one another by the waist and looking brazenly at him. From disgust, or in jest, either to be revenged on his love or to destroy it, Meaulnes followed them slowly on his bicycle and one of them, a sad-looking creature whose sparse blonde hair was pulled back into a false chignon, gave him a rendezvous for six o'clock in the garden of the Archbishopric – the garden where Frantz, in one of his letters, had made an appointment to meet poor Valentine.

He did not refuse, knowing that by then he would long since have left town. And she stayed for a long time at her low window, in the sloping street, waving to him vaguely.

He was in a hurry to get away.

Before leaving, he could not resist the melancholy urge to go one final time in front of Valentine's house. He stared long and hard at it, and stored up a feeling of sadness. It was one of the last houses on the outskirts of town, and the street became a road from there on. Opposite, a sort of patch of waste ground made something resembling a little square. There was no one at the windows or in the courtyard, anywhere – only one dirty, heavily powdered girl going past a wall and dragging two urchins with her.

This is where Valentine's childhood had been spent, where she had started to see the world with her trusting, submissive eyes. She had worked, she had sewn behind those windows. Frantz had come to see her and smile at her in this suburban street. But now there was nothing, nothing left ... The sad evening wore on and Meaulnes only knew that somewhere on this same afternoon, lost, Valentine was looking at this dreary square in her mind's eye and would never return here.

The long return journey that he had in front of him would be his last defence against unhappiness, his last forced distraction before he lapsed into it entirely.

He set off. At the sides of the road, in the valley, between the trees, delightful farm houses at the river's edge showed their pointed gables decorated with green trelliswork. No doubt, on the lawns, there were intense young girls talking of love. One could imagine souls, beautiful souls ...

But for Meaulnes at that moment there was only one love, the unsatisfied love that had just been so cruelly assaulted, and the girl whom he should, above all others, have protected and safeguarded, was the very one that he had just sent to her ruin.

A few hastily written lines in the diary informed me that he had determined to find Valentine, at whatever cost, before it was too late. A date at the corner of a page gave me to think that this was the long journey for which Madame Meaulnes was getting him ready when I came to La Ferté-d'Angillon and upset all his schemes. In the abandoned town hall, Meaulnes had been noting down his memories and his plans one fine morning at the end of August, when I opened the door and brought him the great news for which he had ceased to hope. He was caught up again and paralysed by his old adventure, not daring to do anything or to confess anything. And this was when the remorse, the regret and the grief had begun, at times repressed, at others driving out all other ideas, until the wedding day when the gypsy's shout in the trees had dramatically reminded him of the first oath of his young manhood.

On that same monthly composition book, he had quickly scribbled a few more words at dawn before leaving – with her permission, but for ever – Yvonne de Galais, his wife since the previous day:

'I am leaving. I have to find the trail of the two gypsies who came yesterday to the fir wood and who set off by bicycle towards the east. I shall only return to Yvonne if I can bring back with me Frantz and Valentine, married, and settle them in "Frantz's house".

'This manuscript which I began as a secret diary, and which has become my confession, is to be the property of my friend François Seurel, should I not return.'

He must have quickly slipped this exercise book under the rest, locked his small, old schoolboy trunk and vanished.

EPILOGUE

Time passed, I was losing hope of ever seeing my friend again, and dreary days went by in the peasant school, and sad ones in the empty house. Frantz did not come to the meeting that we had arranged and, in any case, it was a long time since my Aunt Moinel had known where Valentine was living.

The only joy at Les Sablonnières was, very soon, the little girl, whom they had managed to save. At the end of September, she even gave signs of growing up as a healthy and pretty child. She was nearly one year old. Clutching the backs of chairs, she would push them along by herself, trying to walk, not bothered about falling over and making a continual din that would rouse the dull echoes of the abandoned house. When I held her in my arms, she would never allow me to kiss her. She had a wild and delightful way of wriggling and, at the same time, pushing my face away with her little hand held open, all the time laughing aloud. It was as though, with all her merriment and all her childish energy, she would drive away the sorrow that had hung over the house since her birth. I sometimes thought, 'I expect that, for all her wildness, she will be a little bit my child.' Once again, fate would decide otherwise.

One Sunday morning at the end of September, I had got up very early, even before the country woman who cared for the little girl. I meant to go fishing in the Cher, with Jasmin Delouche and two men from Saint-Benoist. The village people from around there would often include me in their great poaching expeditions: fishing by hand or, at night, with illegal nets. Throughout the summer, on holidays, we would start at dawn and not return until noon. For almost all these men, this was their livelihood, while for me it was my only recreation, the only adventures that reminded me of the escapades we used to have. Eventually, I had come to enjoy these excursions, the hours spent fishing along the river bank or among the reeds in the lake.

So that morning I was up at half-past five and waiting in front of the house, in a little shelter up against the wall that separated the English garden at Les Sablonnières from the kitchen garden of the farm. I was busy untying my nets, which I had thrown down in a heap on the previous Thursday.

It was not quite daylight, but the moment before dawn on a fine September morning, and the shelter where I was disentangling my things was half plunged in darkness.

I was there, silent and busy, when suddenly I heard the gate open and the noise of footsteps on the gravel path. 'What's this?' I thought. 'These people are earlier than I expected. And I'm not even ready!'

But the man coming into the yard was someone I didn't know. As far as I could make out, he was a tall fellow, with a beard, dressed like a huntsman or a poacher. Instead of coming to get me where the others knew I would always be when we had arranged to meet, he went directly to the front door.

'Right!' I thought. 'It's one of their friends, someone they've invited without telling me: they've sent him on ahead.'

Softly and silently, the man tried the latch of the door; but I had locked it as I went out. He did the same at the kitchen door, then, after hesitating for a moment, he turned round towards me, with an anxious face, lit by the half-light. Only then did I recognize The Great Meaulnes.

For a long time, I stayed there, frightened, desperate, suddenly overwhelmed with all the pain reawakened by this return. He had gone to the back of the house and walked round; now he was coming back, uncertainly.

So I went across to him and, without a word, embraced him, sobbing. He understood at once.

'Ah!' he said, curtly, 'she's dead, isn't she?'

And he stood there, terrible in his silence and immobility.

I took him by the arm and gently led him towards the house. Day had now broken. Right away, to get the worst over, I showed him the staircase leading to the room where she died. As soon as he went in, he fell on his knees by the bed and stayed for a long time with his head wrapped in his arms.

He got up at last, wild-eyed, swaying, not knowing where he was. Still leading him by the arm, I opened the door between that room and the little girl's. She had woken up all by herself, while her nurse was downstairs, and had sat herself up purposefully in her cot. You could just see her head, turned towards us with a look of surprise.

'This is your daughter,' I said.

He gave me a startled look. Then he grasped her and lifted her in his arms. At first, because he was crying, he could not see her properly. Then, to distract attention from this flood of tears and strong emotions, holding the girl tightly against him, seated on his right arm, he turned towards me with bowed head and said, 'I've brought the other two back . . . You can go and see them in their house.'

And, indeed, when later that morning I set off, thoughtful and almost happy, towards Frantz's house, which Yvonne de Galais had once shown me empty, I saw from a distance someone like a young housewife in a white collar, sweeping the doorstep, attracting the attentive curiosity of several little cowherds on their way to Mass, dressed in their Sunday best . . .

Meanwhile, the little girl was growing tired of being held so tightly and, as Augustin, turning his head to hide and stem the flow of tears, was still not looking at her, she gave him a great slap with her little hand on his moist, bearded mouth.

This time the father lifted his daughter up high, tossed her in his arms and looked at her with a kind of laugh. She clapped her hands contentedly.

I had stepped back a bit to see them better. Filled with wonder, and a sense of slight disappointment, even so, I realized that the girl had at last found the companion for whom she had unconsciously been waiting. I felt that The Great Meaulnes had come back to deprive me of the only joy that he had left me. And already I imagined him, one evening, wrapping his daughter in a cloak and setting off with her for some new adventure.

Notes

1. *My mother took the junior class*: The educational reforms instituted by Jules Ferry (1832–93) in the early 1880s provided France with a system of primary education that was universal, obligatory, free and non-religious. It covered the years from six to eleven, in the *cours élémentaire* and the *cours moyen* (which I have translated as 'junior school' and 'middle school'). Monsieur Seurel was one of a new army of schoolteachers created by the Ferry reforms.

2. *departmental préfet*: The main administrative district in France is the *département*, of which there are ninety-five in France itself, plus two overseas. The chief executive of the *département* is the *préfet*.

3. *Fourteenth of July*: The French national day, a holiday marked by fireworks and festivities. It commemorates the capture of the Bastille prison in 1789, a date usually taken as the start of the French Revolution.

4. *képi*: The cap, with a circular top and a peak, worn by French policemen, military officers and other officials.

5. *standing at a basket-maker's*: Daniel Defoe, *Robinson Crusoe*, chapter XI: 'It prov'd of excellent advantage to me now, that when I was a boy, I used to take great delight in standing at a basketmaker's, in the town where my father liv'd, to see them make their Wicker-ware'. There were several translations of Defoe's novel in nineteenth-century France. Alain-Fournier may have been thinking of one published around 1875 with illustrations by Grandville.

6. *three and a half leagues*: A league is a distance of about four kilometres.

7. *those squally Thursdays*: Thursdays were left free in French schools, and students had to attend school on Saturdays.

8. *Rousseau and Paul-Louis Courier*: Jean-Jacques Rousseau

(1712–78) was one of the most influential figures of his time, the author of works on politics, education and other topics, and of the autobiographical *Confessions*. Paul-Louis Courier (1772–1825) was well known for his anti-clerical views. He wrote pamphlets in defence of the interests of citizens against State and Church, and translated works from Greek, including Longus' *Daphnis and Chloe*.

9. *the men mobilized from the Seine in 1870*: That is, the men from the *département* of Seine mobilized to fight in the Franco-Prussian War.

10. *Talma or Léotard*: François-Joseph Talma (1763–1826) was the leading actor on the French stage in the revolutionary and Napoleonic period. Jules Léotard (1839–70) was a famous acrobat who gave his name to the single-piece garment that he favoured for his work.

11. *the Certificat d'études supérieures . . . the Ecole Normale*: A law of 1882 set up obligatory primary school education in France, leading to a school-leaving certificate (*Certificat d'études primaires*). There were also to be secondary schools of the kind at which Monsieur Seurel teaches, known as *Ecoles primaires supérieures*, which would deliver a *Certificat d'études supérieures*. Some of their pupils might go on to study for a teaching qualification at the *Ecoles Normales* (teacher training colleges) that were to be set up in every *département*.

12. *Brevet simple*: At the time, a school-leaving certificate. But, as we learn from the next paragraph, François is going to study for a further year to obtain the *Brevet supérieur*, which will give him a teaching qualification.

13. *Cours complémentaire*: At the time, a type of secondary school giving general education. The Cours supérieur, mentioned below, was for those pupils who decided to stay on for further study after completing their years of compulsory education.

14. *in seventy*: The Franco-Prussian War of 1870 ended in a rapid defeat for France, the abdication of the Emperor, Napoleon III, the proclamation of the Third Republic and, in 1871, the uprising of the Paris Commune.

15. *Presidents Grévy and Carnot*: Jules Grévy (1807–91) was president of France from 1879 to 1887. He was succeeded by Sadi Carnot (1837–94), who remained in office until his death.

16. *green paper crowns*: Presumably to crown the winners of end-of-year prizes.

17. *Rousseau's . . . George Sand to her son*: Passages from literature

suitable for pupils to write down to dictation. For Rousseau and Courier, see note 8. The passage from Rousseau is a well-known story about a walnut tree from his *Confessions*, Book I. Courier's short tale is based on his experiences in southern Italy. George Sand (Aurore Dupin, 1804–76) wrote many letters to her son, Maurice; it is not certain which is the one mentioned here.

PENGUIN CLASSICS

MADAME BOVARY   GUSTAVE FLAUBERT

'Oh, why, dear God, did I marry him?'

Emma Bovary is beautiful and bored, trapped in her marriage to a mediocre doctor and stifled by the banality of provincial life. An ardent devourer of sentimental novels, she longs for passion and seeks escape in fantasies of high romance, in voracious spending and, eventually, in adultery. But even her affairs bring her disappointment, and when real life continues to fail to live up to her romantic expectations the consequences are devastating. Flaubert's erotically charged and psychologically acute portrayal of Emma Bovary caused a moral outcry on its publication in 1857. It was deemed so lifelike that many women claimed they were the model for his heroine; but Flaubert insisted: 'Madame Bovary, c'est moi'.

This modern translation by Flaubert's biographer, Geoffrey Wall, retains all the delicacy and precision of the French original. This edition also contains a preface by the novelist Michèle Roberts.

'A masterpiece' Julian Barnes

'A supremely beautiful novel' Michèle Roberts

Translated and edited with an introduction by Geoffrey Wall
With a Preface by Michèle Roberts

PENGUIN CLASSICS

SENTIMENTAL EDUCATION GUSTAVE FLAUBERT

'He loved her without reservation, without hope, unconditionally'

Frederic Moreau is a law student returning home to Normandy from Paris when he first notices Madame Arnoux, a slender, dark woman several years older than himself. It is the beginning of an infatuation that will last a lifetime. He befriends her husband, an influential businessman, and their paths cross and re-cross over the years. Through financial upheaval, political turmoil and countless affairs, Madame Arnoux remains the constant, unattainable love of Moreau's life. Flaubert described his sweeping story of a young man's passions, ambitions and amours as 'the moral history of the men of my generation'. Based on his own youthful passion for an older woman, *Sentimental Education* blends love story, historical authenticity and satire to create one of the greatest French novels of the nineteenth century.

Geoffrey Wall's fresh revision of Robert Baldick's original translation is accompanied by an insightful new introduction discussing the personal and historical influences on Flaubert's writing. This edition also contains a new chronology, further reading and explanatory notes.

Translated with an introduction by Robert Baldick
Revised and edited by Geoffrey Wall

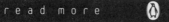
PENGUIN CLASSICS

NOTRE-DAME DE PARIS   VICTOR HUGO

'He was like a giant broken in pieces and badly reassembled'

In the vaulted Gothic towers of Notre-Dame lives Quasimodo, the hunchbacked bellringer. Mocked and shunned for his appearance, he is pitied only by Esmerelda, a beautiful gypsy dancer to whom he becomes completely devoted. Esmerelda, however, has also attracted the attention of the sinister archdeacon Claude Frollo, and when she rejects his lecherous approaches, Frollo hatches a plot to destroy her that only Quasimodo can prevent. Victor Hugo's sensational, evocative novel brings life to the medieval Paris he loved, and mourns its passing in one of the greatest historical romances of the nineteenth century.

John Sturrock's clear, contemporary translation is accompanied by an introduction discussing it as a passionate novel of ideas, written in defence of Gothic architecture and of a burgeoning democracy, and demonstrating that an ugly exterior can conceal moral beauty. This revised edition also includes further reading and a chronology of Hugo's life.

Translated with an introduction by John Sturrock

PENGUIN CLASSICS

AGAINST NATURE (A REBOURS)　J. K. HUYSMANS

'He drank this liquid perfume from cups of that oriental porcelain known as egg-shell china, it is so delicate and diaphanous'

A wildly original *fin de siècle* novel, *Against Nature* contains only one character. De Esseinte is a decadent, ailing aristocrat who retreats to an isolated villa where he indulges his taste for luxury and excess. Veering between nervous excitability and debilitating ennui he gluts his aesthetic appetites with classical literature and art, exotic jewels (with which he fatally encrusts the shell of his tortoise), rich perfumes and a kaleidoscope of sensual experiences. *Against Nature*, in the words of the author exploded 'like a grenade' and has a cult following to this day.

This revised edition of Robert Baldick's lucid translation features a new introduction, a chronology and reproduces Huysmans's original 1903 preface as well as a selection of reviews from writers including Mallarme, Zola and Wilde.

Translated by Robert Baldick and edited by Patrick McGuiness

PENGUIN CLASSICS

AROUND THE WORLD IN EIGHTY DAYS
JULES VERNE

'To go around the world in such a short time and with the means of transport currently available, was not only impossible, it was madness'

One ill-fated evening at the Reform Club, Phileas Fogg, rashly bets his companions £20,000 that he can travel around the entire globe in just eighty days – and he is determined not to lose. Breaking the well-established routine of his daily life, the reserved Englishman immediately sets off for Dover, accompanied by his hot-blooded French manservant Passepartout. Travelling by train, steamship, sailing boat, sledge and even elephant, they must overcome storms, kidnappings, natural disasters, Sioux attacks and the dogged Inspector Fix of Scotland Yard – who believes that Fogg has robbed the Bank of England – in order to win the extraordinary wager. *Around the World in Eighty Days* gripped audiences on its publication and remains hugely popular, combining exploration, adventure and a thrilling race against time.

Michael Glencross's lively translation is accompanied by an introduction by Brian Aldiss which places Jules Verne's work in its literary and historical context. There is also a detailed chronology, notes and further reading.

Translated with notes by Michael Glencross with an introduction by Brian Aldiss

PENGUIN CLASSICS

LA BÊTE HUMAINE   ÉMILE ZOLA

'He was coming to think that he was paying for others, fathers, grandfathers . . . that he had their blood, tainted with a slow poison'

Séverine Roubaud, the pretty young wife of a rail worker, is desperate to escape her marriage to the violent, brutish Roubaud, and becomes drawn into an intense affair with his colleague Jacques Lantier. Lantier seems gentle and sensitive, bringing her true happiness for the first time. But, unknown to Séverine, she is entering a dangerous world far beyond her control. For Jacques Lantier has a fatal flaw: he is a killer, battling with an ill-suppressed urge to kill again. Seventeenth in the twenty Rougon-Macquart novels, *La Bête Humaine is* one of Zola's most dark and violent works: a tense thriller of madness and possession; an attack on legal and political corruption; and a study of the basest human instincts beneath the civilized veneer of society.

Leonard Tancock's powerful translation is accompanied by an introduction tracing the origins of the novel in the disparate subjects of railway life, the judicial system and an individual doomed by heredity to be a murderer.

Translated with an introduction by Leonard Tancock

PENGUIN CLASSICS

DEERBROOK
HARRIET MARTINEAU

'If you do a thing which a village public does not approve, there will be offence in whatever else you say and do, for some time after'

When the Ibbotson sisters, Hester and Margaret, arrive at the village of Deerbrook to stay with their cousin Mr Grey and his wife, speculation is rife that one of them might marry the village apothecary, Edward Hope. Although he is immediately attracted to Margaret, Edward is persuaded to wed the beautiful Hester, and becomes trapped in an unhappy marriage. But his troubles are compounded when he becomes the victim of a malicious village gossip, whose rumours threaten his entire career. A powerful exploration of the nature of ignorance and prejudice, *Deerbrook* proved an inspiration for both Charlotte Brontë and Elizabeth Gaskell. It may be regarded as one of the first Victorian novels of English domestic life.

New to Penguin Classics, this edition of *Deerbrook* contains the full text of the original three-volume novel. Valerie Sanders's introduction outlines the novel's themes and considers its unique position in nineteenth-century women's literature. This volume also contains a chronology, further reading and detailed notes.

Edited with an introduction and notes by Valerie Sanders

read more

PENGUIN CLASSICS

THE SHOOTING PARTY
ANTON CHEKHOV

'Why did I marry him? Where were my eyes? Where were my brains?'

The Shooting Party, Chekhov's only full-length novel, centres on Olga, the pretty young daughter of a drunken forester on a country estate, and her fateful relationships with the men in her life. Adored by Urbenin, the estate manager, whom she marries to escape the poverty of her home, she is also desired by the dissolute Count Karneyev and by Zinovyev, a magistrate, who knows the secret misery of her marriage. And when an attempt is made on Olga's life in the woods, it seems impossible to discover the perpetrator in an impenetrable web of deceit, lust, loathing and double-dealing. One of Chekhov's earliest experiments in fiction, *The Shooting Party* combines the classic elements of a gripping mystery with a story of corruption, concealed love and fatal jealousy.

Ronald Wilks's new translation of this work is the first in thirty years. It brilliantly captures the immediacy of the dialogue that Chekhov was later to develop into his great dramas. This edition also includes suggestions for further reading and explanatory notes.

Translated and edited by Ronald Wilks

THE STORY OF PENGUIN CLASSICS

Before 1946 ...'Classics' are mainly the domain of academics and students, without readable editions for everyone else. This all changes when a little-known classicist, E. V. Rieu, presents Penguin founder Allen Lane with the translation of Homer's *Odyssey* that he has been working on and reading to his wife Nelly in his spare time.

1946 *The Odyssey* becomes the first Penguin Classic published, and promptly sells three million copies. Suddenly, classic books are no longer for the privileged few.

1950s Rieu, now series editor, turns to professional writers for the best modern, readable translations, including Dorothy L. Sayers's *Inferno* and Robert Graves's *The Twelve Caesars*, which revives the salacious original.

1960s The Classics are given the distinctive black jackets that have remained a constant throughout the series's various looks. Rieu retires in 1964, hailing the Penguin Classics list as 'the greatest educative force of the 20th century'.

1970s A new generation of translators arrives to swell the Penguin Classics ranks, and the list grows to encompass more philosophy, religion, science, history and politics.

1980s The Penguin American Library joins the Classics stable, with titles such as *The Last of the Mohicans* safeguarded. Penguin Classics now offers the most comprehensive library of world literature available.

1990s The launch of Penguin Audiobooks brings the classics to a listening audience for the first time, and in 1999 the launch of the Penguin Classics website takes them online to a larger global readership than ever before.

The 21st Century Penguin Classics are rejacketed for the first time in nearly twenty years. This world famous series now consists of more than 1300 titles, making the widest range of the best books ever written available to millions – and constantly redefining the meaning of what makes a 'classic'.

The Odyssey continues ...

The best books ever written

PENGUIN (🐧) CLASSICS

SINCE 1946

Find out more at www.penguinclassics.com